Advance praise for *Skin Contact*

'Elisa Faison's enthralling and unflinching *Skin Contact* gives us an intimate view of an intricately bound cast of characters, finding the hidden places where the real story lies. . . Faison has crafted a story that surprises us with its honesty, its passion, and its intensity'

Kevin Wilson, author of *Nothing to See Here*

'A book that's all hot and bothered, examining intimacy, fidelity, sexuality and motherhood with a backdrop of grief. It explores a network of desire, with peripheral characters intercepting the narrative to take centre stage as they share their own slice of sexy, complicated life . . . Deeply readable, this will be the hottest sluttiest book of the summer'

Alice Slater, author of *Let the Bad Times Roll*

'Sexy and self-assured, *Skin Contact* is irresistible. While exploring the boundaries of desire and fidelity, Elisa Faison's characters ask big questions about the choices we make and how to negotiate what's beyond our control'

Ada Calhoun, author of *Crush*

'*Skin Contact* is so much more than a sharply observed portrait of a marriage, though it is that too. . . This book is the party of the year and I wanted to join in, opening the next door and the next, getting a bit more gossip, sharing just one more story, stealing one more kiss. An absolute knockout of a debut'

Gwen Kirby, author of *Shit Cassandra Saw*

'Elisa Faison's debut novel will captivate you: lucid prose, delicious sexual tension, bursts of heartbreaking intimacy. I loved these characters, their stories, this book!'

Jean Chen Ho, author of *Fiona and Jane*

Elisa Faison is a freelance editor living in Carrboro, North Carolina with her partner and two-year-old twins. She has published stories in *The Missouri Review*, *Electric Literature*, *Smokelong Quarterly*, and more. Her story 'Motherlove' was the recipient of the 2024 Peden Prize, awarded by *The Missouri Review* and judged by Rachel Yoder. Formerly, Elisa worked as a bookseller at Flyleaf Books and the book reviews editor at *The Carolina Quarterly*. She holds a PhD in English from UNC Chapel Hill.

SKIN CONTACT

Elisa Faison

Sceptre

First published in Great Britain in 2026 by Sceptre
An imprint of Hodder & Stoughton Limited
An Hachette UK company

The authorised representative in the EEA is Hachette Ireland,
8 Castlecourt Centre, Dublin 15, D15 XTP3, Ireland (email: info@hbgi.ie)

1

Print book interior design by Marie Mundaca

A CIP catalogue record for this title is available from the British Library

Hardback ISBN 9781399748599
Trade Paperback ISBN 9781399748605
ebook ISBN 9781399748612

Typeset in Sabon LT Std

Printed and bound in Great Britain by Clays Ltd, Elcograf S.p.A.

Hodder & Stoughton policy is to use papers that are natural, renewable and recyclable products and made from wood grown in sustainable forests. The logging and manufacturing processes are expected to conform to the environmental regulations of the country of origin.

Hodder & Stoughton Limited
Carmelite House
50 Victoria Embankment
London EC4Y 0DZ

For Wil
and
In memory of my mom, Sharon

Motherlove

"I'M REALLY SORRY. NO one told me you were here." That was the first thing Lily ever said to us, that she hadn't seen us. But now she was looking me right in the eye, with a little pleading smile, and I softened—as I always did when I felt someone needed something from me.

Ben and I had been seated for fifteen minutes. For the first five minutes, we had luxuriated in the wait, reading to each other from the menus on our phones and sinking into each syllable. "Duck confit," I said, letting myself lean a little Frenchy at the end.

"Heirloom carrot," Ben said. "Yuzu. Turnip. Honey." If you didn't know whether it was an entrée or a grocery list, it would be either delicious or tiny but almost never both.

For the second five minutes, we discussed how unpretentious the décor was. "These chairs look like our chairs," he said. "And I like our chairs." I shared my opinion that tiki cocktails were too trendy—though I dreaded the day that I'd have to pretend to like bourbon and smoke again.

For the third five minutes, we tried not to notice the lingering silences that began to pepper our inanities. The big sad thing we were trying not to think about. "Maybe I should say something," he said.

"Maybe."

She came and saved us from the shame of requesting something.

"The hostess is new," she explained as she set down two glasses and a carafe of water.

"Don't worry about us!" I said, and wrinkled my eyebrows together in a show of sympathy. I repressed an urge to tell her that I had once worked in service. I liked to be an easy customer, liked to cultivate a rapport with waitstaff—authentic or not—and liked to leave 25 percent tips when I was sober and 30 percent tips when I was drunk. I sometimes imagined that my waiters thought of me after I'd left, remembering my easiness fondly and with relief.

"We really just sat down," Ben lied.

She told us her name was Lily, which I thought was a beautiful name. Her face was smooth and shiny in the right places, like she hadn't put on any face makeup or like she knew the best makeup to buy. Her eyebrows were thick and dark and straight, above brown eyes and a nose with a little bump in it. Her lips were full, with a big dip at the top, and painted not quite nude, a little burst of light pink next to the white of her skin, like a lily, which was my mother's favorite flower.

A year or so ago, I would have thought of her vaguely as "our age," but now I realized that she was younger than we were, maybe twenty-four. I was thirty, no longer the youngest kind of adult you could be. I had kinky gray hairs that broke up my wall of bangs. I had college-ruled lines of wrinkles across my forehead that I hated and covered up with the bangs. I had wide parentheses around my mouth that used to appear when I laughed, but now lingered like unwanted guests long after the dinner had ended. I had begun to fear that my eyes were shrinking, that the hood of flesh under my eyebrows was succumbing to gravity and slowly subsuming them, the way my mother's had before she died last month. People used to comment on my big eyes, which were blue even though my hair was dark. But all the strangers had gone silent lately.

I supposed I should be grateful to be alive. My grandmother's sister, Frances, for whom my mother named me, was dead by thirty. Dead before her hair went gray, and her forehead got lined, and her neck began to sag, and her eyes began to shrink, and her mom began to die. People noticed her for her whole life.

"Early Valentine's Day?" Lily asked.

"No," Ben said. "Yes," I said. I wasn't sure why, except that to say yes seemed light and festive, which I wanted to feel. In fact, I hadn't even realized it was February. I'd celebrated the New Year in big stupid 2020 glasses, a glittery zero around each of my eyes, and two days later, I got the call and chronology stopped. Time had become one gray blob that I merely floated back and forth in, like an astronaut in space, unmoored, homeless.

"Sort of." Ben laughed, and grabbed my hand across the table. "Just thought it'd be nice to get out for a date." Nice to get dressed, nice to leave the house, nice to be a person in the world again, who loved and was loved. I had woken that morning wanting it out of nowhere, with a desperation that startled me.

We ordered cocktails. Cognac, ruby port, spiced Demerara syrup, allspice dram, lemon, orange. We ordered snacks. Nori, enoki, shoyu. Fried potato, kimchi dip. We started to get a little silly and a little horny.

"What about them?" I asked, tilting my head to the couple at the table next to us. He was an enormous blond with a squashy face, and she was a bony redhead with thin shoulders. He was drinking red, and she was drinking white.

Ben gave them an appraising look. "Never. Once a month at most."

"And only when the kids are with their grandparents," I said. "If they're there, she can't stop thinking about them. If she remembered to turn the night-light on. If they're warm enough."

"Which is a problem for him, because he has a fantasy of getting caught."

"Gross! No."

"He can't help it. He caught his parents as a kid. Don't kink-shame him."

I shrugged, sucked on the edge of my cocktail glass, and popped a fried potato into my mouth. The kimchi dip was hot and tangy—almost sweaty, like Ben after his morning run. He nodded at something over my shoulder. "What about them? The glasses behind you, to the left." I looked up into the mirror behind his head.

It reflected a man in glasses who had a turtleneck under his blazer and a clean-cut taper fade. His eyes were warm and open, and he laughed at something the man across from him said. I could only see the back of his head, but I liked the squareness of his hand cupping his glass. "All the time," I said. "Look how they're looking at each other."

"Maybe. Unless they only get turned on when they're out together. And when they go home, all they want to do is watch TV on the couch and wrap up in a blanket."

I nodded. That was a thing. A thing that was sometimes our thing, and I felt the need to protect it. I said, "Glasses likes that, though. He likes the way his husband's butt looks in sweatpants. He gets all hot and bothered when their hands brush against each other when they reach for the remote and he can't help himself. They always have sex on the couch, never in the bed."

We ordered a bottle of wine: orange muscat, Izydora Natural Amber, Cimişlia, Moldova, 2019. When Lily brought it over, she said, "This is a *really* good bottle. It eats really well." She reached into the pocket at her waist and brought out a bottle opener and used it to slice the neck of the bottle. As she crushed the wrapping in one fist, she brought her other hand up to her forehead and smoothed back a swath of errant baby hairs. Her fingernails were short and perfunctory, but each was painted a different color of the rainbow. My mom and I had sometimes done my nails that way, when I was a kid. I must have been staring because Lily balled her hand into a fist as she brought it down from her face.

"It eats well," I said to Ben after Lily had walked away, lifting my glass and tilting it slightly toward him. I had liked the way it sounded in her mouth, and I wanted to remember to say it about other wines. It was syrupy and rich, and I held it on my tongue for a few seconds before I swallowed it.

We ordered duck confit, mushroom, cippolini, cannelloni. The whole fish, allium mignonette, fresh greens. We started to get a little sad and a little lovey. Ben held my hand across the table and ran one finger up and down my palm, and I found myself talking about Lily's fingernails, offering up flashes from my mind for him to make sense of: some slumber party, hot pink silken pajamas smooth on my skin, my mother's pursed lips blowing a soft stream of air onto the tips of my fingers, my palm in hers.

Lily arrived to remove some of our empty dishes, the fish plate covered in the bones that we had licked clean. I wiped my face roughly with my palm, and I couldn't tell if she saw or not.

Lily. There was no end to the proliferation of things that made my mother seem more dead.

"I'll be right back," I said to both of them.

I went to the bathroom and made a face in the mirror that I had a feeling I only ever made at myself in mirrors. I had seen the faces other women made in mirrors, and I never recognized them as existing in nature. I pulled the skin under my eyebrows up and thought how pretty I must have looked in my twenties. I went into the stall and luxuriously let three big tears fall out of my eyes, not sure if they were for my mom or for myself five years ago. *I miss her miss her miss her miss her miss her miss her miss her miss her miss her miss her*, I repeated to myself. Meaning both my mom and the me who still spoke to her mom every day, who still like a child thought that her mom might be her soulmate. What did you do when you found yourself, happily married at thirty, suddenly missing half of your soul even though your husband was right there, his hand on your back for hours and hours? I let two more tears fall and thought, *I miss her miss her miss her miss her but this has to be the end of this, please.*

Afterward, I thought about sending a picture of my tits to Ben to make myself feel better, but I chickened out.

As I walked back to the table, I passed the open kitchen. Lily's hand was on another waitress's shoulder, and she was whispering something to her with a smirk on her face. When I sat back down, I said to Ben, "What about Lily?" I put my cocktail face back on, a sly crimp at the corner of my mouth.

"Lily," he said. "The waitress?"

"Server," I said, though I realized I'd been calling her a waitress in my head.

"Oh yeah, yeah," Ben said, shaking his head as though to knock the word out of it. "What about her?"

"I don't know," I said, risking more wine. "I bet she has a boyfriend waiting for her at home. And he's always complaining about how she has to work on the weekends and gets home so late. But she's full of energy when she gets back from seeing so many people and maybe finishing their nice leftover wine at the end of her shift. She wakes him up to have sex."

"Yeah. He's always pissed off at first, because he just fell asleep. But he gives in and then he's glad he did."

"She can't help it." I felt a hot flush come into my cheeks. It was the end of the story, per the expectations of the game, but I wanted to keep going. It surprised me, to feel pulled back into my body. I wanted to stay there. "She likes it when her customers flirt with her, even though she knows she's supposed to be annoyed by it. She complains about it to the other waitresses when she's drinking their wine, but she doesn't mean it."

"Servers, Frances," Ben said, and I frowned at him and rolled my eyes. "Don't be sexist. Which reminds me—Lily especially likes it when the women at her tables flirt with her."

I let the sip of wine sit in my mouth. It was more like honey or sherry than wine. I thought about Lily saying that it had eaten well, and I felt a giggle in my chest. "I have sort of a crush on her," I said after I swallowed, only realizing it as I said it.

"Really?" Ben's eyes went wide, and he leaned in to look into the open kitchen. "She's not really your type." I always made a point of preferring women who were taller than me and fatter than me and had bigger boobs than me. I wanted to be smothered in womanness.

With men, I always became maternal in my expressions of lust. Even as a teenager, when I started to fall in love with a boy, I'd find myself cradling him in my arms, kissing the top of his head, smoothing the wrinkles down the back of his shirt. It could excite me, even five years ago, to picture myself doing these things with men. I thought that it set me apart from other women, whose attentions I pictured as more surface than mine, less encompassing. Now, at thirty, I had begun to feel ambivalent about this tendency, worried that it was another way I was aging myself. I wanted to be sexier, dumber, more bodily.

I said, "Mm. I don't know why."

"I do," Ben said with a grin. "She looks sort of like you."

I let out a laugh—an almost harsh *ha!*—which I hadn't consented to. "No, she doesn't! Does she?" The idea swelled up in me, a balloon. I thought of her pastel moon of a face, smooth and shining.

"She has brown hair, she's sort of tall, thin . . ." He shrugged. "Like you!"

I couldn't suppress my smile, but I didn't want him to know how much he'd thrilled me. It seemed ridiculous. "Oh, no," I said, and took an erratic drink of wine, savoring the taste of loss that lives somewhere between the first honeyed scent and the warm tartness at the back of the throat. "I don't think so. Is that a thing?" Ben shrugged but kept smiling. I felt like he was seeing something hidden in me that I hadn't known was there. I said, "What were we talking about before? Before I went to the bathroom, I mean." After I asked, I realized that it had been Lily's rainbow fingernails.

If he remembered, he picked up on my tone and pretended not

to. "That was forever ago; I don't know. Maybe how fucking good the duck is. You should have the last bite," he offered.

"Oh, no," I said. "I'm too full. You should have it."

"You sure?" Ben asked, already reaching for it. When I nodded, he picked up the meat and melting fat with his hand and popped it into his mouth, licked his fingers. I smiled. Ben was always pretending he didn't want something and getting it anyway. It felt good to me in a way that hit deep in my belly.

When Lily came back, she said, "I know you two are going to get dessert." Her voice shimmered as she said this, and I wondered if she really would drink our leftover wine as she talked about us with the rest of the staff, her mouth where our mouths had been. I leaned toward her just in case she really did like it especially when the women flirted with her and asked what she recommended. We ordered Cognacs and the olive oil cake, lemon preserve, fior di latte ice cream.

"Thanks," I said, breathy and drunk, when Lily came back with our order. Her fingers brushed against mine as she handed me the tiny, warm glass, and I seemed to feel them trill down my spine. *Hi*, they said, *hi, hi, hi, you're still here, in this body.*

As we were paying the check, Ben said, "Should we leave her our number?"

"What?" A disconcerting ache shot through me. "Like, wait, for real?"

Ben leaned in and ran his hand down my shoulder. It felt like ten hands. I realized, looking into his eyes, that he was drunk and excited and happy again, too. He looked like himself, and I must have looked like myself, because he said, "Why not? I mean, we'll leave before she sees it. The worst that will happen is she'll have a fun story to tell her boyfriend later."

"Oh my god," I said. I felt giddy, like a girl. "Okay, let's do it."

Ben turned the receipt over and scrawled his number. He read to me out loud as he wrote above it, "'We think you're cute. Give us a call if you'd like to get together sometime.'"

"Perfect," I said. But then: "No, wait, did you already write it?" He nodded. "Fuck. I feel like we should have said 'text,' not 'call.'"

"Same difference," Ben said, folding the note.

"That's really old of us to say 'call.'"

"You're not, like, *ancient*. My question is: What are we going to tip? Like, we can't give an enormous tip, which I know you want to, because then it will seem like we think she *owes* us a call."

"A text," I say. "Yeah."

"But obviously we don't want to under-tip her because we're not, like, assholes."

"No, yeah. Okay. What about just, like, twenty percent? That's normal, right? Not bribery?"

"Yeah, yeah, good call."

We threw on our jackets like we were shoplifting them and practically ran from the table. But once we were outside, Ben grabbed my shoulder and said, "Wait!" He turned me so that we were both looking through the big front window at Lily, who had the note lifted in front of her face, her hand pressed tightly to her mouth, her eyes smiling, unless I imagined it.

We were hungover Sunday morning, surrounded by our shoes and the piles of clothes we had clumsily ripped off each other when we got home. I had told Ben to use me like a thing, so he had pulled my hair, but I hated it and it turned tender and caring in the end. We'd drunk too much, and neither of us came.

I rolled into his body and pressed my throbbing forehead against his neck. He kissed me on my ear and said we had to start ordering coffees with our desserts.

I said, "It was fun, though."

"When Lily saw the note. That was cute," he said. Cute. It made me feel tender toward him, and I curled myself up tiny into his arm.

"I wonder if we should go back," I said after a few minutes of silence. "We didn't get to try the artichokes."

He rolled to his side so that our noses were touching, and he studied my face. "You want to see her again? For real?"

"Yes," I said. I thought of how it had felt, to imagine her life, to brush my fingers against hers. The rush of heat, the idea of something yet to come. I wanted to keep feeling it. "Don't you? Or—"

He smiled. "I think she's going to call."

"She'll text," I said. "Maybe. Maybe not."

"Why are you so worried about how young she is? She doesn't seem very young."

"Well, how old do you think she is?" I asked him.

"I don't know, twenty-four?"

"I regret to inform you that that's almost a decade younger than you."

He shrugged. I felt an irrational hot flare of anger at him. He had never looked better to me than he had over the last year. His face was tanned and lined like he'd been working outside, though he never had been. His hair was longer, and his beard was flecked with patches of silver. His shoulders were broad and strong. Men really did look better older, more solid and defined. I had a deep sense that I, on the other hand, was smudging, that soon I would be nothing but a splash of pale color.

At the same time, I wanted his body pressed into mine. I wanted it to press past mine so that we were one body. I wanted him. Or I wanted to want him and felt the failure of want animate my body instead, my desire transmuting into a more primal need to be soothed.

"Don't be worried, Franny," he said as he brushed my bangs out of my eyes. He let his hand linger in my hair and ran his thumb back and forth across my forehead. I closed my eyes, and for a second, his hand became my mom's hand, pulling my hair back into a barrette.

A blood vessel had burst in her brain and she had died.

That was all it took to leave me here without her.

On Sunday night as we were prepping the coffeepot and putting away the dishes, Ben's phone buzzed. Before we clicked the notification, my heart began to thud against my breastbone. At that point, it was the promise of Lily, not Lily herself, that excited me. The promise of a new kind of sex, vibrant and weird and unexpected. The promise contained in her single text:

Hey, it's Lily from last night. I'd definitely be interested in meeting up!

The galaxy of subtext contained in the little winky-faced emoji.

* * *

On Monday, after Ben left to teach a seminar, I lay in bed late into the morning, as I had been doing for a few weeks now. But that day, I drank four cups of coffee and watched lesbian porn. I imagined all the women as Lily, round cheeks, her sly smile, her dark hair, the tiny divot on the bulb of her nose. The way, I thought, her shoulder blades might curve under those satin straps. The way she might look at the woman she wanted to fuck.

Even though I was already behind schedule for the memoir I was ghostwriting, I did the same thing the next morning and, later that night, heard myself tell a truth and a lie: that I was feeling more like myself, and that I felt I'd been very productive. I ordered a new dress that reminded me of one I saw on one of the porn stars, tanned and drunk, hopefully fake drunk. I wanted to wear it on Friday, and I wanted Lily to see me in it and eat me alive. I had it rush delivered.

On the third day, I tried to watch threesome porn, but it invariably disappointed me. I hated the loud whiny sound that is ubiquitous in porn involving men and that I—like every girl—had imitated for several years in my early twenties in lieu of having actual orgasms. Twice, I flung my phone away in disgust and closed my eyes and imagined Lily instead. At first, I would lick her and bite her and touch myself while Ben watched, unable to keep himself from coming. But then I would find myself lying next to her in bed, our faces underneath white sheets, the morning sun seeping through and making her skin glow beneath my hand. I would run my fingers down the side of her cheek, feeling her dewy skin. I would lean into her and kiss her forehead, soft under my lips, her hair smelling like rosewater and dry shampoo.

Our brown hair intermingling on the pillow so that I couldn't tell which was mine and which was hers.

On Friday, I fretted and puttered around the house. I washed the sheets and then realized I'd probably wash them again tomorrow. I bought fresh flowers and put them out and then worried that they made us seem too domesticated. I considered booking myself for a full Brazilian, because what if she had one? I never worried about my pubic hair. I had practically forgotten it existed. Ben didn't care how wild it was, or at least he said he didn't. But now there was going to be a direct comparison. In the end, I didn't book the appointment because I was afraid that I would seem overeager, like I had overprepared. And maybe it was cooler to be natural. Also, I was scared that all my skin would come off. I watched a YouTube video about how to use a man's beard trimmer to trim pubic hair. I watched a YouTube video about how to go down on a woman in case I had forgotten. I watched a YouTube video about how to pair cheeses with wine.

At six thirty, I put on a thong and then took it off and put on black lace underwear and then took it off and put the thong back on. I put on the new dress and cut the tags. I set out a cheese tray: Camembert, bleu, manchego, prosciutto, soppressata, fig butter, olives. A bottle of tempranillo and a bottle of cava, both of which I was assured by YouTube would eat well. I lit a candle.

At ten 'til eight, Ben emerged from the shower and put on his regular clothes and ate a slice of cheese and kissed me on the top of my head. "You okay?" he asked.

"I'm okay," I said. "I'm nervous. I'm excited? It's going to be fun." He looked at me for a long time. "*Really.* I promise." I shrugged and laughed. "New thing!"

He laughed, too, and said, "All right. Fuck yeah."

Lily arrived in a white T-shirt and black cutoff shorts. I felt ridiculously overdressed. Ben shook her hand, and I gave her a hug. I was overcome by the worry that this was how her parents would greet her. The warm hug my mom always gave me.

But she smiled and laughed and made herself at home and said to me, quietly, while Ben was getting the champagne flutes, "You look *incredible.*" I grew hot all over. We drank the cava first, and she popped a slice of Camembert into her mouth with her fingers. Her nails were baby blue. I imagined her hand in my hand, my mouth blowing a hot stream of air onto those nails.

We sat down at the table, and I wished we hadn't. It felt like a formal interview: Ben and I across from Lily, who, at first, sat up straight as she answered our questions: How old was she? She was "twenty-three and a half," she said, which was almost worse than if she had said something like twenty-two. What had been her major in college? Film, with a minor in gender studies. I felt myself blush when she said that. When we'd been in college, it had been called "women's studies," and to major in it was vaguely pitiable. "I picked them to sort of piss off my dad," Lily clarified as she finished her first glass, the bubbles rising in her throat to form an adorable hiccup. Ben laughed then, which meant I could laugh, which helped me relax. "And because I just wanted a break, I think. I'd taken a gap year to work beforehand. Actually, though, I ended up really loving film and things. I take photographs now, just part time."

As we chatted—about the restaurant, about her post-college experience—she began to lean progressively forward toward us, to laugh louder and longer at Ben's ill-advised puns. The sleeve of her V-neck top slid incrementally down her right shoulder to confirm that she hadn't worn a bra. I was thrilled by her body language—which years of reading women's magazines had taught me was strongly indicating her sexual interest in us. But I also began to worry that I might not be kinky enough for her. Sex had changed maybe. At least, it seemed like it had, based on what I had been reading lately. Could I bring myself to scratch her if she wanted me to? Or choke her? Or hit her? These thoughts terrified me. But I knew that it was okay to hit now and that many women liked it, had lifted it from its context of heterosexual abuse. I wanted to want it.

We drank the tempranillo and moved to the couch. We started to get a little sexy and a little close. Lily draped one leg over mine, and Ben ran his hand across it. She said, "This is embarrassing, but I was talking about you guys with my friend the other night."

"At the restaurant?" Ben asked, and I could feel both of our bodies go electric.

"Yeah," she said. "We thought you seemed really cute. Some married couples are so sad to wait on. They, like, have nothing to say to each other."

"Well," I said, unsure how flattered I should feel by the compliment, "we like each other."

She reached over to the cheese tray, grabbed an olive, and said, "Well. I liked you, too." Then she leaned forward and placed the olive on my tongue and kissed me before I had swallowed it. The move felt rehearsed, but not necessarily like she'd done it with another woman before. More like she'd seen it in a movie and practiced it in the mirror. Maybe she'd been as nervous as I was. Maybe she'd put on a dress, and then taken it off, and then put on a bra and the top, and then looked at herself in the mirror and decided to take off the bra.

I pulled her into my lap. Her mouth was hot and salty and smaller than I'd expected. I leaned back and breathed heavily, and turned to Ben. He gave me a big, slow kiss on the mouth and whispered, "Don't worry about me."

Lily laughed and kissed him, too, before she looked back to me and ran her hand down the strap on my dress. She became fast and erratic, like she couldn't wait. Or like she was used to pretending to be more turned on more quickly than she really was. All of it was hot, but it also made me want to rub her back and tell her that she could slow down, that she didn't have to pretend for anyone.

I surprised myself by saying, "Let's go to the bedroom."

We took our clothes off, and I took her in. She asked, "What do you think?" in a voice that was almost sultry, but which contained a base layer of insecurity that touched me. She was curvier than me, cute and clean. I smiled at her. I was thrilled by the spray of freckles across her stomach that seemed to emanate from a splashy birthmark at the top of her left hip. I breathed in heavily and, before I had even decided to, felt myself leaning in and kissing her birthmark, my hand behind the small of her back, pulling her hip up to meet my mouth. I thought about how this brown spot had always been in this exact place on her body, even as all the rest of her had been woven and unwoven over time. I felt that I was in contact with the very core of her, a spot that her own mother had seen on the day she was born, and then day after day for years, and then, very suddenly, maybe ten years ago, for the last time, without realizing it. I moved my hand so that my thumb could trace the edges of the mark as I kissed my way down to her clit, which tasted to me like something my mouth had lost along the way and had been missing.

She was gasping regular, affected squeaks that reminded me unfavorably of the porn I had tried to watch in this very spot a few days ago; but when I put two fingers inside her, she went totally silent, and for a second, I worried that she might have stopped breathing. But then I realized that it was just that she had stopped performing for me. Stopped thinking about me at all and started thinking only about herself. *Take from me*, I thought. *Just take this from me*. I wanted to tell her that by the time she learned to take the things she wanted, they might have disappeared forever. I kept licking her and was overcome with something indescribable when she gasped again and shuddered hard against my mouth. It was something like joy, like fullness, and as I lifted my face to look at her, I wondered if I had tears in my eyes.

"Fuck!" Ben said as he came. "Fuck, oh my god." Lily giggled. Ben looked at us sheepishly and said he'd go get a towel. I looked at her pale face with pink splotches, smooth and shining. Brown hair like mine. A little bump in the nose like mine. I wondered if I had ever looked as new and perfect and unspoiled.

"What do you want?" she asked me, low and quiet. I saw myself when I looked at her, younger and more desperate to please, to be valued by what I could give to someone. What did I want? I wanted to tell her to flip me over and get on top of me. I wanted to tell her to eat me out while I watched Ben fuck her from behind. I wanted to tell her to hit me. Or I wanted to want those things, and maybe I just wanted emptily, without object.

I said nothing because I couldn't say, "Let me just look at you, and look at myself, and remember being bouncy and whole and twenty-three." I lay down beside her and pulled her back into my stomach and wrapped my leg across hers. I nuzzled my face into her hair and kissed the top of her head, kissed the lobe of her ear, kissed the back of her neck. Maybe this was all I wanted from her. Maybe this was all I ever wanted from anyone. The realization both disappointed me and calmed me, a loss, but of something insubstantial. "Sweet girl," I whispered to her as I ran my hand down the side of her face. "Sweet girl," and I took her hand in mine and lifted it up to my mouth and kissed the tips of her sweet blue fingernails one by one.

The Hug

THE APOCALYPSE BEGAN THE year after we graduated from college. Class of 2019. Because we were girls, we knew that growing up could only mean walking a narrow path toward thinness and defeat. So the whole pandemic thing felt almost mundane to us at first—pretty much expected, as though our own aging had propelled the world into its sick, runny future.

We'd spent our post-graduation months feeling sly and a little uncomfortable, like we were cheating our fates, because our own moms had turned twenty-two and become mirages of themselves, most of them already married and some already pregnant with us. Annie's mom was already raising children at twenty-two. But that summer, we still clung to our bodies, to wholeness, to one another. It was hard to let go.

In the fall, we'd evolved a little, as was expected of us. For instance, we stopped living together when our lease ran out. We all lived with our boyfriends now, except for Annie, who got married in October and moved in with her husband. He was a doctor who had scooped Annie up senior year while he was still married to another woman. We tried not to feel sad about living apart. We were lucky because we all still lived in the same town, unlike a lot of groups of college friends. For a while, we were taking spin classes together twice a week and always went out for drinks after. We'd hang around each other's apartments all the time, and it never felt like a special occasion or anything. We wouldn't wash our hair before getting together. Or we wouldn't change after our workouts. We would drink from each other's cups and leave them on the counter still dirty. We would get high and have cartwheel contests on our front lawns. It was a lot. Maybe it was a little childish.

It seemed impossible that our moms had ever wanted to touch anyone the way we wanted to touch each other. When we were little, we had watched them in their bathrooms getting ready to go out, one hand with a round brush, and the other with a hair dryer. We saw their hair float up around their faces and their eyes go blank. After we'd heard them click-clacking to grab their purses on their way out the door, we would sneak back into their bathrooms and grab the hair dryers and turn them on full blast. When we used them, we became bigger and we could annihilate the ghouls that were hiding behind the shower curtain. Back then, we were hot meaty things and our moms were just a trace of scent in the air. When they got home, they'd smile and kiss us, and then they would vanish as they clicked out our night-lights. We had talked about that, how little they seemed to exist.

So in March, the news felt kind of funny. Like the universe was telling us to grow up. When our local government recommended that we wear face masks, Annie messaged the group and said, They think we look like hags! I told you guys we should have started using wrinkle cream.

When they issued a stay-at-home order, Michelle texted, Gov wishes we had all gotten our MRS degree like Annie.

Lily joked about it most of all, saying God was punishing her for the super gay threesome she'd just had, forcing her back home with her boyfriend so she could learn to cook and keep her plants alive. We wanted to laugh. We had disappeared just like our moms! It was about time.

But now it was July 2020, and we felt lonely and vaporish. We were no longer sure that we were going to survive. We were fragile and afraid of getting sick. In short, we had become adults and it sucked. When Annie, the baby of our group, invited us to celebrate her twenty-third birthday at her new house, which used to be the house her husband had shared with a thirty-year-old woman, we felt a sense of bodily want we hadn't quite known we were capable of. We all said yes, even though it felt risky. Even though it felt like a step backward, in some way we couldn't have explained back then.

When we arrived at Annie's, we felt overwhelmed by how big the house was. We had forgotten. We were all struck, imagining Annie's body rattling around alone while her husband worked long shifts. We imagined her mixing herself a Manhattan, using the bar cart that the ex-wife had left behind. We imagined her sitting down on the couch to watch a movie alone—the couch the ex-wife used to sit on. We imagined her unmaking the bed at the end of the day without having said a word to anyone but the husband's dog, which used to be the dog he'd shared with the ex-wife.

For a second, we wanted to surround her, hug her, and fill the space up tight, but we didn't. We were nervous. We had coached ourselves in our cars on the way over. *No matter how much we want to, we can't touch each other. Not even after we start drinking. We are adults! We can control our impulses!* We had thought this would be hard, that we'd have to bite our lips tight to keep from reaching out to each other. But maybe we had gotten used to the distance. Plus, we had never really hung out here before, preferring our old college haunts. The house was too adult, too complete. It seemed like it was looking down at us, keeping an eye out to make sure we behaved. It said, *A doctor lives here. Don't get too close. Trust me, it's for your own good.*

Instead of hugging, we waved at each other. It felt natural. We had put on masks as we pulled into the driveway, to show we were serious about science and compassionate toward other people. We took them off simultaneously, in front of one another, and smiled as we raised our voices an octave and called, "Happy Birthday!" Something felt off between us, and we went quickly around back to set up our lawn chairs and individual coolers six feet apart from each other. We measured the distance by imagining the husband lying on the ground between us.

After a drink or two, though, it became easier to be around each other. We still didn't want to touch, but we relaxed in our chairs and began talking over one another. It soon became clear that the house wasn't entirely imposing, even though it was one of those places that was more a collection of features than a home. Granite kitchen island. Picture window. Statement piece above the fireplace. The ex-wife's parents had left behind a few things that had character, though, like a distressing number of lawn sculptures, and nine koi, which lived in an aboveground pool on the back porch.

"Wait," Lily said, pulling her beer from her mouth. "This house used to belong to the ex-wife's parents?" She wiped her chin and then rubbed her hand on her bare thigh.

"Oh yeah," Annie said, looking around at us as if to confirm that she had told us this before. "That's how she and Chris were able to afford this place during residency."

"Okay, but like...why isn't this her house now?" We were all wondering the same thing, but we didn't like the way Lily asked, as though she had something sour in her mouth.

Annie blushed and said, "I don't know. Something about the divorce agreement. She had to move for her fellowship anyway. It was, like...mutually beneficial. We wanted it, I mean. To stay here."

We had a feeling that when Annie said "we," she meant "the husband," because we were pretty sure that he already owned the house by the time they became engaged our senior year. But we couldn't blame her for exaggerating her agency. Lily's question had seemed weirdly condescending. We hated it when she got like that, like she knew something we didn't. She was probably just jealous. Because actually, the more we thought about it, the more we realized how lucky Annie was. We pictured our own one-bedroom apartments, our galley kitchens with electric stoves, our rickety fire escapes, which tried but failed to give us access to the outside world. Something roiled through us.

To change the subject, we asked if we could see the koi. Annie got up excitedly to lead the way, but Lily stayed where she was. "You guys know I hate fish," she said as she cracked open another beer. We all wanted to roll our eyes. She got into moods sometimes.

As we peered into the pond, we saw that most of the koi were, in fact, hate-able, pale and anemic, with scales a color so reminiscent of our own pinky flesh that they seemed somehow peeled. But some of them were beautiful, we thought: a beach-sunset orange with shimmering ghostly tails that chased them down.

"Those red-spotted ones are the ones we could sell for, like, a thousand dollars," Annie said.

"Are you *serious?*" Michelle asked. "For a fish?"

"Are you going to sell them? You could use the money and turn this into an actual pool. It's big enough," Gracie said. "Oh my god. Have you thought about that, though? You really should do that."

Lily was walking over now, as we knew she would. "Well, I'm not coming over to swim in an old fish pool," she said. "That's gross." She was sort of kidding this time, trying to be funny so that we would forget that she had actually been sort of a bitch.

"It would be different water," said Leah. "They're not so bad." She reached her hand into the pond, and a lovely bright one swam up to her fingers and touched them. She pulled away like she had been burned.

"I was *totally* going to sell them. It felt like kind of a waste of money to keep them. But Chris thinks they really add something to the yard, so . . ." She shrugged. "Anyway, now I kind of like them. I think they're cute. Is that weird?"

"Are you going to become a *koi person?*" Michelle asked, splashing Annie.

We were dog people, and even though we hadn't been asked what our favorite animal was in fifteen years, that mattered to us, because it meant that we were friendly and sincere and loving.

"Sweet Annie, you're so easily swayed! I can already picture a huge koi tattooed on your calf." Lily laughed. It was an odd thing to say, but she was trying, and we decided to cut her some slack.

We had all been alone for a long time. And more than any of us, Lily hated to be alone.

"I feel like I should be offended, but they're sweet, and if I got a koi tattoo, it would be two or three little guys. Look, they love each other." Annie raised her still-full wineglass at the corner of the pool, where a cluster of them had become bunched together, and she took a tiny sip in mock cheers. The mucousy bodies of the koi were rubbing up against one another in the tight space. Annie looked down at them fondly, with bright eyes. Two of them squeezed a third's body between them, and it wriggled to escape.

"Okay, that *is* gross," said Gracie as she turned away and finished her own drink. "Sell these and get a pool."

We followed her back to our chairs, and Leah said, "If only you'd done it right when you bought the place. You'd be the only one of us who could actually get some exercise these days. Even if you were just, like, dog paddling." She was right. Sometimes we did yoga videos at home, but only if our boyfriends were out or asleep. We had tried running, like our moms, but it was too hot and too boring. We missed our spin classes, the other breathing, sweating bodies next to ours.

We felt guilty for noticing, but we did all seem to have extra pouches of flab around our bellies and arms. When we first arrived, we had all taken a quick inventory of one another, letting our eyes flit to those parts of each other we didn't normally look at. We were nervous that the fat made us look younger. Weren't you supposed to become gaunt and willowy as you turned into a woman? Well. At least it was happening to all of us. We were all still in the same proportion to one another.

Annie told us, excitedly and maybe nervously, that her husband had bought her a Peloton bike for her birthday.

"Are you fucking *kidding me?*" Leah asked. "Those things are like three thousand dollars!"

"Oh my god, I know," she said. "It's way too much. And, like, the commercial! It's so dumb, and I told him not to because who knows if it will even be a good workout? But I feel like it's better than nothing, you know?"

Lily looked like she was about to say something, but she shut her mouth. I had a feeling I knew what she was thinking: If Annie had a Peloton, it meant that she wouldn't be coming back to the studio with us once it reopened. Which meant that maybe we would stop seeing her every week, even when the world went back to normal. It was always going to happen at some point, that someone would become too busy or move away or marry a rich doctor who would shower her with gifts. We had been telling ourselves to expect this.

"Can you put it outside and let me try it? I wish I had one," said Michelle.

"That just seems crazy to me. Not being allowed to exercise is, like, the only perk of this whole thing," Gracie said.

"I'm so tired of being trapped inside," Lily said. "If I could go back in time, I'd rent us a giant cabin or something so we could all be together in the woods. We would have had so much fun." We had all imagined something like this, especially on Friday nights, right at the moment we switched off the Zoom call when we would find ourselves still silly and drunk, but suddenly alone with our own unknowable boyfriends.

"No more pandemic talk!" Gracie yelled about an hour later. She began to rummage through her purse. "It's Annie's birthday and

I think we should play a game!" She pulled out a handful of pens and a bunch of torn-up pieces of paper. "Horny Bowl?" We had invented this game out of desperation one night in our sophomore year. No parties were happening. We'd had no Solo cups to play flip cup with or cards to play kings with. All we had were our school supplies. It was dumb but it became our favorite, a regular Friday night pregame event. All you had to do was nominate a few celebrities you wanted to sleep with, put their names in a bowl, and draw them out at random to put on a bracket. Michelle always drew the bracket because she was the one who liked sports. Once the bracket was filled out, we all argued about who was hotter than who until we lost our voices. We loved it, loved imagining our wild future sex lives, loved screaming and cackling at each other.

"Wait, wait, wait!" Lily said, her face shining with alcohol and a secret. "I have a surprise for Annie. Well, actually, it's for all of us." She reached into her cooler and produced an enormous pink Tupperware and a fistful of plastic spoons. "Voilà!"

"Lily, *no!*" said Michelle, thrilled. "That is not a Jell-O shot." We collectively shrieked. They were easy and lethal, just vodka and cherry Jell-O, another of our college traditions. We never owned enough shot glasses to portion them out—and we were too lazy to mold and cut them into dainty squares we could pick up and slide into our mouths. We ate them out of a big bowl, sharing the same spoon.

"Right in one," Lily said, peeling the top off the Tupperware. "I almost brought a candle to put in it, but I thought it might melt the Jell-O."

"Plus I'm not, like, extra sure we should be eating something someone has just spit all over. No offense, Annie, I'm sure your spit is super cute."

"*Anyway!*" said Lily, dunking a spoon in and holding the shot out toward Annie. "I brought everyone separate spoons, yay me."

Annie grabbed it from her but didn't immediately take a bite. "Wait...sorry, but are we really going to eat this? Me and Chris don't really—I don't really drink vodka anymore." She wrinkled her nose, and we felt our stomachs fall.

Lily looked like she had been punched in the face. Before she could open her mouth, Leah said, "It's for old times' sake! You can go back to drinking your fancy Negronis and shit tomorrow."

"Ugh, this stuff makes me act so stupid," Annie whined. "This is one hundred percent why I smashed my head into the corner cabinet that night." Her hand jumped up to the little white scar above her right eyebrow, and she rubbed at it.

Lily knit her eyebrows, and Leah took a long swig from her beer. Gracie said, "That *was* really scary!" Michelle rolled her eyes.

Lily kept looking at Annie. She said softly, "I like your scar. It makes me think of us when we were nineteen. Right?" She looked around at all of us.

"Okay," Annie said. She set the Tupperware down and began to pick at her nails, something she only did when she was nervous. "I didn't want to say anything, but I'm kind of cutting back because...well, we're trying to get pregnant. I got my IUD out last month." She let a smile creep onto her lips and began to look around pleadingly.

Trying to get pregnant. It felt like a joke to me. To all of us. You were supposed to try *not* to get pregnant. You were supposed to sort of do a bad job of trying not to get pregnant. It had always felt like we were lucky, untouchable, promising young women when we squeaked by every month! Either that or we were barren, but that was a problem for future us. We couldn't imagine wanting a pregnancy. What did that mean? That we still didn't know how to act our age?

Or, worse, did it mean that we were somehow cold? Because as Annie looked around at all our faces, it came to me—to all of us, I think—that we were glad she wasn't pregnant yet. We loved Annie's body just the way it was. We were used to it. We had touched it thousands of times, hugged it as she cried, snuggled into it as we slept, held it in mock slow dances. The imaginary baby would balloon her out, break her apart, and come out half-husband. It would take her from us and then toss her aside. At some point, we had cast our own mothers aside as easily as wiping the morning crust from our eyes.

"I'm excited!" she said, a little too loudly.

"Wow!" Michelle said. "So... did it hurt?"

"The IUD? No, not even close to how much it hurt going in."

"Congrats, Annie. That's so exciting," Gracie said, reaching for the abandoned Tupperware and sticking her own spoon into it.

We should feel excited for her. We shouldn't feel left behind. It wasn't her fault. It was up to us to catch up. So we all said congratulations and we smiled. Except for Lily, who began to look around incredulously. She scoffed and grabbed the Tupperware for herself.

"Lily?" Annie said.

"*Annie*," she answered, looking hard into her eyes. Then she looked around the circle at each of us, slowly and accusingly. "What's *wrong* with you guys?! The house?! The dog?! The koi?!" She began to gesture wildly, small globs of Jell-O flying off her spoon.

"What are you trying to say?" Leah asked, irritated, clearly trying to tell Lily with her eyes to cool it.

"Do you not get it? He gets whatever he wants. He's old and he's ready to have a family, so okay? You just *have a baby?* Today is your twenty-third birthday!"

"What does that have to do with the—"

"Because he wanted the house and the dog and the koi and *whatever* and he just got it! It didn't matter that it was his ex-wife's house! He just takes what he wants! I mean, ugh!" She threw her hands up dramatically. It would have been funny if she weren't so serious. "Annie doesn't want all this stuff. It's so... boring! Being a little wife in a big house? It's so ..."

"Oh god, here we go again," Michelle said, rolling her eyes. "Is it *heteronormative*, Lily?"

Lily had had a threesome with a married couple about a month before the pandemic started, and hadn't shut up about it. It had been "eye-opening," or something, a way of claiming control over her own body, instead of letting Lucas, her boyfriend, be in charge of it. She had been insisting it had taken their relationship to a new, enlightened level, but we were all pretty sure they were only still together because they were each other's Covid bubble. She never talked about Lucas, but she talked about the couple all the time, and how excited she was to see them again when the world went back to normal.

She looked around, outraged. "For real, you guys? Are you all forgetting what happened? Tess?"

Her eyes met mine, and I felt a hot wave roll through my body. "Don't look at me," I said.

Lily rolled her eyes, let out a kind of growl in the general direction of the group, and continued, "He got sick of his wife, who was, like, an appropriate fucking age for him and, like, a fucking doctor herself, and he just took Annie, who's young and sweet and—sorry, Annie, but it's true—you're a pushover! He can take anything he wants from you, and he knows it, and it's because he has money!"

We all drew back in our chairs. Annie had been a scholarship kid, and never talked about money, or her family really. Lily must have known more about it than we did, because Annie had been her freshman year roommate, but she hadn't let much slip, except that she'd paid for most of their alcohol and shared her clothes a lot that year. Annie's face went white, and then almost cartoonishly red. Whatever discomfort we had felt before, thinking about pregnant Annie, made us feel sick now. Lily was taking it all too far, as she always did. We wanted to distance ourselves from her, to make this whole conversation go away. This wasn't us. We always had each other's backs, for the real stuff anyway.

"Lily, I don't think—" Gracie began.

"The fucking *Peloton!*" she screamed, her face now entirely red. "He's isolating you!"

Annie was still looking pointedly at her lap. She was picking her fingernails more intently than ever. We knew they'd be bloody later. "He's not isolating me," she said. "We're *in isolation*. Everyone is!"

"He wants you and he's taking you, Annie! Just because your mom was eighteen doesn't mean twenty-three is old enough for—"

Annie looked up fast, and we were surprised to see how wild her round face looked. "Taking me from who?! From you? I'm not yours, Lily!"

Everyone went silent. We could hear each other breathing, especially Annie. Her breath came out loud and pointed. She and Lily were staring at each other like they had forgotten we were here. I became suddenly aware of how far apart from one another we were sitting. I found that I didn't mind and curled into myself. Lily let out a loud sigh and tore her gaze away from Annie's, which we knew meant she was about to cry. She hated it when we saw her cry, almost as much as she hated crying alone. We wanted to feel sorry for her, but it was Annie's birthday. She shouldn't have said anything.

Finally, Gracie said, "Seriously, you guys? Are we getting drunk and having a fight? Are we in high school?"

After a minute, Lily said *sorry* to a patch of grass to the right of Annie.

"Whatever," Annie said, peeling off a cuticle in one long string.

"Come on, Annie," Leah said encouragingly. "It's been a long few months. That's all."

"Here," Michelle said, grabbing the Jell-O shot from Lily's feet and shoving it toward Annie. "Don't be a sucker. You're not pregnant yet. Just eat the fucking thing."

Lily caught Annie's eye. "It's your favorite flavor," she said, giving her a small, teary smile.

"Fuck all you guys," Annie said. She shoveled an enormous, jiggling corner into her mouth.

By the time the sun started to go down, we felt punchy and untamed. We had tried to smooth over the rough edges that Lily had carved into the party by drinking twice as much and playing absurd versions of Horny Bowl. We played "Horny Bowl: Cartoon Characters" and then "Horny Bowl: Foods." Leah made a convincing argument for Pop Rocks being the food most likely to give you a literal orgasm. After the game, we were all starving and a little wasted. One by one, we called our boyfriends and instructed them to have takeout for us when they picked us up.

It dawned on us then: a surprising, collective sense of dread. Annie had been last. We were all twenty-three now, and we were separating, and the next time we saw each other, we would be two-dimensional and shaky and pixelated, speaking to each other through our laptop screens. And maybe Annie would be pregnant.

Lucas arrived first. He called as he was about to pull in and we saw Lily's face flatten. When she heard him in the driveway, she moved herself a bit closer to the koi pond to be hidden from view. She was still looking at Annie. She smiled slightly and started doing the robot. Annie took a small step forward, then stepped back and also robot-ed. They let out a laugh.

Lily whispered, "Annie. Can I please hug you?" She was looking at her desperately, like she needed to be saved. She glanced around at the rest of us but didn't seem to care what we were thinking. We were all packing up our things, but I was listening, even if no one else was. Lily thought she was being a lot quieter than she was. Her question annoyed me. It made me feel like I had been tricked, because I had been sitting awkwardly far from the other girls all day and refusing sips of the infinitely more appealing drinks that they had brought because I thought we had to, that we had all agreed to that.

Annie whispered, "Is it allowed? What do you think?" Her face was suddenly glowing with the kind of flushed boldness I remembered from when we were eighteen, deciding to pelt our frat boy neighbors with snowballs. It came to me that she was drunk, maybe drunker than we were. I felt guilty that we had pressured her into the Jell-O shot.

"I think it's okay just this one time. Please. I really need to," Lily said. I thought maybe she was about to cry again.

"It's my birthday!" Annie said. "Take what you want." And then she let out an almost feral laugh. We all looked up and watched her double over, that way she always did when something just cracked her up. We weren't sure quite what was going on, but for a second, we all thought *fuck it* and imagined how it might be to forget that we were going to die. We were all smiling, and all about to get up and grab on to each other without a care, but then Lily's boyfriend honked his car horn. We all screamed girlishly, but stayed put.

Except for Lily, who clapped her hands and hopped closer to Annie. They wrapped their arms around each other in a big bear hug and then started swaying side to side like they were at a middle school dance. It was dumb but cute. We were just happy that the fight was over.

Then they stopped swaying, but they didn't pull apart and laugh and say *shh* to each other like we thought they would. They just stood there, like they could never get enough of hugging each other. Lily's fingers began to move like spiders tightening around Annie's arms, and Annie turned her face into Lily's hair and began to stroke her back. They were quiet and still and entwined and unhurried, and they forgot we were there.

When she finally pulled back, Lily placed one hand on the side of Annie's face, the tips of her fingers laced with pieces of her hair that had come loose in the heat. She beamed at Annie, whose face took on that nebulous, lighted quality of a beautiful thing being looked at. Slowly, Lily shifted her thumb to graze across that little white scar above Annie's eyebrow, twice. She made a little, private, shameful sound that we couldn't identify.

We averted our eyes.

Suddenly, our stomachs felt too fat, and our backs felt too sweaty, and we felt too drunk. We were disgusted by the beads of mucus they were breathing into each other's hair. We were repulsed by the sticky noise that Annie's hand made as it rubbed against Lily's bare, pinkish skin. When Lily removed her hand from Annie's face, we could see that the jagged scar had gone slightly red and raised from the pressure. They smiled almost shyly at each other.

In our heads, all of our moms said, *Indecent*. The whole thing made us want to puke.

When we got back to our unimpressive little rooms that night, we drank some water, and took off the jumpsuits that we couldn't remember why we had worn, and sat by ourselves until our boyfriends came in and put their hands on us, those familiar, unmottled things that gave us modest, sanctioned touches. We suddenly loved knowing that they were the only hands that had touched us for months, and that they were the only hands that would touch us maybe ever again, and we felt proud of ourselves for how well we were following the rules. We told them that the party had been nice and that was all we said about Annie or Lily before we turned out the lights.

Group Sex

FRANCES AND BEN WERE in their sweatpants on a Saturday morning in September. He made the coffee, as he always did. She drank more than her fair share of the pot but, as always, offered the final half-cup to Ben. They were sitting on the couch, a green velvet sectional. New. They'd needed a change, after almost two years of being stuck in their living room. Ben's legs were stretched long across the love seat. Frances's were tucked into her body, which she pressed tightly to Ben's side. They were looking at Ben's phone.

"This is the app I read about," Ben said.

"It's better than Tinder?" Frances asked, the steam from her coffee fogging up her glasses. Warmed, she leaned her nose farther into her mug. She looked younger in the morning—unformed—her face puffy from sleep, her edges soft.

Ben looked at her. He said, "I think so, for what we're looking for anyway. I mean, according to the internet."

Ben and Frances had never online-dated before. They met in college through Frances's ex-boyfriend. The general abundance of possible hookups on campus rendered sites like OkCupid irrelevant to them, a joke. Tinder didn't exist. Still, both had bemoaned the tragedy of online dating with their single friends. It was shallow, they said. It was robotic, they said. It was the end of romance, they said. When they were alone together, though, they sometimes expressed a secret longing to have the experience. "Think of the good bad date stories we're missing out on!" Ben would say, imagining sharing them with his friends over a beer. "Think of all the people we won't meet!" Frances would say, imagining the myriad ways in which she might have been adored.

"So, what happens? I make a profile and you make a profile?" Frances asked.

"Or maybe we could do a joint profile? I think there's an option to do separate profiles and sort of link them. But since we're only seeing people together, I think that makes the most sense. Package deal."

The profiles had been years in the making, seeds they'd been cultivating since the threesome they'd had with Lily. It had been exciting, for Ben, to see Frances with Lily. To see her anew, as Lily had seen her. He had been satisfied to have her in their bed. But he had also been satisfied to watch her leave. The next morning, in the warm glow of their private relationship, he kissed his wife on the forehead, which appeared slightly changed to him, its wrinkles smoothed out, fresh. She lifted her face without opening her eyes and kissed his mouth. Her lips broke into a big smile, and she said, "We should do that again."

For as long as he'd known her, Frances had been a presence. When she walked into a room, she became a solid, foundational part of it—so much so that you might wonder how the room had held together before she arrived. It was something about being sure of herself, he thought. Something about the certainty of her personhood. It was something he admired, perhaps what had attracted him to her in the first place. When her mother died, though, Frances was snuffed out, as though she'd lost the necessary oxygen to keep burning. Even now she tended to fade, sometimes quietly, into the background of her life, sometimes chaotically into her compulsions and anxieties.

But that morning, after Lily, her wide smile, the morning light on her cheekbones...He'd felt his own face brighten as he said, "Yeah, definitely." If he noticed the little pang that went through his chest, it felt less important than the fact that she was his Frances again, just for a minute.

Initially, they'd planned to reach out to Lily again. But the longer they were isolated, the more time they spent fantasizing: new people, new configurations, a whole world out there. "She was so young," Frances said. "If she's still interested in dating a couple, she'll be on here. It feels too desperate, to text after all this time."

And so here they were, almost two years later, making profiles for a dating site, pressing the final button Ben hoped would keep Frances whole, forever.

"What are we looking for?" she asked, turning the phone toward him. He looked at all the boxes you could check, each a tiny want that might be satisfied. *What are we looking for?* he thought. He felt suddenly overwhelmed by the question. By the number of options, which felt both too many and too few. He had a tendency to do this, to make the smallest thing existential.

"What are we looking for?" he repeated, as if he didn't understand the question, even though he did.

"Yeah, like, singles? Couples? Women? It wants us to specify."

"Well, a woman, right?"

"Yeah," she said. "For sure. But I was thinking, if you're into it, what about a couple? I feel like everyone is just looking for a woman. It's a little... I don't want to say cliché but maybe? And it would be nice for there to be an even playing field, so I wouldn't have to worry about whether the other woman feels left out or alone. You know, since we're together and she'd be single. I could let that distraction go."

"So it would be us with two women?"

"Yeah, sure. Or a woman and a man. Obviously, I mean, if you're into it. It wouldn't have to be, like, the two of you. We could just see what it's like. Swap or whatever, if you'd prefer. In the same room. It could be fun." She said all of this very fast.

Ben was surprised. He had expressed only the most basic, surface-level attraction to men before, mostly to seem open-minded and cool to Frances. He heard himself say, perhaps for the same reasons, "Yeah, I'm open to trying anything once."

Frances beamed at him.

Together, they made a profile that said that they were interested in men and in women, in singles and in couples. They uploaded a photo of themselves that they took two years ago when they were in Italy with Ben's family. They thought it made them look adventurous and not too pretentious. When they hit "Publish," they felt like a team.

Frances had had a hard time writing lately. She was a freelance ghostwriter, currently contracted to finish the memoir of a B-list child actor who had starred in a popular sci-fi show in the 1990s.

She had always been a good ghost. It thrilled her, actually, to explore someone else so intimately. To understand them from the inside out. She liked to disappear into the bodies of others, to snuggle in tightly.

Or, at least, she used to like this. Lately, she had felt uncomfortable about her work and the ease with which she let herself vanish into it. She recently came across a memoir that she'd partially ghostwritten in a bookshop and perused it. In the acknowledgments—from which her name was omitted—the official author had referred to the book as her "baby." *That's my baby*, Frances found herself thinking. *Mine*. Her face had flushed angrily underneath her mask, and then, just as quickly, she felt her eyes well up with tears, overcome by the memory of packing away her mother's books last year, the handwritten name plates in the front of each bearing her mother's name: *Rose. Rose. This book belongs to Rose.* She left the bookshop, confused and tired and wishing she could control her emotional impulses, as she had once been able to do.

Her grief for her mother had felt hot at first, an animating force. But even that had gone cold. She was just one of thousands of people who had lost a parent in 2020. Nothing special. She tried to write, but she felt too empty, bereft even of the child star's memories.

She reached for her phone and pulled up the dating app. A man. A man and a woman. A man. A man. Two women. She swiped and swiped, each flick of her thumb a lifeline. Each "like" a way back into the heat of her body.

Ben was in a faculty meeting when he felt his phone buzz in his pocket. He looked down as surreptitiously as possible and saw a text from Frances: SOS.

A hot rush of panic before he opened her next text. She had sent him a screenshot from the app, a picture of a man and a woman with their faces blacked out above a wall of text:

GF and I are ENM couple (32M, 21F) looking for
singles to play with, GGG & 420 Friendly!
Looking for MMF, FFM, FF, FWB
In the bdrm: BDSM, mostly D/s, sometimes switch,
DP, Ropes
Sag sun, Cap moon, Cancer rising, 8x7, Fully vaxxed!
If this sounds like u, HMU!

A follow-up: I am wading through alphabet soup!!!! What does this LITERALLY MEAN?!

He snort-laughed and covered it up quickly with a small cough. The director of Graduate Studies, who still wore an N95 mask to work each day, scooted loudly away from him.

He texted back with one hand under the table, Will bring home decoder ring.

Thirty minutes later, she followed up: In a near-future world, humans have all but disappeared. The earth has burned. Only bulls and cuckolds and brats and daddies and cumbeggars and sugarbabies remain. This summer, find out if Ben and Frances, the last regular human married couple in the world, have what it takes to survive.

Ten minutes later, also featuring unicorns.

Over the next few weeks, they put their heads together, waded through the soup, and made meaning of the bios. Ben read books about ethical non-monogamy. He read *More than Two* and *The*

Ethical Slut and *Polysecure*. He wanted to understand the concept logically before he experienced it emotionally. He left these books on Frances's desk for her to read when he finished them.

Frances did not read them. Instead, she put her energy into navigating the app. She picked out the unicorns, a word that she now understood to mean bisexual women who were open to threesomes—rare, shining creatures who fascinated her. She picked out the normal-seeming couples whose profiles were written out in words, not in letters. She clicked "Like," she refreshed her app to see if she had been liked, she sent flirty messages. She received a dick pic. She was repulsed—and then ashamed when the image popped into her head right before she came later that night while Ben ate her out. She stood in front of her mirror and took selfies. She learned how to angle her hips so that her butt appeared round and shapely. She sent her first-ever nude to a woman called Jae, a "pansexual woman in an ENM relationship looking for feminine energies." She felt her heart leap when Jae responded to her pic with a pic of her own. She wanted to laugh. She had forgotten that a heart could actually leap, that this was more than a turn of phrase. She hadn't felt the sensation since she was twenty years old. She was thirty-two years old and she had a crush!

A few nights later, she had a dream that Ben died. At his funeral, she wore thigh-high leather boots and a corset. Everyone looked at her. She woke up the moment that she wrapped the whip around her own throat.

When Ben was at work that day, she sent him the selfie that she had planned to send to Jae.

She and Ben met Jae for cocktails. They laughed and flirted and navigated the awkwardness of a three-way make-out session in the parking lot when the bar closed. At home that night, tipsy and buoyant, Frances said, "She was a really good kisser, don't you think?" And then they both cackled because they couldn't remember the last time they called someone a good kisser. The next morning, they couldn't find Jae on the app and found they had no way to get in touch with her again.

"Ghosted," Frances said, bereft, the feel of Jae's mouth still on hers.

Their friends began to wonder if they were okay, why they had disappeared. They received a text from Ben's best friend Max that said, **Where are y'all?! If you're hiding because Frances is pregnant, STOP! I promise to ignore that she's not drinking.**

"I'm not ashamed of what we're doing," Ben said over dinner that night.

"I'm not ashamed either!" Frances said. "Not at all."

"It's perfectly normal that we might want to explore before we start a family."

"Totally. If not now, when?" Frances had thought about that a lot. Her parents had separated when she was four years old, and her mom hadn't dated again until after she went to college, and even then, half-heartedly. She had liked to think that she was different from her mom, in that way. That if it had been her, she'd have fallen in love again, and again, and again, even if she'd had a child at home. But her mom had always said, *I love you, and that's enough.*

Remembering this, Frances's body tingled with something like anxiety. Shouldn't she want to be satisfied with what she had, as her mom had been? Wasn't that, actually, a better way to be?

"We should tell people what we're up to," she said, to stop herself from spiraling.

"Yeah," Ben agreed. "It's not for them anyway; it's for us."

And a quiet voice in her head, before she could stop it, whispered, *It's for me. This is mine.*

A Few Questions and Helpful Comments from Frances's Book Club

Wow. Honestly, I thought y'all had, like... the perfect marriage. I'm a little relieved. Nothing is ever as good as it seems from the outside, you know?

So Ben gets to have sex with *any woman he wants* but it's not cheating? How did he convince you to let him do that? Ted has been trying to get me to have a threesome for, like, *forever.*

A lot of couples think they can save their marriage by opening it up, but really it's just a Band-Aid. You should be careful. Don't waste your prettiest years on this.

I cheated once. Bernard knows. To be honest, I don't regret it. It made me appreciate him more.

Listen, your marriage is between you and you. I just know that *I* could never do it. I'm *way* too jealous. It's hard work, but we just wake up and choose each other every day.

God, I miss it. That new relationship feeling. Is it as fun as I remember?

It's not possible to love more than one person. Not, like, *really*. I mean, sure, I love my friends, and I love my kids, and I love my husband. But that's not the same thing.

Sorry but isn't it a little naive to, like, "not believe in ownership"? It sounds like something one of Ben's students would say! And anyway, is it so wrong to want to feel owned? We all want to belong to someone.

I dated a woman once in college and I never knew I had so many feelings. So. Much. Communication. Kill me. We're all crazy.

Aren't you, I don't know, a little afraid that you might be gay? I know the Kinsey scale says everyone is a little bit gay, but what if you realize you're gay *now?* In your *thirties?*

Obviously Ben isn't *really* interested in men. He's just doing whatever you want. He'd do anything for you. He loves you *so much.*

Frances was making a risotto. Ben was sitting at the kitchen table flipping through the newest issue of *Bon Appétit*, which arrived in their mailbox that morning. They still subscribed to it and were unsure whether they should feel guilty about doing so.

Frances, rummaging in the miscellaneous drawer for a wine bottle opener, said, "Do you ever imagine me dead?"

Ben closed the magazine calmly and pretended to think. He said, "Hm. Only when I masturbate."

The cork came out with a loud pop. "Ben, what the fuck!" she said, tilting the bottle of pinot grigio over the Le Creuset, smothering the toasting rice.

"I have to kill you off before I sleep with all those naked women. It doesn't feel fair otherwise."

"Ben," she said, turning to look at him.

"Frances," he said seriously.

She narrowed her eyes at him, smirking. She wiggled the wine bottle in the air and asked, "Want some of this?"

"Sure," he said, and got up to take two wineglasses from the cabinet.

Frances poured the wine. They clinked their glasses together. She added a ladleful of warm stock to the pot.

"Franny. Why are you asking me if I ever imagine you dead?" Ben asked, standing just behind her, letting himself linger in the buttery scent of the softened onions. He ran a hand through her hair and then down her back.

She paused for a moment and then shrugged.

"Because of your great-aunt?"

"What?" Frances spluttered. "No!" Her great-aunt Frances had been killed when her mother was only a child. Murdered, most likely because of the extramarital affair she'd been having, though her case remained unsolved. When she was younger, Frances had found her name old-fashioned and morbid; now she cherished it, imagining that it conferred upon her some kind of preternatural romanticism, an inability to be hemmed in by societal constraints, a willingness to die for love.

"Because, to be clear, I'm not going to kill you for sleeping around."

"That's such a fucked-up thing to say."

"I thought that's what you were getting at."

"No, it's just... I imagined your funeral the other day."

"Oh, comforting."

She turned to face him. "That's not weird. People imagine funerals."

He shrugged.

"Haven't you thought about mine?" she pushed.

"Sure. I've thought about it," Ben said, and took a sip of wine.

"Well, how do you see yourself at it? I'm just curious. Do you imagine yourself in a suit in the front row? About to get up and make everyone weep with, like, a perfect eulogy about me? Or do you think you'll be a mess? And everyone is worried about you because maybe you showed up in your sweatpants or something."

"Honestly, I don't think I'll be there. Unless I'm haunting you. Statistically, men die younger."

"That's not fair," she said, surprised to feel the quaver at the back of her throat. "You don't get to claim dying first, just because you're a man."

"But it's, like, the only privilege men have."

When she glared at him, he said, "Fine. If I'm there in the flesh, I'll probably be in my boxers, with Dorito dust all over my fingers, and I'll cause a whole scene because I'll run up to your casket and wail into it and leave big orange fingerprints all over your dead body." He took a long drink of wine. "You should probably just let me go first."

Frances wiped at her eyes and took another sip of wine, too. She smiled and said, "You know. You don't have to kill me off in order to sleep with a bunch of hot women in your imagination, either. That's the whole point of this whole thing."

Ben shrugged, kissed her on the top of her head, and grabbed a wooden spoon to give the risotto a stir. "I know. It just feels wrong."

She took the spoon from him and said, "I'd rather be alive."

One morning, they woke up to find that they had connected on their app with a couple—a man and a woman named Adam and Celeste, who identified themselves as polyamorous and both bisexual. "We're very much in love and will prioritize our primary partnership. We are looking for another man and another woman in a similar situation to connect with sexually and emotionally," their profile said. They appeared to be in their mid-thirties, a bit crunchier than Ben and Frances. Adam was white with shoulder-length dirty-blond hair slightly wilder than Ben's. He had a neck tattoo of a butterfly and an eyebrow piercing. His flannel shirt partially concealed a chest tattoo. Celeste was racially ambiguous. Her skin was slightly darker than Adam's and was freckled across her nose and cheekbones. She wore no makeup, and her long hair was wavy and untamed, falling over her linen dress. Both were lovely, Frances thought, but her eyes were drawn to Adam in the photo. This made her feel complicated, sitting next to Ben. She felt a pulse of attraction, imagining her fingers running down the lines of the tattoo, discovering its final shape.

"What do you think?" she asked.

"I mean . . . they sound like us. It sounds like what we're doing, right?"

"Sort of. Yeah. I mean, I hadn't really thought of this as, like, polyamory. It feels a little"—Frances gave a grimace and a fake shiver—"mushy."

"Ha. Yeah, I know what you mean. Like, I don't want to go out and *hold hands* with two other people at an outdoor concert."

"Gross."

"But also...I think that's a pretty reductive picture of polyamory. Because we *do* want to try dating another person or another couple together. And we *do* want to like them. And get to know them. And not just, like, *wife swap*. Or *swing*."

"Grosssss."

"Yeah. I mean, those just feel pretty cold. And pretty hetero."

"Are you...are you definitely open to a guy?" Frances felt herself hoping.

Ben put on his professorial face, the one he affected whenever he had been thinking hard about something and had decided it was finally ready to voice. "Yeah. It's been on my mind since you mentioned seeing a couple. I feel like...honestly, I feel like you can't know what you like until you really try it. And whatever I fucked around with as a kid doesn't really count. I think if we're going to do this, we should really do it. Like, really try new things and experiences together."

Frances was still surprised, sometimes, when Ben was exactly who she hoped he was. She felt lucky, undeserving. And she also loved getting what she wanted. "So...group sex. A foursome is group sex, right?"

"I think so. Yeah. Group sex."

She scooted her body closer to his in the bed, brushed her fingers along his arm. "It'll be hot to see you with another guy."

He laughed, grabbed her hand, and kissed her fingertips. "Is it weird to say that I also think it'll be hot to see you with another guy?"

Still touching his mouth, she said, "Not weird. Hotter." She set down her coffee. They fucked and forgot to message the couple until hours later.

Whenever Ben and Frances had sex, it was intimate, connective. They felt closer afterward, as though their bodies fit together more comfortably. As though their skin had become magnetic. But whether their sex had ever been "private" was up for debate. When Ben kissed Frances, his mouth was on Frances's mouth. But he was also kissing a version of Frances who existed only in his memory, a little less lined, a little rounder in the face, as she was when he met her. When Frances ran her hands down Ben's back, she was touching Ben. But she was also touching a Ben who existed only in her imagination, a little more confident, a little more dominant, a little less inhibited. They fucked each other, but they also fucked a thousand other versions of each other who came and went unbidden. And sometimes, when they fucked each other, they were also fucking other people: old boyfriends, old girlfriends, their hot yoga instructor, the guy from that show, the people from that porn that once got them off, an accidental friend who might walk in. In the room, they were alone. They worked to make each other come in the ways that only they knew exactly how to do. But it happened all at once, every time: The doors burst open. Behind their closed eyes, they were suddenly surrounded by bodies, watching, touching, being touched; being just a bit prettier, a bit sexier, a bit dirtier than the real Ben or Frances. It was hot, having group sex. They did it over and over again. And then they came and the other people vanished. Their counterparts coalesced, once again, into one self, one body, a little older and a little worse and infinitely more lovable. They looked at each other, their faces sweaty and wrinkled around the eyes where those younger selves once laughed, and they saw each other. They pulled together, tight.

They met Adam and Celeste for drinks after a week of texting.

"Do I look okay?" Frances asked as they got out of the car. She was wearing a skirt and Doc Martens, a look that she hoped would read a bit queer and not as a grown woman trying to look young.

"You look perfect. Do I look okay?"

Ben looked, as he always did to Frances, unacceptably better than her. In his glasses and sweater, he reminded Frances of those Oscar Isaac thirst traps in *Scenes from a Marriage*. Her heart swelled with pride and contracted with envy. She grabbed his hand, and they walked in together.

They had agreed that, most likely, nothing would happen between the four of them that night. They wanted to get to know them first. They wanted to establish healthy, clear boundaries. Tonight, they would just get a feel for them. That was the plan.

But they were perfect. More magnetic than their photos and exuding an affection for one another that had the strange effect of enveloping Ben and Frances, too. Celeste was a music teacher and waxed poetic about her students and her favorite classical pieces. Adam, it turned out, was the co-owner of a brewery where Ben and Frances, in their mid-twenties, had played weekly trivia with their friends Gina and Bernard. To all four of them, this felt—improbably and after several cocktails—like fate. "We must have met you before!" Ben said, twice.

When Adam and Celeste walked up to the bar to pay their tab, Ben turned to Frances and asked, "Do you think they like us?"

Frances, flushed and giddy, said, "Totally. We've been a delight!"

"We *are* a delight!" Ben agreed.

"They're talking about us," Frances whispered into his ear, looking over at the bar, where Adam and Celeste were bent low over the check.

"Checking in? About tonight?" Ben speculated.

"Probably."

"Well...what do you think?" he asked, his eyes bright. She had seen this look before: It was the same one he had when they left their number for Lily.

"I'm game if you're game. I feel comfortable with them," she said.

Ben nodded frantically.

When they returned to the table, Celeste said, "So...no pressure, but do you want to come over for another drink at ours?"

They barely made it through the door before Celeste ran her fingers through Frances's hair and kissed her. "Is this okay?" she asked. Frances nodded, her words lost in the sudden, overwhelming physicality of her own body. A brief intrusive thought: *Will Ben be okay kissing Adam?* When she imagined having sex with the two of them, she thought that she would kiss Adam first. It was both deeply exciting and pragmatic to her. Ben would feel more comfortable starting with Celeste. But now, with Celeste's mouth on hers, watching Ben grab the back of Adam's neck, pragmatism felt ridiculous. She might have laughed if everything hadn't felt so urgent, so immediate, so encompassing.

When they talked about it afterward—all four of them, still naked, trying to remember who did what when, how they ended up in bed, and then on the floor—they found that they had no idea how any of it happened. It felt, to Frances, like dissolving into a feeling and then watching herself be reassembled again, sweatier and more content.

The sky was a light gray-purple when Frances and Ben got home. They crawled into bed together. Before they fell asleep, they had sex again, their bodies still brightly alive.

A Few Questions and Helpful Comments Their Friends Have About Adam and Celeste

How'd it happen anyway? Were you just trying to spice things up and it got...I don't know...out of hand? No judgment! We don't have sex nearly as much as we used to, either.

Okay, help me out. If you like them, and they like you, and nothing ever goes wrong, and you fall in love, what happens? Are you going to, like, move in together? Raise kids together? Like...what's the *goal?*

A foursome just feels like a lot of legs.

But, Frances, how pretty *is* Celeste? I feel like I would want her to be uglier than me so that I wouldn't have to worry about it. Like, worry that her boobs are bigger or that she's skinnier or whatever. I'd want to be the hot one. Although I guess at the same time, I want her to be super hot, since we're having sex. I don't know. Are you attracted to Celeste, like actually, or do you just wish that you looked like her?

Is it weird, to see your partner with someone else? I feel like it could be sort of hot.

What kind of protection are you using? Condoms? What about, like, herpes? It's just that it seems like they're the kind of people who have sex with a *lot* of other people.

Could you two stop touching each other? We get it. You've had some kind of sexual awakening.

So were you *always* bisexual and just didn't realize it? Or is it something you're just kind of...trying out? Like a kink?

I hope this isn't weird to say, but I haven't seen you this happy in a long time, Franny. It's nice.

After they had been sleeping together, the four of them, for about a month, Celeste texted Frances and asked if she wanted to come over to watch a movie because Adam was out of town. **Totally cool if it's not where y'all are. But we're feeling comfortable with same-gender one-on-one hookups since it's what we originally planned on.**

They had told Ben and Frances, a week or so before, that they hadn't intended on dating together. Celeste wanted to date a woman, and Adam a man. But they liked Frances and Ben, and so they adjusted their plan.

When she read the text, Frances felt herself flush. She had been dying to see Celeste one-on-one. She loved the group sex, loved how it strengthened her bond with Ben, as though they were one side of a regular couple, a singular person with shared quirks and insecurities and desires. And it was hot—hotter every time. But she found herself, once or twice, frustrated when she was pulled away from Celeste by Ben or Adam. She had become desperate to figure Celeste out: to learn exactly how she liked Frances to touch her, and where and when.

When she showed the text to Ben, she downplayed her desire, worried that he wouldn't be willing to cross this particular boundary. But Ben only shrugged and said, "Hm. Kind of weird, don't you think?"

"What do you mean?"

"I don't know. It's not risky to go one-on-one with the same gender, but it is risky to go one-on-one with the opposite gender? It's a little bi-phobic, right? It privileges heterosexual relationships as more meaningful than queer ones."

Frances hadn't thought of it that way, but she agreed instantly. "Totally."

"Like, it's the same old thing, just in woke language about personal boundaries. The basic idea is that two women together can't be anything more than fun and sexy—because their 'real' desire will always be for men."

As he spoke, Frances found herself getting worked up. It annoyed her, suddenly, the idea that Celeste felt comfortable dating her, but not Ben, because she was somehow nonthreatening to

Celeste's primary relationship. She would be as likely to leave Ben for a woman as for a man, she thought to herself proudly.

"...And just on a personal level, I feel differently." Ben was still speaking. "Maybe I'd be jealous if you were on a date with Adam. But it wouldn't be any different than whatever jealousy I might or might not feel if you go hang out with Celeste. It's just about me feeling left out either way. And that's my problem, not yours—and definitely not, like, *our* problem. Because in the end, you would never leave me for a woman or for a man, equally."

"Right," Frances said, and leaned in to kiss him. "I was just thinking almost the exact same thing."

The first time she spent the night with Celeste, Frances was unsure of herself. When they were alone, Celeste felt like Frances's friend. They opened a bottle of wine and popped popcorn and watched *Bridget Jones's Diary*, the lights from Celeste's Christmas tree cocooning them in a reddish glow. They argued about whether Hugh Grant was sexy or gross. They pretended to swoon over Colin Firth. Frances had had dozens of the exact same night with her friend Gina, who was straight and married, with a one-year-old daughter. The more comfortable Frances got, the more she feared that she and Celeste were kidding themselves, that they were just playing queer.

But then there was the way Celeste leaned into her shoulder when she laughed. There was the way she turned her face so that her lips brushed against Frances's jawline. There was the way she traced her finger down the knobs of Frances's spine. *Bump, bump, bump.* It felt to Frances like Celeste was walking into a dark house and hitting light switches as she moved down the hallway. She felt her body buzz into bright, hot light. She pulled Celeste into her lap, spread her fingers wide around Celeste's hips, and traced her thumb back and forth across the freckles at her hip bone. She slid her hands up Celeste's shirt and experienced something like awe when her nipples hardened against her fingertips, amazed that something her body did could change the very structure of another woman's body.

Her heart stopped, briefly, when Celeste pulled away from her. Her chest and stomach, which were hot and sweaty, now seemed cold and wet, exposed to the air. "Just a sec," Celeste whispered. She went to her bedroom and came back with a small blue vibrator.

"Is this okay?" she asked.

"Oh," Frances said.

"It's not you," Celeste said quickly. "It's just a lot easier for me to come this way. Alone, too."

"I want it to be good for you," Frances said, unsure. Celeste smiled, clicked to the setting she wanted, and handed the vibrator to Frances.

"Stay here," Celeste said as she leaned back into Frances and pushed Frances's hand down between her thighs. She held it with her own, pressing it hard. Frances felt Celeste relax and loosen in her arms. *This is what Celeste looks like when she's alone*, Frances realized. She felt like a ghost, watching something that ought to be private. It occurred to her that this was a good feeling. She wondered if Adam had ever seen Celeste like this. The thought lit her up again, and she grabbed Celeste's other hand and bit into the soft curve between her thumb and forefinger, sucked it like an orange slice. When Celeste turned around and went down on Frances, she came almost immediately.

Afterward, she asked, "Do you use that with Adam, too?"

Celeste let out a small laugh. "Yeah, I do now. It's pretty easy to use during sex. I have another one that's specifically for partner play."

"I've never used a vibrator with Ben. Honestly, I don't really use one at all. They're too strong or something. I don't know. I'm a little vanilla, I think."

"So vanilla you're having regular group sex," Celeste said, and Frances laughed. "I didn't use it with Adam for a long time, though. He was weird and jealous about it at first, like he wanted to prove he could be better. It sucked. It just meant I had to fake it to have a good time with him. He came around, obviously. It doesn't matter how you come; it's just nice to do it together."

"Yeah," Frances said. "I agree." But inwardly, she felt herself flinch. Had Celeste been pretending when they'd had sex before, in a group? Frances had faked plenty of orgasms in her life, even sometimes with Ben, though the shame she felt afterward usually eclipsed any of the performance's convenience. Would she be able to recognize a fake orgasm, even if Ben or Adam couldn't? The idea that she might have missed something so basic unsettled her.

Her discomfort must have colored her face because Celeste asked, "You okay?"

"Do you...can you *only* come with the vibrator? Because I thought..."

"Oh god," Celeste said. "Sorry! I shouldn't have mentioned faking it. No, I don't *need* it. It just helps sometimes. Especially if I'm feeling nervous."

"I make you nervous?"

Celeste smiled. "In a good way." She kissed Frances, more tenderly than usual, and touched her cheek. "Wow," she said. "That was way easier to explain to you for some reason."

A List of Frances's Worries

1. That her friends no longer believe she has the perfect marriage.
2. That she no longer has the perfect marriage.
3. That Celeste feels like what they are doing isn't sex but foreplay.
4. That maybe she isn't attracted to Celeste but only wants to look like her.
5. That she might not ever be able to untangle the difference between being attracted to women and wanting to look like them.
6. That when her mother died, she lost the only experience of total, full, unhesitating love she would ever be granted.
7. That she might always be doomed to love people more than they love her.
8. That, by wanting to be loved by other people, she might be less lovable to Ben.
9. That she might end up alone.
10. That she might, currently, be the happiest she has been in a long time.

Ben had been preparing, for the last three weeks, to get fucked in the ass.

He and Adam had been on one solo date. They drank beer and played pool at Adam's brewery and, eventually, talked about their past experiences with men. Ben's were confined to his childhood—group masturbation with other boys, the occasional shameful blow job, and once, when he was fourteen, a painful attempt at anal sex. Adam did these things at around the same age, but then, in his mid-twenties, he became curious about his sexuality and had, for about nine months, been the secondary partner to a married gay man ten years his senior. They talked about shame and confusion and desire until, after he had shut down the bar, Adam pushed Ben backward into the pool table and blew him. "I like you," he had said to Ben. "I like you a lot."

A List of Ben's Worries

1. That he might be bisexual.
2. That, by being bisexual, he might be less attractive to Frances.
3. That he might not be bisexual.
4. That, by not being bisexual, he might be less attractive to Frances.
5. That he is boring.
6. That, at some point, Adam and Celeste will realize that he is merely an uninteresting person who is married to an interesting person.
7. That, when Frances also realizes he is an uninteresting person, he will be left behind.
8. That he might end up alone.
9. That Frances might, currently, be the happiest she has been in a long time.

* * *

When he got home from the brewery, flushed and exposed, Ben got into bed next to a sleeping Frances. He pulled up Amazon on his phone and ordered the anal training kit that Adam recommended.

To his surprise, he liked it, liked the feeling of being full, liked the depth of a prostate orgasm. He wondered if that was what it felt like for Frances when she came when he was inside her.

Try this next, Adam texted him. It was a link to a vibrating butt plug. **I like to use this with Celeste too**.

Ben had never really liked taking the dominant role in the bedroom with Frances. It felt unnatural to him. In their regular life, Ben found pleasure in succumbing to Frances's whims, to letting her be in charge. He liked being at Frances's mercy. And so, in some ways, lying face down on their bed while she pushed a vibrating butt plug into his asshole felt perfectly comfortable, perfectly right—like something he had been wanting to do without knowing it.

"Is this okay?" she kept asking as she pushed deeper into him. He felt that he ought to be put off by her timidity, but he wasn't. He liked saying, "Yes, it's good." He liked being the one to determine whether or not it was okay and good, even as he lay ostensibly powerless. He liked her hand on his back, pressing down softly. He liked it when she leaned forward and lightly kissed his shoulder with the final push. He was not sure whether his pleasure came from the almost motherly way she was attending to him or from the sense that she might violently rip him open. He didn't really care.

The next time the four of them had sex, he found himself drawn to Adam, wanting to be grabbed by him, to be pushed face down on the bed by him, to be crushed. But when Adam turned around and asked Ben to fuck him, Ben lost his erection. He wasn't sure why, and though Adam redirected him kindly and with care, he was ashamed. He came that night with Frances on top of him, his eyes on her face the whole time.

He still wanted Adam. But he found himself making excuses not to get together with him alone. Adam didn't push it.

Upon Reflection, Their Friends Have a Few More Thoughts

Actually, I think it's really smart of you and Ben, getting it all out of your system before you start having kids. You won't have time for stuff like this after. Trust me.

What if Frances gets pregnant? I mean, won't you always be worried it isn't really yours?

You *will* stop seeing them—and anyone else—when you start trying to get pregnant, right? It's a sacred time for the two of you. It really feels special.

How could Ben *possibly* be okay with someone else having sex with you when you're *pregnant?!* Aren't you worried you'll get an STI? That's, like, really, really bad for the baby.

You guys seem so happy right now, though. And you're still young, you've got a few more years to waste. No problem with just having fun for a while. Kids can wait. The whole thirty-five thing is really a myth!

What are you going to tell your kids? Kids see everything. You can't keep an open marriage hidden from them. What if they tell your parents? Kids will say *anything!*

I don't know. It takes a village, right? Trust me! I could have used a few extra sets of hands.

It's just that this stuff can be really confusing and damaging for kids. I've seen it. We have some kids like that at school.

You know, historically, children reared collectively were more likely to survive. In prehistoric societies, babies were breastfed by multiple women. Is there a filter on your app to find lactating women? Ha!

Ben began to feel like the odd one out. Since the holidays, he'd barely seen Celeste. Frances got together with her while he was teaching his evening class, or on nights that he had plans with Max—relaxing nights that felt like the only ones that weren't focused on sex and dating. It seemed to Ben sometimes that Frances was in an intimate relationship with her phone. Rather than plugging it in by the bed when she got home, or tossing it somewhere and forgetting it, Frances began to keep it on her in the house. In the pocket of her sweatpants or within eyesight, on whatever table was closest to her. When it vibrated, her body vibrated with it. Ben felt he had become just another human body, warm in the night. He tried to be okay with it. He didn't want to spoil anything for her. He could tell that her phone was making her happy.

Sometimes, when Frances opened the phone and found that little word on her home screen—Celeste—she closed it immediately, not wanting the moment to be over. She wondered for a few minutes what the text would say. She tried to keep from smiling.

In spite of herself, and despite the fact that such a text would be in patently poor taste, she couldn't help herself from thinking: *Tell me you love me, tell me you love me, tell me you love me.* It felt subversive—more subversive, at this point, than the sex itself. Celeste never did say it, though sometimes, Frances thought, she hinted at it. When she texted, I can still feel you on my skin, for instance. Or, I was thinking about last night all day. One of my students asked me if I was smiling so much because I had a crush <3. Texts of this sort could buoy Frances for days at a time.

Did she love Celeste? She wasn't sure. She knew that one evening, when she was in bed with Celeste after they'd both come, she was bursting with the word. She was facing Celeste, their heads on one pillow, her leg draped over Celeste's hip, her wet thighs still pressed hard into her skin. The word was taking up all the air space in her lungs, and she felt like she might suffocate from wanting to say: I love looking at you. I love the way that curl sticks to your forehead when you sweat. I love the way your hair feels in my hand. I love the acne scars on your back, a little constellation. I love the way your nipples get hard in my mouth. I love the softness of your stomach. I love the first time I reach my hand up your skirt and feel how wet you are. I love the way you taste. I actually, unironically, think you might be the most beautiful woman in the world.

Instead, she breathed, hard and fast and eager.

Was this how Aunt Frances felt, before she was killed? Did she die, feeling like she was finally living?

She knew all the jokes about lesbians—What does a lesbian bring on a second date? A U-Haul. Ha ha—and she began to wonder if women fell in love more easily than men. Or were women just more likely to mistake infatuation for love?

"It's called limerence," Ben told her one night when she couldn't hold it in any longer. They'd made fish tacos for dinner and, at the last minute, decided to have margaritas. It was surprisingly temperate for a January evening, so they ate on their back porch, wrapped in their coats. Frances was at the mercy of the warming air, the sour-sweet alcohol, the bright tang of a lime. Her second drink had the effect of reminding her not only of how much she wanted to touch Celeste's body, but also of how much she trusted Ben. He understood her, she thought, and could help her.

"Limerence?" she asked, savoring the lilting syllables. It was a word that sounded like salt on a rim, like sparkles on the hem of a dress. She didn't know what it meant, but she knew instantly that it was what she felt for Celeste.

"Yeah," Ben said, sitting up straight and beaming that way he did when he knew something that Frances didn't. "I read about it in that book on polyamory and attachment styles. I think I left it out for you."

"Oh right!" Frances said, unsure if this was one of the books she had pretended to have read. "Remind me."

"It's that really intense feeling you get at the beginning of a relationship, when all you can think about is the other person. It can feel like love—or like romantic love anyway—but it's more obsessive. You're fixated on the other person and your feelings for them, and all you want is for them to reciprocate. It's really normal. Nothing to, like, worry about." He was saying this to Frances, but also to himself. He had been telling himself not to worry a lot these days. He let the words play on repeat in his head.

"So it's basically just a crush?" Frances asked, disappointed.

"Yeah, but they didn't want to make you feel like a teenager, so they invented a new word."

"Honeymoon phase?"

"They also didn't want to be heteronormative." Ben crossed the porch and ran his hand through her hair. "Don't worry," he said quietly. "It's intense, but it'll be over soon." And it was worth it, he thought, to see her this happy again. This energetic. *It will be over soon*, he repeated to himself.

She began to grieve almost immediately.

The more she thought about it, the more she realized that, of course, she was not in love with Celeste. Celeste really pissed her off. She reminded herself of this often. Celeste was nitpicky and defensive. She corrected Adam all the time, in front of everyone. She appeared to be jealous of Frances when the four of them had sex together, breaking in when Frances was with Adam. She believed in astrology. She thought cilantro tasted like soap, or pretended to think cilantro tasted like soap in order to have a thing. She talked about people's auras. She was a dog person. She kept her house at a sweltering 75 degrees.

But the thing is: She kept her house at a sweltering 75 degrees because she liked to be nearly naked at home, liked to appreciate the difference between her couch's soft velvet and her dog's scraggly fur on her legs, liked to feel the vibrations of her guitar against her belly, the hum of the earth as it carried her slowly through space.

Frances knew these things, and knowing these things made it impossible for her to stop thinking about Celeste. In the time it took Celeste to type out a text, Frances could imagine their entire life together at home in their bras and panties. A future contained in three little dots.

Perhaps it didn't matter whether she loved Celeste. What mattered was that feeling—amorphous and tender, sororal and sexual—of being held by her. She lived in it, fully, for the next two months, trying to savor, and not to define, the warmth of eating dinner with Celeste in her kitchen, of sharing gossip about their friends with Celeste's hand on her inner thigh, of watching TV naked under a blanket together, Celeste's head on Frances's shoulder. A happiness that couldn't be anything but good, no matter what anyone else thought.

Two weeks passed in which there was little to no contact between the four of them; all but Frances were busy with work. No one seemed as willing to spend time on one another as they once were—as Frances still was. She sat at home and hoped her anxiety would transform into the almost-manic, obsessive state from which she produced her best ghostwriting.

Instead, she spent two weeks sending careful, casual texts to Celeste every other day or so, to remind Celeste that she existed. Sometimes they were links to songs she was listening to, which she thought would make her seem interesting and which, if closely considered, contained hidden hints of longing. Sometimes the texts said things like, How did your meeting go? Sometimes they were just emojis—hearts, a sun hat with a bright green ribbon around it. One day, in a fit of daring and melodrama, she sent a snippet from a letter that Virginia Woolf wrote to her lover, Vita Sackville-West, in 1927: "I like your energy. I love your legs. I long to see you." Frances received perfunctory responses that were perfectly amicable, and perfectly devastating.

She worried that she had done something wrong, that she had come on too strong for Celeste. She had been told hundreds of times in her life that she was an "intense person," and indeed she thrived on emotional brinks. *Not everyone is like this*, she reminded herself. Celeste savored her independence more than Frances did. Frances savored the feeling that her heart was between someone else's teeth.

"I'm sure it's nothing," Ben said. "She's busy at work, I bet."

On a Saturday morning in mid-March, Frances woke up to a text: Free for a coffee? Her heart began to race. Yes, she responded, and though she had typed the word, she felt out of breath, as though she had screamed it. She blinked and refocused her eyes. The text was from Adam, not from Celeste. Something shifted in her belly.

She left Ben on their green velvet sectional, no longer quite new, to have his coffee alone. Ben didn't mind the solitude. He definitely didn't. He rarely had the house to himself, since Frances so often worked from home. He settled in to enjoy his book. He read a sentence, took a sip of coffee. He read the same sentence again, and then again. He stood, ran his fingers through his hair.

He liked to be alone in the mornings, liked to stretch out across the couch, liked to put on whatever music he wanted. He definitely liked this. He put his half-empty coffee cup back in the kitchen, blaming the caffeine for his inability to concentrate. Eventually, he gave up and went to the grocery store.

Frances and Adam got out of their cars at the same time.

"Hi!" she said, walking up confidently to hide her nerves.

Though she was not sure she wanted to, Frances kissed him quickly on the mouth.

They each ordered a large black coffee at the counter. Adam pulled out his credit card and insisted on paying. Though it was only a $2 cup, Frances felt uncomfortable letting him, though she couldn't articulate why, even to herself.

Once they'd settled into a quiet table in the corner of the coffee shop and completed their requisite pleasantries, Adam said, "Frances, I don't know how to start."

A hot wave of something rolled through her body. "Just say it," she said.

"I . . . well, I guess I want to say . . . I don't know . . ."

To Frances's surprise, Adam's eyes filled with tears. He saw her notice and wiped them. She felt a burst of affection for him, this sweet man. She remembered the first time she saw him, on the app. Suddenly, she longed, as she did then, to reach out to him, to run her hands along the lines of his tattoos. She wished she had made more time for him as an individual.

"Adam," she said, keeping her hands in her lap. "It's okay. Whatever it is, it's okay." She had no idea if this was true, but she couldn't keep from saying it. She wanted to enfold him in promises.

"I need to ask you . . ." He wiped his face again and then

let out a loud, surprising growl of frustration. "Sorry. This is embarrassing."

"It's not."

"It is. I... I'm here because... I need to ask you to stop. To stop seeing Celeste. Please." He said this to his coffee cup and then picked it up, took a long drink.

"I don't... what do you mean, stop?" Frances knew what he meant; but if she pretended that she didn't, perhaps he wouldn't be able to articulate what he wanted her to do, and she wouldn't have to do it.

"It's... affecting us. Her seeing you. I feel... well, we've been fighting. Please. She knows I'm here talking to you. She's... well, she agrees with me. It's become too complicated. She's... I don't know how to... She's more emotionally invested in you than she wanted to be. She's always had a hard time separating sex from... well, you know."

From love, Frances thought. She allowed herself to think it, just for a second. *She loves me. The whole time she has loved me.*

"Wait," she said, willing her mind to catch up. Willing her body to sit still. "Are you breaking up with me? For Celeste?"

"I think it's more... I think we need to focus our energies on just each other for a while." Adam ran his hand through his hair. "I'm sorry this is so weird. We were up all night. She said she couldn't do it, not yet. See you, I mean."

"When can I see her?" The pull felt so strong suddenly. If she could only see her, she thought, Celeste would change her mind.

Adam looked alarmed. He looked into her eyes for the first time all morning. "I don't know," he said. "I think... I think I'm asking you not to see her."

"Do I have a choice?" she asked, her heart beginning to fall, her mind beginning to catch up.

Adam hesitated. "Yeah," he said. "But please."

For a second, she felt angry. She had no power. Adam knew she had no power. Her choices didn't matter at all. She never got to keep the things that kept her alive. To her horror, she felt her own eyes fill up with tears. She felt her hand shake. Her anger dissipated as quickly as it appeared. She was suddenly afraid she would crumble.

"Okay," she said, getting up, leaving her full cup of coffee on the table. She began to leave, but then turned around. "It's your responsibility to tell Ben. I'm not doing it."

Ben received a text from Frances: Please don't talk to me when I get home. As he was reading it, Adam called him. He walked through the produce section, weighing his options, as Adam explained. He felt, as he selected a bunch of bananas—not too ripe and not too green—a wave of relief wash over him. The feeling surprised him—and then it didn't. He wouldn't have to be the one who called off the relationship. He could remain, in Frances's eyes, the open-minded, non-jealous husband he wanted her to have. He feigned sadness and disappointment for a while and then hung up the phone. He paid for his purchases.

Without looking around, Frances went straight to the bedroom when she got home. She sat down in front of her mirror and watched her face contort and redden. She got a text. Celeste. Her heart pulsed. She put her phone down. She waited. She picked it up and opened the text. Im sorry. This is hard for me too. It made her sad. It made her angry. She wanted to respond, I am the one who this is hard for! Me! But she didn't have the resolve. She began to cry. She wanted more: more time, more Celeste. She spun through hundreds of ways that she might have been able to hold on to these things—had she behaved differently, said something differently, lived differently. Ghostly versions of Celeste's body brushed up against hers in her grief. She would never touch Celeste again.

I am heartbroken, Frances thought. These words actually rolled through her head. She let them sit in her mouth, unsaid. She savored their taste. *I am heartbroken. I am five years married and I am heartbroken.* She looked at her phone, opened her contacts, and scrolled down to M♥M. A heart emoji between two M's, the way her mom had written her name on the notes in Frances's lunchbox, the letters she sent to Frances at college. The longing that she felt to tap on that small pink heart, to press her phone to her ear, to hear her mom's voice on the other side—that longing eclipsed every other feeling in her body, and she doubled over in big, thick sobs that stopped her breath in her throat.

When her tears finally began to slow, she lifted the phone in one hand and took a picture of herself in the mirror. She was not exactly sure why she did this, except that she wanted some kind of evidence. Proof that this thing had happened to her. Proof that she was a ruined, messy, brokenhearted person who maybe fell in love with the wrong person and who hadn't, yet, died. "You're still alive," she said quietly to her reflection. "You're more alive." Then she got in bed.

When Ben brought a bouquet of lilies and bottle of wine home from his grocery run, she hugged him hard around the neck and sobbed, again, into his shoulder. He kissed her on the top of the head, and she folded herself into Ben's steady, warm body. He exhaled, and with Frances's face safely pressed into his chest, he allowed a shameful smile to creep across his face. It was just the two of them. He settled in.

The Angel Gabriel Aesthetic

MAX'S FEET WERE IN a pair of compression socks, which were in a pair of running shoes, which were tied just a little too tight. Max liked his shoes to be snug, the arches of his feet to be pressed securely against the cushioning insole. The outsoles of his shoes were hitting the ground alternately. Heel to toe, heel to toe. He knew that he ought to try to hit the ground toe first. It would take the pressure off his knees and shins. He worried about these things more now that he was in his thirties. Shin splints. IT band issues. He wanted to stay as he was—healthy, able-bodied, alive—for as long as possible. But that wasn't how he'd learned to run as a child, and he had never been able to make his feet do it. He had stopped trying to change his technique by now. He didn't like to be reminded of the fact that his body could revolt against him, that his muscles could jump and not be caught.

It was unseasonably chilly, especially in the woods. Max's back was sweating but his fingers were stiff with cold. The sun filtered through the trees and hit his skin in polka dots of momentary warmth. It was quiet outside. And Max was quiet. His breathing was measured. His pace was consistent, even when he had to navigate around puddles and rocks. He didn't listen to music, and he held up his hand silently as he passed the occasional hiker.

Inside his head, though, it was loud. In there, Max was replaying a conversation he'd had with Ben the night before.

Yesterday, Ben had met Max in his office and suggested that they grab a beer at the graduate student bar across from campus. This wasn't entirely unexpected. On Thursdays, they both taught seminars that ended at roughly half past five. Actually, Max had only gone to his office in hopes that Ben might meet him there. He'd packed his satchel with the papers he needed to bring home before heading to class. Why had he done that? he wondered now. Packed his papers in advance. As though he wasn't going to go back and wait for Ben, when he always did.

It had become a favorite tradition of his, albeit an unnamed one. Maybe that was why it felt so special. As he and his friends entered their late twenties, it went out of fashion to stop by someone's apartment or call with a last-minute invitation. It was expected, now, that plans would be made two weeks in advance. That someone would play host and that said host would put serious effort into cleaning the house first. Lockdown had only intensified this trend. Whenever Ben dropped by his office and asked him if he had time for a drink or maybe to catch a movie while his wife, Frances, was at her book club, Max felt... something. What was it? he wondered as he ran. Young? No, that wasn't exactly a good feeling for Max. It was a privilege to make it past nineteen.

To worry about IT band issues and shin splints. Perhaps it was something like feeling worn-in. Like favorite shoes, something to throw on easily, without worry or discomfort. It was intimate, to inhabit a space with someone outside of scheduled time.

Ben and Max had walked together across the quad, watching the sun descend, and had talked about nothing.

Once they'd sat down with pints in the booth where Ben had written most of his dissertation before Max knew him, Ben let a grin take over his face. "I've been wanting to tell you for so long. You're gonna love this."

Max had prepared himself. Ben and Frances had been a bit elusive lately. He and Daniel had wondered if Frances might be pregnant. How silly, he thought now, his cheeks growing a shade warmer in the cool breeze. He'd been so excited to receive the news. Like he himself was going to be a father, or an uncle.

But instead, Ben, looking like a teenage boy, had said, "Frances and I are dating. Well, I mean. I don't really know how to say it. We're still trying to figure out what we're really doing. Language-wise, I mean. Sorry, I'm rambling. I mean, we opened up our marriage! Or we're trying polyamory, or whatever." He'd taken a big slug of beer, all proud.

Maybe it was the discrepancy between Max's expectations and the reality of the garbled news, but for some reason, Max had felt his heart sink. And then it had begun to pound, almost like it did whenever he had to call his father. The effect had been unsettling.

"You're gonna love this," Ben had said. As though, because Max was gay, he was into non-monogamy. Or into gossip. Running, he let a righteous anger rise up in his chest and, in his mind, informed Ben, in a measured way, that it was all fine and good for him and Frances to sleep around; they were a white, straight-passing couple. But if he were to do it, he'd be a stereotype. Sex-obsessed, irresponsible, unclean. The way his father thought he was. In his head, he made the slew of confident, clear, and convincing points to Ben that had eluded him the night before. He won the argument, kept Ben from fucking up his marriage and his life, and went home to his own spouse, his Daniel, who loved him and only him.

Max told himself that he felt better now. He had been angry, and he had every right to be. He'd explain his feelings to Ben tomorrow when they grabbed their usual coffee before Max's office hours and Ben's 101 class.

A woman whom he saw regularly on the trail passed him. She was pushing an enormous empty stroller in front of her. Max used to wonder sadly about this all the time until, one day, he and Daniel had passed her as they were hiking. They'd stopped to chat, and Daniel had asked about the stroller. Max had wanted to melt into the ground. You didn't ask about people's losses. But the woman had laughed and said her son had outgrown it but that pushing him during the first year or so of his life had given her Michelle Obama arms. Max waved to her, mouthed an awkward hello, and kept running.

Daniel would have stopped to talk to her. Daniel got along easily with strangers. Everyone liked him.

Last night, when Max had returned home from drinks with Ben, he hadn't felt confident the way he had in his imagined, alternate history. He had felt nervous. He'd passed the kitchen and seen that Daniel had his AirPods in and was making tteokbokki, Max's childhood favorite, a recipe of his maternal grandmother's. The sight had made his heart clench tighter. Daniel always cooked for him, even if it was too late for dinner. It relaxed him after his long, stressful workdays.

Frances liked to cook, too. She and Daniel shared recipes, sometimes took cooking classes together and prepared multi-course dinners for him and Ben. Max had always thought that Frances and Ben were happy. One of the happiest couples he'd ever known. Like him and Daniel.

Watching Daniel soaking the rice cakes in hot water, he'd found himself grabbing on to the doorframe, desperate to steady himself. He hadn't thought he was that drunk. But he had felt suddenly unmoored. He'd walked up behind Daniel, patted him on the shoulder so as not to startle him, and then pulled his body back into his, buried his face in Daniel's shoulder.

How could you ask your husband, after a year and a half of marriage, to please not decide to sleep with someone else? To please never, ever leave you alone again.

You couldn't. Or at least, Max couldn't. Instead, he'd become snarky and judgmental, telling Daniel about Ben and Frances's decision as though it were all a big joke.

"It's ridiculous!" he had yelled, mixing himself an ill-advised Negroni at their bar cart. "They're dating some *polyamorous couple*, a woman and a man. They're sleeping with them! And, like, having *brunch* with them. And Ben...Ben thinks he's, like, *bi* or something now! It's fucking absurd."

He wished he hadn't said the last part. He felt a roil of shame flow through him now as he turned onto his favorite trail. Daniel was bi, and was particularly touchy about his sexuality, which he felt Max tended to erase.

Daniel's face had reddened. "So what?" he had asked, his voice sharp. "Is that so impossible?"

"No, it's just... he just *isn't*. I know him."

"Sounds like he's trying something new," Daniel had said, taking the Negroni from Max and drinking half of it down.

"Well, why now?"

"You mean, why not three years ago, with *you?*" Max had felt himself flush. With anger or embarrassment or the deeper shame of being seen, he didn't know. He hadn't said anything. He'd reached for the Negroni but Daniel had said, "You don't need this," and finished it.

They'd looked at each other for a long time. Max had begun to grow terrified of what Daniel might say next. Terrified of how bad he would be at answering it. He hadn't wanted to be in a fight with Daniel. He wanted to be back in the kitchen, holding Daniel securely to him. He wanted to crawl out of the hole he had made without anyone ever realizing he'd fallen in. Maybe his helplessness had shown on his face, because Daniel's had slowly softened.

He'd said, "Do you think you might be so angry because you're feeling a little jealous? It's normal, I think, if you are."

Was he jealous? In the moment, to Daniel, he had denied it. "I've never felt that way about Ben," he had said. He'd meant it. But he couldn't help wondering, now that he was alone. He loved Ben. He loved feeling chosen by Ben. Perhaps he resented that Ben had chosen another man to share his most private desires with first.

Maybe—pathetic, Max told himself—he was afraid of losing him.

The image of the first boy that he lost surged into his mind, almost stopping him in his tracks. That boy was still nineteen; which is to say, he wasn't any age at all anymore. He was a picture that drew itself onto Max's brain long ago, and that occasionally flooded with color.

Crooked smile. A dimple on only one cheek. Curling blond hair. "It's the Angel Gabriel aesthetic," his friend Marie had called the look when a giddy Max had shown her his picture on Facebook, so many years ago. "No wings, though," she had added with a slight frown.

Not now, Max said to that picture of him, with a shudder. He returned to the argument he was trying to have with his friend, the one who was, for now, still with him. Still sitting upright, looking at him from across the table, not splatted on the street outside his studio apartment.

"I mean... wow," Max had said to Ben after he'd waxed poetic about the couple, who were "also bisexual" and "so experienced" and "so similar to us!" He'd finished his first pint. "It sounds like you're really into them. In a big way."

"Yeah, I know!" Ben had said, also finishing his drink. "I don't know, maybe it's fast, but it's felt good, you know, to just jump right into it. Headfirst, you know. I never do stuff like that!" Max's breath catches, remembering. Ben had looked so proud as he'd said it. He was smiling—a little sheepishly, sure. But collected. It was an expression that didn't match the words. How could you be sure you'd be able to come up again after you jumped? Gravity is unyielding.

Perhaps it was the phrasing that had bothered him, Max thought now. Perhaps he was overreacting because of those words, not what Ben had meant by them. He thought of the boy's mother's voice as it came through his flip phone. "He jumped." Max hadn't spoken to him in six months by that point, but his mother must have known who he was.

"Why not see what else is out there?" Ben had asked Max. "Not something better, I mean," he'd clarified. "I can't imagine something better than what Frances and I already have. But just… I don't know. We're getting older. We might try for a baby soon. Why not try something new while we can? Have more?"

He had once said something like that to the boy. That they could have more, be more to each other, more than friends. As if he wasn't already the most of anything Max had ever had.

No wings, though. That was the thing Max remembered most about the boy now.

Max wasn't paying attention to the trail. He was running too quickly. He hit a root at the wrong angle and he fell forward. "Fuck!" he yelled, breaking the silence around him. He felt a sharp sting on his knees and on the palm of his right hand, which he had thrown out automatically to catch himself. He felt tears spring to his eyes. It hurt, to scrape your knees. "Fuck!" he yelled again, louder.

"I get that you're worked up," Daniel had said to him at the end of last night. Max had been crying then, too. They had sat down next to one another on the couch. "Just sleep on it. That'll help."

"Yeah," Max had said. "I just…I don't know what to do about it."

Daniel had laughed. "I don't think you need to *do* anything. I don't think it's a good idea to do anything, except support your friend. It's Ben's thing. And Frances's. Not yours." He'd grabbed Max's hand then and said, "Or ours." He'd arched his neck, trying to catch Max's eye. But Max had found himself averting his gaze, embarrassed that Daniel had seen that hidden insecurity.

"I don't want anyone else," Daniel had said. "Probably not ever. Is that enough for now?"

Max had felt his eyes well up again, to his shame.

"Max? Does that sound like what you want, too?"

What Max wanted was to tether the people he loved to the security railings lining their rooftops.

But he hadn't said that. He hadn't known how. Instead, he'd nodded and said yes and let himself be led to their bedroom.

And now, he was lying sprawled in the dirt. A grown man, crying because he'd scraped his hands and knees. *Pathetic*, Max told himself. The word mixed cruelly with Daniel's *probably*. He let out a choked sound and then looked around, panicked, to see if anyone had heard it. No one. He was pretty sure no one had seen him fall, either. Max wiped his eyes. He got up and brushed the dirt off the back of his shorts. He shook loose and then began to run. Inside his head, like a metronome, Daniel's words repeated. His feet hit the ground, heel to toe, again and again, keeping time with Daniel's *for now, for now, for now.*

A Sex Fantasy as I Fall Asleep Next to My Husband

IT STARTS LIKE THIS: I open my front door and there you are. I'm wearing a dress. It's casual: gray, ribbed fabric, racerback top. My shoulders are tan, a little broader and more toned than my real shoulders. That's okay, this is just a fantasy. If my shoulders looked like that, I'd have short hair to show them off. Alexa Chung's haircut. I'm a bit thinner in the face—that makes sense, I'm grieving. The dress has a slit up one side.

I'm pregnant, of course. That's why it's so tragic. When I open the door, I place one hand on my belly, which is perfectly round. As I consider you, I run my hand up and down as though I'm protecting the baby, or using it as a talisman to protect me from you.

Oh, I say. It comes out as a breath. The rims of my eyes are red, but not puffy. I have summer freckles across my nose. My eyes would be puffy, though. I'm really sad. Depressed. Forcing myself, every day, to push through.

It's okay to imagine my eyes wouldn't be puffy. It's just a fantasy.

But it's important that you see how hard this has been for me.

And it would be hard, wouldn't it. Maybe too hard. How would I even survive? If Ben died when I was pregnant, before he got to meet the baby? Maybe there shouldn't be a baby. And I could be wearing black. In the summer, though? It could be winter.

No, there has to be a baby. I have to have a reason to be alive. If he died, I'd kill myself. I'd convince everyone I was fine so that they would leave me the fuck alone in my own goddamn house and then I'd do it. Maybe pills. No, not pills. I hate throwing up. You can die from sodium poisoning if you drink enough soy sauce. I like salt. But still, throwing up. Maybe a gun. It's easy to buy a gun. I'd tell whoever was babysitting me I had errands, something innocuous. Books I had preordered. A quick shot to the head, easy. A blip.

You would be sad if I died. You would be the one grieving. Ha.

I might not do it, if there were a baby. Ben's baby. I would love it, because it was him. And me. My baby pictures. That little girl on the beach, holding a Hi-C, her curling hair in a messy ponytail. With his brown eyes. The slight gap between his front teeth.

Maybe he could stay alive long enough to meet her. Couldn't she be there, a toddler, grabbing on to my leg as I open the door? That would give him time to have a longer death. Maybe he gets sick when the baby is a newborn. And he has time to explain to me about our investments. If he died suddenly, when I was pregnant, in a car crash or something, I'd be in shock. And I'd seem like an idiot because I'd have no idea about our money and things.

But the shock is important. Why would I say yes to you otherwise? When you show up at my door and are going to ask me what you're going to ask?

How could I watch him die and then give even one fuck about you? I would hate you.

Anyway, I would open the door and say, *Oh*, like a breath. There you are. You're sorry about Ben. About everything. You've come to realize that you didn't treat me the way I deserved to be treated. That you shouldn't have ended things the way you did. Your eyes are puffy, and your hair is a mess, and you're in a T-shirt and cutoff shorts. But that doesn't matter to me, because you're beautiful. Later, after you've said what you came to say, we'd be in bed, the pink sheets over our faces, the sunlight shining through so that we're both glowing rose. I want to cry, looking at you, the way your wild, curling hair falls against your forehead, your bare arms.

In the doorway, you say something like, Hi. Maybe you're actually wearing that white shirt, the band one, the one that cuts off right at your belly button. You say something like, I know this sounds crazy, but...

This is so stupid. It's okay to just imagine spending a day with you without all this bullshit. Maybe we just run into each other somewhere, like both of our flights were canceled and we can't get home and we decide to pretend that you never hurt me, never left me, for just tonight and no one has to die or be born because of it.

But imagine if you said to me, I know this is crazy, but I've been thinking about it, and what if we did this, together? What if you let me help you and love this baby and love you forever? What if you let me watch rom-coms and eat dinner on the couch with you for the rest of your life? Because I love you and I loved you then, even though I never said it. You don't ever have to love me as much as you loved him.

If you said that, I would move my hand from the door, take a step back, and let you in. You would cry and fall to your knees and wrap your arms around me and kiss my belly. I would get down on my knees, too, and grab your face in mine and say something like, Everyone will think we're crazy.

It usually ends like that. It's implied that we have sex, but I only imagine the sex if I'm in bed alone and feel like masturbating. Even then, I don't get very far before I just put on porn. The best part is the clothes, and the grief, and knowing I am getting what I want and doing nothing wrong.

A Little Stranger

WEEK 6: The baby is the size of a sweet pea!

HI! OKAY, I HAVEN'T kept a diary since I was about ten, but I *have* to get it out—I'm pregnant! And I've already made it one week longer than I did last time! I just have a feeling. This one's going to be it. I'm dying to tell my friends, especially Lily, but Chris thinks we shouldn't tell anyone until twelve weeks, just in case. Just thirty years ago, I wouldn't have known I was pregnant yet, he said. Pregnancy tests are so much more advanced these days. That's why there are so many miscarriages now, apparently. Not *actually* any more; we just know about them now. Don't think we're just getting our periods late or whatever. So he said I should try my hardest to not really even consider myself pregnant yet. Just to spare my own feelings, you know. Because I got really upset last time, and I could avoid that this time, like he did before.

But I had my first bout of nausea! Eee! And I went ahead and put in my notice at the bookstore. I didn't say why. But it felt good, to be able to do that. To know I can focus on just me and the baby. We're so lucky Chris can take care of us. Watching Angela trying to shelve books when she was so pregnant was awful. I just started doing all the low ones for her. Imagine if Mom had been able to stay home. Probably a lot of things would be different.

Still, I thought it might be nice to have some kind of creative outlet. Lily's always pushing me to write again. She read all my stories when we lived together. Helped me think of ideas sometimes. Hers were so much funnier than mine. But it's hard to write, without the deadlines for class. Maybe this will get me back to it.

We had this historian come in to talk about her book maybe a month ago, a kind of memoir/history hybrid about how maternity changed over time. She said it was a fad for pregnant women in Victorian times to keep journals while they were pregnant because it was important to elevate their minds when their bodies became so visible/embarrassing. They said things like "I'm awaiting a little stranger" instead of "up the duff," or whatever. Pretty cute, actually. Not too different really from the mommy blogs that were everywhere when I was, like, thirteen. I liked to look at them sometimes, and imagine my own family in a pretty house one day. I googled some of the ones I used to read, and they're all corporate now, with ads and lots of contributors. Oh well. I did find a cool little thing that tells you how big your baby is each week, though:)

Okay, not much for now except...I'M PREGNANT!!! It's so fun to say!!

WEEK 7: The baby is the size of a blueberry!

I threw up in the employee bathroom Wednesday after I looked at my grilled chicken salad. I canceled my dinner plans with Lily that night, which made me feel terrible. It's been a little while since I've seen her, and I've been kind of worried about her. I used to see her almost every day, told her stuff like what I ate for lunch and weird looks the grocery cashier gave me. But we never really got back in the groove after the lockdown. Or maybe after Chris and I got married, I don't know. I miss her. She still texts me all the time, random stuff that happens in her day. But I have Chris to share those things with now. She'll find someone soon.

Anyway, I told her I was coming down with something and then I slept for fourteen hours.

But that's all great news actually, because Google says that you're less likely to miscarry if you're feeling early symptoms like nausea and fatigue!

I'm trying to listen to my body, so I picked up Taco Bell for dinner tonight, yuck, I know. I was just driving by and it looked good! "Yo quiero Taco Bell!" Ha! When I was a baby, the mascot was a Chihuahua wearing a sombrero who always said that. You could get away with anything in the '90s. I'm glad the baby's being born now, not then. Better world!

My friend Harriet had a dog like that. We ate cinnamon twists in the back seat of her mom's station wagon once. It might have been the first time I had Taco Bell, actually. Harriet poured the cinnamon sugar from the bottom of the bag down her throat after she'd finished them. She looked so cool. I'd wanted to be like her so badly. House with a dog. Mom with a car she could get cleaned, not clean herself.

WEEK 8: The baby is the size of a kidney bean. Maybe a refried bean.

I tried to eat a bowl of cereal this week and I threw up. I tried to eat a sandwich this week, and then I remembered that I can't eat lunch meat unless I heat it, so I unmade the sandwich and watched the pieces of turkey spin around in my microwave and then I threw up. I thought about eating nothing this week, but then I got hungry and the hunger made me throw up.

But I went back to Taco Bell, and it was so good, I cried in the car and turned around and went back for another quesadilla.

Lily texted me and asked how I was feeling. I did something bad. I told her I tested positive for Covid. She got really worried and asked me all these questions, which I know was nice but I just didn't want to talk at all. She kept saying things to try to make me feel better, like this variant isn't supposed to last as long as the others, and at least I got it now so I'll be fully recovered before our appointment. We've got our friendiversary coming up, and the spa is finally back up and running like usual, so we're doing our tradition again. She's really excited about it, I can tell, which sucks, because it means I can't cancel, even though right now I really want to. If I'd been thinking straight, I'd have saved the Covid excuse.

I guess she told the other girls what I said, because they all sent me an Uber Eats gift card. I used it to order Taco Bell a bunch of times.

I ate a Baja Steak Chalupa. I ate a Cheesy Roll Up. I ate a Crunchwrap Supreme. I ate two Doritos Locos Tacos. I ate a Cheesy Gordita Crunch. I ate a Power Menu Bowl. I ate a Bell Breakfast Box. I drank a Wild Cherry Breeze Freeze. I drank a Brisk Mango Fiesta. I drank a Baja Blast. I ate packet after packet after packet of fire sauce. I didn't throw any of it up. I loved it.

Except for my ultrasound, the minutes I was eating Taco Bell were the only good minutes of my week. That sounds sad, writing it down, but honestly, I don't really feel anything.

In the ultrasound, I sort of thought Chris might sit next to me and hold my hand like the dads do in the movies. But he just stood and watched the computer thing from behind the tech's head. He pointed out the placenta and the baby's heartbeat, which I guess was helpful. My heartbeat. Your heartbeat. You. Who are you?

Your heart was so small and going so fast, it made me want to cry.

WEEK 9: The baby is the size of a Chihuahua's bugged-out eyeball.

Everything salty was disgusting this week. Chips. Cheese. Chris's cum. I felt a little bit better yesterday so I said yes when he wanted to have sex and even the smell of him getting close made me want to be sick. I gagged when I went to pee afterward.

God, I just realized how much a Victorian pregnant woman would never say that. I should be thankful to have honored the "first pledge of matrimonial love" or whatever.

Even though I felt grossed out all the time, I was still starving all week. Chris and I thought it would probably be the healthiest choice to get my sugar naturally from fruit. But then I ate a whole pineapple for breakfast one day, and afterward, I read on the internet that the enzymes in pineapple can soften your cervix and trigger contractions so I spent the rest of the day on the couch panicking about how I had probably killed the baby and its tiny heart.

The next day, I ate an apricot and then an orange and then a mango and then a pear because Google told me they were the top four best fruits for pregnancy.

They all tasted good while I was eating them, but I never got full. I didn't really feel hungry, either, just empty, like there was nothing inside my stomach or my brain.

Finally, two days ago, I gave in. At the drive-thru, I said, "Just three orders of cinnamon twists, please." And then for some reason, I added, "Kids just finished soccer practice," like I was one of those mommies from the blogs.

The board called me "ma'am" and said they didn't carry cinnamon twists.

"Maybe they're called something different now," I said. "It's the cinnamon dessert thing."

"Do you mean the Cinnabon Delights? They're part of a partnership with—"

"No, I don't mean the Cinnabon fucking Delights. If I wanted a Cinnabon, I'd go to a Cinnabon. I mean the cinnamon twists. They're like a churro but Styrofoam." My voice was really loud, and I could feel the blood pounding in my neck and on the side of my head. Apparently, you gain four pounds of blood when you're pregnant, and your veins get all thick and visible. Maybe it started to happen to me right then.

The board said they had been discontinued.

Then this really fucked-up thing happened. I lifted my hand and hit the steering wheel really hard, like *really* hard. I screamed at the thing: "Can I speak to your fucking manager?!"

Instantly, I wanted to die. My stomach was full of nothing, and my head was full of blood. "Sorry," I said. "Don't get your manager. Sorry. Fuck. Kids, you know?" I forced out a laugh, like I was a frazzled but good mom. "They want what they want. I'll have a small Baja Blast instead. Wait, no, sorry, I'll have a large Zero Sugar Baja Blast."

I found some sunglasses and crammed them onto my face and didn't look at the woman who took my money.

Harriet died when we were thirteen. That's a real thing that happened to me. She had an aneurysm and her mom left a message on our machine. She used to get migraines when she ate hot dogs. Ten years old was really young to get migraines. We should have noticed at the time. You could get discontinued even if you were really good and no one thought there was anything wrong with you.

I pulled into a parking spot and tried not to hate myself as I googled the Taco Bell Chihuahua. It turned out she was named Gidget and she played Bruiser's mom in *Legally Blonde 2: Red, White & Blonde*. I'd seen that movie, and I hadn't even recognized her. I chugged my entire Baja Blast and then opened my car door and threw it up with my seat belt still on. The puddle of vomit was so blue and bright that I thought I might cry. When I started to leave, I got a text from Lily that just said, love you so much.

WEEK 10: The baby is the size of a fucking Cinnabon Delight.

Every day this week, I woke up feeling like I'd eaten ten Crunchwrap Supremes and drunk a pitcher of margaritas the night before, even though I mostly ate only black bean power bowls with water. I didn't really leave the house, except to get the bowls. I go to the farther away Taco Bell now. Everything and everyone I saw on the drive exhausted and annoyed me. On top of everything, there's a spot on my back that's already hurting, and I can't reach it. Isn't that supposed to happen later?

Chris sat me down one evening and said he was worried about me. I hated him and how he smelled and how he had the energy to go on a jog every day. But I knew that if I wanted him to leave me alone, I needed to tell him something.

"I feel really bad," I said after a minute. As usual, my fucking eyes welled up with tears. This time, they were sort of helpful, though. "It's... it's hard to be pregnant. I'm really... tired."

"Oh, babe," he said, and put an arm around me. His sweat made me want to gag. "I get it. I remember being so tired in residency, I didn't have the energy to do anything after work."

"Right," I said. "But it's also like... it's hard because I feel like nothing is making me feel... Don't worry or anything, but I feel like nothing is making me feel very happy anymore. Like I'm sort of only happy when I'm eating a taco and then, when it's over, I hate myself."

Chris laughed. "I always feel like that after I eat fast food. Maybe we should try some meal prep at home, yeah? Give you something to do?"

Something inside me started to boil. I didn't really trust my mouth to be controlled by my brain anymore. "No," I said in the calmest voice I could muster, "I'm saying the tacos make me happy. They're, like, the only thing. But I... all the rest of the time, I just feel sad and angry."

He asked what I meant with a kind of disgusted look on his face, and for some reason, I told him about the cinnamon twists.

"It was horrible," I said, crying again and wiping my nose.

Apparently pregnant women produce more mucus. I blow out about ten pounds of snot every morning. "I was a *Karen!* I...I think I was a racist!!"

"Annie, you're overreacting," Chris said, and laughed and petted my head. "You didn't even see the person taking your order. They might not have even been a person of—"

"I'M A WHITE PERSON!" I screamed, snot flying wildly from my nostrils. "AND THAT'S ALL THAT MATTERS!"

In a low, measured voice, he said, "There's no need to yell. Don't you think...and don't be mad at me for saying this ..." He raised his hands like *don't shoot*. "Don't you think this might just be your hormones?"

For a second, I actually did want to shoot him. *Of course it's my hormones! I'm not an idiot!* The internet told me my body's producing the progesterone equivalent of 500 birth control pills a day and those things make you crazy. I was the bitchiest fourteen-year-old alive for the first month I was on them. Although maybe that was because of Harriet. Not long after.

Anyway, just because my feelings are being caused by my hormones doesn't make me not feel them! That was the whole problem. I'm trapped inside a big, fat, meaty, diablo sauce emotion machine and I can't get out.

When I met Chris, he was thirty and I was twenty and he was divorcing his wife because he woke up one morning and realized he didn't understand her at all. They'd known each other since they were sixteen. She would get mad at him for no reason, he said. She would cry and cry at night even though they were perfectly happy and he provided everything she could possibly want. "You're so much easier," he said to me the first time we slept together. I remember he pushed a piece of my hair behind my ear and kissed me on the tip of my nose and I felt almost powerful.

How can I expect him to understand me if I can't understand myself? What if I keep getting mad at him for no reason, and crying every night for no reason, and he realizes this is too hard, that I am too hard? He will leave me alone with my body and whatever it's producing. Some little stranger.

I wish I could talk to Lily about that so bad it hurts, even worse than that fucking stupid spot on my back. She would understand. She always understands what I'm trying to say. Always knows what to do, when to give me a minute or when to give me a hug or when to distract me from whatever I'm worried about. But if I told her what my stupid fucking hormones are making me think right now, she'd just hate Chris more than she already does and it wouldn't help at all. She would want him to leave, even if she didn't say it. She'd think my life would be better. But it wouldn't, and I know that for sure, because I definitely couldn't afford to have a baby on my own just with my job at the shop. Anyway I won't be like this forever, I won't.

On top of that, it's too soon. The whole pregnancy might end up being over tomorrow.

"You're right," is what I ended up saying to Chris. "I think I'm just hungry, too."

"Why don't I make us a healthy dinner?" he said, like he had offered to self-immolate for me.

WEEK 11: The baby is probably the same size as the piece of taco shell I found on my sweater this morning and ate.

I ignored all of my texts and eventually they stopped coming. Last one from Lily: Hey, can you just confirm I'll see you next week? Don't want to lose deposit. The friendiversary. The couples massage, which is supposed to be fun, and funny, and something I'm excited about. I can't even deal with it.

I can't stop thinking about the Chihuahua, Gidget. Her energy. Her charm. How well she could pull off a hat. How confident she was about what she wanted: *Yo quiero Taco Bell.* How she always got it!

And then she grew up. She became Bruiser's Mom, and no one even knew it was her. She got lost in the role. Being Bruiser's Mom was the last thing she ever did. She didn't even die until 2009. She had just disappeared. That was going to happen to me. Like it happened to my own mom, who just worked and worked and slept and slept, just because of me.

What did I *quiero?* I never even tried to figure it out. And now here I am.

I had an appointment with my ob-gyn today. I didn't want to, but Google told me I should, so I told her that I was feeling depressed. I was worried that if I was experiencing prenatal depression, I would also experience postpartum depression. She offered a knowing, compassionate sigh. She was a woman, too, I thought.

"How much do you exercise?" she asked.

"I used to take five spin classes a week," I said.

"And now?"

I didn't say anything.

"You should get outside more. Some easy cardio can make such a difference. It doesn't have to be a hike, or even a long walk. Just a thirty-minute stroll around your neighborhood counts. Your body is working hard, even if you can't feel it. Eat lots of good protein, too."

"Good idea," I said. "Thanks."

She pulled up my chart or something on her laptop and spoke out loud while she typed, like an idiot: *Encouraged patient to exercise to relieve symptoms of depression.*

What I want is to feel pregnant, not sick and fucked up. I want to feel powerful. I want to feel impressive to Chris, like I'm doing a big, special thing that he can't do. I want him to look at me with awe. I want to feel enlightened. I want to be amazed by the amount of love I can hold. I want to feel proud. I want to walk through the grocery store with my hand on my belly and watch people smile at me. I want to feel selfless. I want to make sacrifices and not mind, because the baby is all that matters. I want to feel like I have a special secret, something just for me and a whole new little person inside me. I want to stop feeling alone in my life and in my house and in my body. I want to feel closer to life, not farther away from it.

Or maybe what I want is to not be pregnant, if being pregnant is like this. I hate it. I hate it hate it hate it. But I ordered it and it came and now I have to pay for it.

WEEK 12: The baby is the size of a lime.

On Saturday, I met Lily at the spa. They'd done an upfit while they were closed. It used to be pretty basic, which was why we went that first time, only sophomores, pretended to be a couple so we could get the cheapest option. Called each other "honey," giggled. No way they believed us.

I felt okay, just guilty and off. And my back still hurt, which was honestly the reason I didn't flake. I'm really glad I went, though, even though we didn't stay long.

They had us back in this big room with two tables next to each other. It looked dim and nice, but when we walked through the door, it felt like walking into a Bath & Body Works, like I was going to throw up and then drown in cucumber melon. I must have made a face, because Lily wrapped her arm around my shoulders and said, "Hey, you okay?" I nodded, but she kept her arm where it was. Maybe just to seem like we were a couple, but I was glad it was there. It felt good to be close to her, and good when she gave me a little squeeze.

We lay face down on the tables, and I noticed that my stomach felt weirdly hard, like there was a uterus in there, and maybe even a baby, and not just a bunch of chalupas. For a second, that felt good, but then I started to panic a little about whether you were allowed to lie on your stomach and get a massage if you were pregnant. I guess she massaged my neck and shoulders, but I barely even remember it because of the worrying.

But then she got to that lower back spot. She pushed on it, and I felt a muscle in my back jump. I got a swoopy feeling from it, like being on a roller coaster, and I almost laughed. But then the muscle jumped and jumped again, and it hurt so badly, I thought I might scream. And then she pressed again and it just settled. Like it had never been there. I only realized I was sobbing when I heard Lily say, "Can we stop, please?"

The masseuses left the room and we both sat up, wrapped in

our sheets like soft tacos. Lily asked me if I was okay, and I didn't say anything, just let out another huge sob, and she came over and sat next to me on my table. To myself, I was saying, *It's too early, it's too early, it's too early.* To Lily, I said, "I'm pregnant."

She smiled so big, I couldn't believe it. I think part of me thought she'd be mad. She hugged me, and I got to tell her how far along I was, and about the ultrasound, and how I'd have my twelve-week in a few days. Telling her that stuff, I felt normal again for a minute. Excited about there being a baby, for the first time in a long time. Then she said, "Chris must be so happy."

I felt my lip start to shake. I said, "Yeah, I think he is. It's kind of... it's weird right now, because I'm not that far along, so it doesn't really feel real yet. It's just kind of, something weird going on with me. Like it's just my thing right now."

She said, "That sounds lonely." And I nodded. Then she said, "Are you happy?" And I told her, "I'm really scared that I might not be."

I told her how bad I've been feeling, and about the doctor, and about all the Taco Bell. She laughed about the screaming-at-the-window thing. I think I laughed, too, but then I cried again and eventually I was just saying, "I'm sorry, I'm sorry, I'm so sorry."

Finally, she said, "I don't think you're bad for not liking being pregnant. It doesn't mean anything about what kind of mom you're going to be. I bet everyone actually hates it, and they just don't say it because you're not supposed to. So you're not as alone as you think, I bet."

Before I could stop myself, I asked, "Do you feel alone?"

She looked surprised. She kind of shrugged, and looked down at the floor, and said, "Sometimes."

Then she looked up, and her face changed. Smiled. She didn't want to be serious about her own thing, I think, so that I could be the one having the hard time. She tilted her head toward the door, and said, "When she was massaging my calf, she sort of lifted my leg up so that it was pressed against her chest, and I could feel my foot against her collarbone." She raised her eyebrows. "That was the sexiest thing that's happened to me in a long time."

"Ew," I said. And then I wondered when *was* the last time she'd had sex. Had she, since Lucas? That had been in early Covid. She hadn't talked to me much about dating, even though she must have been, now that it was safe again. "What about that couple? Didn't they call you, after the quarantine was over?"

She laughed. "Nah. One-time thing, I guess." But she looked so sad. And then she said, "They're married, you know. They have each other, don't need me."

I thought, *I'm married, and I need you.* I should have said that.

There was a knock on the door, and one of the masseuses came in and said, "Ladies. Um, your massage session is coming to an end."

That made us laugh. Lily said, "Thank you, it was very romantic." And we laughed again.

"So," she said when we were outside and dressed again. "I'm guessing our traditional bottle of wine is out."

"Honestly, I want to vom just thinking about it," I said.

"Kind of same," she said. "I could go for a Baja Blast, though." Which obviously was exactly what I needed to hear. We went to the faraway one, even though she wanted to see who I'd yelled at.

I've been thinking about that knot on my back, and how the masseuse pressed on it so hard, she made it go away. Maybe I'm in the hard part, the part that really hurts, and I just have to keep lying here, not pulling away even though I want to, and then everything will be okay. Better than it was before, even, with me and Chris and the baby, too, whoever they are. I just have to wait, and not move, and then we'll be fixed, like there was never anything wrong.

Bread and Jam

"HI, MA," ROSE WHISPERED, the softness of her voice at odds with her set jaw, her firm stance in my doorway. She had a small duffel bag hanging from one elbow, and her daughter draped across her shoulder, asleep. Frances's legs hung on either side of Rose's body, several inches longer than I'd last seen them. One foot had lost its shoe. "Can we come in?"

"Of course," I whispered, trying to modulate my voice. "Are you okay? What's happened?"

"Let me just lay her down, she *finally* fell asleep again. We drove most of the night."

I nodded and then looked down at myself, still in my nightie at nine in the morning. I smoothed the front down and pressed myself into the wall, trying to give her room to pass. She walked through the door confidently, and moved down the hall, toward her childhood bedroom. I went back to the kitchen, my hands shaking, bewildered. Something must have happened to Peter. Had he been hurt? Were they running from someone? I shook my head from side to side. Surely that was a bit dramatic. I'd always run that way, excitable. Besides, things like that didn't happen to a person twice in one life.

"Oh," I said, feeling the color rise to my cheeks. I'd left the freezer open. I'd been just about to thaw a slice of cake I'd taken home from little Jason's birthday party last weekend. *You'll kill yourself if you keep eating that way, Ma*, Sam had said, seeing me wrap it up. I shut the door and opened the fridge, glad Rose had not seen.

I measured out a quarter cup of cottage cheese and topped it with fifteen grapes, which I sliced slowly and precisely down the middle, trying both to distract myself from all the horrible reasons Rose might be here and to prolong that lovely moment: being about to eat. That moment where you can imagine that you will be satisfied.

My boys, Sam and Walt, lived nearby, both very successful, Sam a doctor! They called or visited weekly, and Walt often brought Jason and Haillie to swim in the pool on weekends. I hadn't seen Rose since Christmas. She had moved to New York City to be with Peter soon after they became engaged. He worked at a publishing house and couldn't relocate. I never believed she wanted to move, though she assured me she did. That was what you did when you became a wife; you made sacrifices, pretended that they weren't sacrifices. I had helped her pack up with pride. I had done that right. I remember thinking so even at the time. Despite everything, I had raised my children right.

I heard quiet footsteps coming down the hall, and then Rose entered, wiping her hand across her forehead. She looked exhausted, ten years older than she had mere moments ago. She must have been holding herself up with glue for Frances's sake. *Frances*. My own little sister's name on that sweet girl. What a thing to bear.

"Oh, baby," I said, putting my bowl on the counter. Rose moved into me, her head in my neck just as Frances's had been in her own minutes before. I felt her hot tears and said, "*Shh, shh, shh*," as I had thousands of times when she was a child. Then something extraordinary happened. I was struck by the *rightness* of my body. How correct it felt, to envelop her. How orderly, to find myself still bigger than my daughter.

Finally, she pulled away from me. Her absence lingered, cold and wet, on my shoulder. As quickly as it had come, that good feeling, it went. Silly me. Dangerous to think that way. Sam's voice in my head, all the time. There was a term for what he said I'd be. Morbidly obese. *Morbid*. The word burrowed into my bones and shook them. I knew he needed to tell me these things, that it made him feel valuable, important. But I dreaded it, and dreaded disappointing him. So I counted my servings, knew my food groups, memorized how to exchange one serving for another within the same group. I could do it all in my head now! I had graduated from using the exchange checklist months ago.

I cleared my throat and stood up straighter. "So are you going to tell me why you're here?" I grabbed my bowl and began to guide Rose into the living room. "Oh, I'm sorry. Are you hungry? Do you want—?"

"I don't want anything," she said, and kept walking. What a thing, not to want. I put the bowl back down, so as not to eat in front of her. "It's Peter," she said as she crumbled onto the sofa. My heart raced, imagining his body. A heart attack at his desk, head in a bound manuscript. Bloody in his car, head pressing against the horn, which screamed and screamed. Stabbed, over and over again. *Don't think about that*, I instructed myself.

"How did it happen?" I asked, pulling a throw pillow onto my lap and pressing it in.

"I... what?"

"How did he die, honey?" I put my hand on her knee, looked her in the eye.

She laughed then. I was almost startled out of my chair. "Ma! He didn't die. He's cheating on me." She laughed again, with a real smile this time. "Wow, I'm sort of glad you thought he died."

"Don't say that."

She shrugged. "Perspective. You can't be mad at a dead guy."

That was true, and didn't I know it. Don had died almost fifteen years ago. Drinking. Alone in the car, thank goodness. My heart still constricted, just imagining if... well. No one was mad at him anymore. No one had ever been as mad at him as they ought to have been, even me. But I shook that out of my head. He had been my husband. The father of my children, after all.

"Baby," I said, "are you sure that Peter—"

"Yes. I... I followed him. I just had a feeling. I acted crazy, like Meryl Streep in *Heartburn*. I knew I was being like her at the time, like I was watching myself do it. I even copied what she did! I looked through his office drawers, at his receipts. Remember we went to see that? When you came to visit that time?" She shook her head, frazzled. "Sorry, I'm tired. I..."

"Take a breath, honey. I'm sure it's all—"

"It's *not* all fine. You always...!" She let out a sigh. "I followed him. I left Franny with our neighbor; she's this sweet old lady who always brings over pierogies. He was looking around, all shifty. He had told me he had a meeting with some agent, but I didn't believe it. Those were always lunch meetings. He went into this building and . . . Ma?"

"Mm?"

"Is it okay if I just tell you? I don't really have . . . not in New York . . ."

"You can tell me anything, honey." Nothing could shock me, I told myself, not anymore. It wasn't a proud thought. It devastated me.

"Okay. I followed him into this building; there wasn't a doorman. Another guy was coming out and he let me through. I saw him go into a room at the top of the landing and I sat outside. I was there for an hour, just getting shakier and angrier. I didn't have a plan. I thought I might hit him. Or one time, I thought about leaving, thought I might just sit at home with his dinner and see if he would tell me. But I couldn't decide so I did nothing. And then I heard the door unlock and I got up and ran and stood behind the corner. And then I saw them. Him and some woman. She was tall, taller than him, and older, too, or maybe it just seemed that way, because he looked different. His shoulders were all crunched in, and his neck hung down. He was fiddling with his hands. Even before I heard them, I thought, *He looks like a little boy.* He got up on his tiptoes and kissed her on the cheek—she had turned her head, craned her face out for it. And then he said"—she swallowed and her cheeks reddened—"he said, *Do you love me, Mommy?*"

I felt my face go hot, too. I pulled the pillow in closer and adjusted myself. "Is it possible he finally made contact with her? It would explain why—"

"No, Ma." She shook her head, like I was being stupid. "She wasn't his mother."

I knew she wasn't. I had finally learned that my brain wasn't as empty as people thought it was. But I understood the role I had to play. Rose needed me to misunderstand, to disbelieve that Peter might visit a prostitute. "If she was older …"

"She wasn't old enough. And she was wearing …" She ran two hands down her sides, mimicking something like a corset. "Trust me, it was clear."

"Oh, honey."

"It was—" And to my surprise, she started to cry again. Not the angry, exhausted tears she'd shed before. Sad, pitiful tears. The kind that she'd cried as a child, when she lost her little Tigger at the state fair. My baby girl. I put my hands up to her face and wiped them away.

"The woman," she continued. "She said, *Oh, Peter. You know I'm very fond of you.*" She shook her head. "And the way he looked, when she turned her face away from him. It was … it was the saddest thing I've ever seen."

I loved my sons. Loved and loved them. But when Rose was born, at only thirty-six weeks, I felt something different. Love mingled with guilt, a desperation to make it all up to her. She was so small, only five pounds. I could still feel it, her fragile, sweet body in my arms. The soft blond hairs that grew on her shoulders, which should have been shed before birth. *You should still be safe in there*, I remember whispering to her when we were alone in the room. *I'm sorry, I'm so sorry.* I felt that still sometimes.

"Mommy!" A shout from the bedroom. Frances was awake.

Rose sat up straight and rearranged her face. "She shouldn't be up yet. She hasn't gotten any sleep." She stood up, wiped off her face, and said, "Can you tell?"

Of course I could, but I said, "She'll never notice."

"I'll be right back, I'm sure I can get her back down."

I went into the kitchen, after she left, to get my cottage cheese. I ate it in about twenty seconds, and then it was over, that good moment. I wouldn't have another one until lunch. I could have the cake, I thought, my heart rate ramping up. It wasn't a normal day, after all. If I ate it, it wouldn't mean that I would *always* eat it.

But just as I'd made the first move, I heard the bedroom door slam. To my surprise, it was Frances who walked into the kitchen, holding a small bag with a stuffed bunny peering out. "Hi, Grandma," she said as though she lived here.

"I thought you were taking a nap, honey."

She shrugged and said, "I won."

"Franny!" Rose said, coming in behind her. "Don't talk like that, please." She looked angry and exhausted again, and wiped her hair out of her eyes.

But Frances just shrugged for a second time, then threw her bag onto the ground and said, "Read me my book, Grandma!"

"What book, honey?"

"*My* book, *my* book!"

"She means *Bread and Jam for Frances*," Rose said, riffling through the bag and pulling out an old paperback with a badger on the front.

"You like this old thing?" I asked Frances, taking it from Rose and guiding them back into the sitting room.

"Yes, yes!"

"What's it about?"

"It's about Frances and she's a badger, which is like a raccoon but not, and she only wants to eat bread and jam, which is like jelly but not, and her mom gives her all of the bread and jam that she wants but then she eats it *too much* and she *cries!*"

"Poor Frances!" I said, and gasped and clutched my nightie as

I sat back down. But I thought, *Lucky Frances.* I supposed that the little badger stopped wanting bread and jam after that, that she began to eat her vegetables, as the mother intended.

"Yes!" she agreed, nodding seriously and sitting down on top of me. "Poor Frances!"

"Do you like to eat bread and jam, too?" I asked. My voice quavered for some reason, so I cleared my throat.

"Yes, but I want to eat all kinds of foods, probably all of them. You're soft, Grandma," she added, and began to bob up and down in my lap. I caught Rose's eye and felt myself flush with shame.

She said, "Frances."

But Frances only said, "*What?* I *like* it," and burrowed her face into my breast. I tried to smile, and shook my head slightly at Rose, hoping she'd understand that it was okay, that I knew what I was.

"Frances, what if I put on *The Little Mermaid*, hmm? Do you think you might want to watch for a little while, while I talk with Grandma?" Frances shrieked and jumped out of my lap as quickly as she'd jumped into it, and followed her mother to the den.

Would it have worked on me, the bread and jam trick? I thought of Mother, measuring my waist, my thighs. A different kind of trick, but still intended to teach her little girl not to want too much.

They're all born bleeding, baby girls, even the ones who came out on time. I had been terrified when I saw. But the doctor explained it to me. They take on your hormones, bleed menstrual blood for their first few days. It would go away, he told me, crying like a child, bleeding myself. I had had trouble believing it. But he'd been right, of course. It had stopped, for a lovely fourteen years.

To be born a girl is to be put together with Scotch tape.

It was a blessing, too, Frances had told me. My own Frances, when she had visited me in the hospital, bringing the boys to meet their new sister. "She has all her eggs already, just like you did. You've never lived without her, or the boys, not really; and she'll never be alone, either."

"Does he know you're here, baby?" I asked, once Rose had settled back in next to me.

She shook her head. "When I got back to the apartment, I couldn't even look at him. I was so mad at him. And I was so sad for him. It was all so pathetic. Just because you don't have a mom doesn't mean you can... There's no excuse. I thought about it the whole drive. He's not the person I thought he was, if he could do that."

Death is almost never the first time you grieve someone you love. I lost Don years before he died. When he came back from Vietnam, he wasn't the same. And after Frances died...

I shuddered.

"How long do you plan on staying?" I asked, to clear out my thoughts.

"I'm not sure. I don't know when I'll be able to find my own place."

"Your—what?" That surprised me. At first, I wasn't even sure what she meant.

"I'm leaving him, Ma." And she looked angry, like she'd already had this discussion with me. Maybe she had. Maybe we'd argued all night, in her head, while she drove.

"You can't leave him," I said. "He's Frances's father."

"I knew you'd say that." She stood up and began to pace. Looking down on me, she reiterated, louder, "I *knew* you'd say that."

"Honey. I know you're angry right now, and hurt. Trust me, I know how—"

"I *know* you know how I feel. We *all* knew! Just because you stayed, and kept staying and *staying*—" Her pacing became more frantic, her voice shakier. And then she looked at me, a stare like a knife. "How could you have done that? How could you have stayed, and let us have that childhood? And let *Sam* have that childhood? Dad was—"

"Dad was *your father*," I said, finally angry myself. I thrust my pillow to the side and got to my feet. "You don't leave the father of your children. Men are—"

"Men aren't *different*. They're just spoiled. You can't let them—"

"If you think I let your father do anything—"

"But you *did!*" she shouted. "You didn't leave him! And you knew! You...you deserved more than that, Ma! We deserved more than that! *Franny* deserves more than—"

"Than what? More than a life with a mother and a father? A home?" I was trembling. I had known, known more than anyone thought I knew. Known more than Rose, or Walt, or even Sam. But you can never predict how men will react when you try to limit them. The best you can do is keep them stable, keep your house stable, keep your children stable. Measure out enough to live on and try to feel satisfied.

"Yes!" She threw her hand down from where it had been in her hair, making her point. "When you're married, you should feel...like enough!"

"But you never are, are you! Men always want more and more, and you just have to let them have it until, God willing, they get old enough to realize they've had too much of a good thing and—and they stop! Just like that... *stupid badger!*" I was loud, louder than her. I couldn't remember my voice ever sounding so loud.

"Ma," she said, stopping in her tracks. "Ma, it's okay."

"What?" I asked, and I heard it in my voice. I was crying. I hadn't even noticed.

"It's okay," she said. She opened her arms and then tried to wrap me in them. I was so much bigger than her. I tried to remember that feeling I'd felt before, that sense of rightness, but I couldn't.

"I should be the one hugging you," I said into her neck.

"Ma, I'm going to leave him." Her voice was measured this time, quiet.

"Honey—"

"No, Ma. I can't go back. And I'm going to be okay."

"I know," I said again. She was so much stronger than I was, my five-pound baby. I had done that. No matter what she said, I knew that it was my choices, my sacrifices, the things I had pushed down and buried, that had made her.

She didn't want to hear me say it, so I didn't. But inside, I knew I had been right, to do what I had done. To stay small and keep quiet. She needed me to support her, so I would. I pulled myself together, sat back down, and listened. Once we had made a plan—she would tell Peter where she was, at my insistence; but then she would stay, and try to find a place in town—I settled her in the den, on the couch with Frances, who fell asleep with her head in Rose's lap. Then I went to the kitchen, opened the freezer, and put the slice of cake into the garbage disposal.

Catfishing

IT HAD BEEN HOT all summer, but nowhere had the heat pressed into our skin the way it did in Budva. We were on fire, all four of us, and our apartment had no air-conditioning. It was Europe. We fastened the shutters during the day, threw open the windows at night. The salty air, the tiny biting bugs, and the scent of fried fish from a nearby street fair all intruded into our beds.

We had arrived three days ago, fresh from the breezy bay of Kotor, where we had wasted away on the edges of the land, our feet in the cool water, our souls held intact by the watchful blue gaze of the church on the island in front of us. Our Lady of the Rocks. "Give me my ladies *on* the rocks," Ben had said with a raise of his eyebrow, two or three cocktails deep. It didn't make sense, but it made us all laugh like idiots. Our cocktails—Adriatiques all of them, we loved a theme—sloshed into the sea. Liam laughed loudest of all—or maybe his laugh just stood out to me, took up more space in my head.

We'd felt light, buoyed on the sea air. Now, in Budva, our bodies were burning back into incarnate life. It was gorgeous and we were miserable. The glue binding Izzy's paperback had melted on the beach the day before, scattering words to the wind. Trash across the earth. I was thirty-three years old, Jesus's age, sweating and a little drunk at the end of the world.

It was the last day of our two-week vacation across Croatia and Montenegro. Ben and I were celebrating our sixth wedding anniversary, Liam and Izzy their second. Mostly, we'd just wanted an excuse to travel again, now that borders had reopened and it felt safe enough. We were college friends, and together, we felt nineteen again. Back then, Izzy and I had shared a single room, our twin beds pushed up on opposite walls, our faces, more often than not, directed toward one another across the small chasm of concrete floor and discarded clothes, gossiping and giggling. Sometimes, Liam was there, his body pressing into my back, his face into my hair as I smiled at Izzy. He had spent six months of our sophomore year as my boyfriend, before I met Ben. He had been Izzy's husband for four times as long, but here, all of us together again, he felt like mine.

We decided to spend our last day at the beach again. It was too hot to leave town to go hiking—unthinkable to organize a ride in a sweltering van to the surrounding mountains. And we had walked the old city walls on our first day in town. I was usually tempted to wander through old churches and monasteries. I wasn't religious, but the decadence of old-world churches—the gold leaf, the blue-and-red frescoes, the emotional intensity of the icons—often brought me to tears. To be in a church like that was to be subsumed into devotion. I wanted to know what it would be like to be so utterly sure of and passionate about something that you were willing to offer every precious thing you had just to decorate it. My mom had had a friend who was a Catholic nun for a while, who would sometimes speak about the paradoxical comfort of being only a tiny piece of a larger good. By indulging in aesthetic excess, I could feel what actual believers did: an immersion into a more heavenly benevolence. But the magic of churches had worn off for me a few days ago. My sensations and desires had become baser. My body had adapted to hangovers by this point in the vacation. I'd been reduced to an essence of hunger, thirst, and heat.

Everyone was exhausted, a little irritable, and ready to get back to normal life. Izzy was clearly ready for some time alone. Ben wanted to get back to his routine, to eat less and drink less. Last night, in bed, he had said, "You know what I want?" I had rolled into him and batted my eyelashes and said, "Me?" And he had laughed and said, "I want to watch TV. I never thought I'd say it again after 2020." The more listless we grew, however, the more determined Liam became that we have a wild time, like he wanted to squeeze the vacation between his hands to collect every last drop of juice. It thrilled me, the way he was always able to get us to do what he wanted.

Liam and I had met in our freshman philosophy class, a class that Ben was in, too. But he sat in the back, had been quiet, had actually cared about what we were learning and so had paid attention to it. We hadn't made friends with him until later. I'd developed a crush on Liam immediately—the way his dark hair swooped into his eyes, the way he'd shake it aside with a twist of his head, the way he scratched deep underlines in his textbook with a thick black pen, the way he lifted a cheeky eyebrow when he answered a question, as though it didn't matter to him whether the professor agreed. I'd spent a summer pining over him—emailing Izzy my long fantasies about our future together—before we started dating the next fall. Our time together was short but fierce. I remembered it with increasing longing, the older I got. We saw him rarely now, only once a year or so. But each time, a little part of me only wanted to see him again and more. It was the way he looked at me maybe. Like he knew something about me that I didn't know.

Since I had turned thirty-three, I had become greedy. I had heard of the fabled sexual peak that women supposedly hit in their mid-thirties, but I hadn't thought that it would overtake me quite so literally. I was having more orgasms—alone and with other people—and they were all better than I'd ever had in my life. I felt like a teenage boy. I wanted and I wanted and I wanted more, like I was an empty vessel that only got bigger and emptier. There were a lot of theories going around about why this was happening to me. Ben thought that, when we opened our marriage last year, I had had a sexual awakening. The idea embarrassed me. It felt trite. My friends suspected that I was trying to fill up the gaping hole left behind by Celeste, who had dumped me a few months earlier. The best way to get over someone, my friends instructed me, was to get under someone. A phrase that I felt presumed the someone to be a man, a boring man who would fuck me in the missionary position. To be honest, even that turned me on.

My theory—the most embarrassing one of all, actually, and

the saddest—was that I *missed my mommy*. Christ. She had died more than two years ago, entirely without my permission, and left an even bigger gaping hole than Celeste had. She had also had a man do the dirty work for her. My father had told me over the phone. He almost never called, so I had answered immediately, eagerly. Humiliating.

All in all, and despite the existential threat of it, I preferred to think that something biological was happening, that my body was making a last-ditch effort to induce me to have a child before I went sterile. Whatever the cause, the effect couldn't be denied. I wanted to fuck and be fucked, all the time.

Liam was in the lounge chair next to me. We'd decided to shell out today for access to a private portion of the beach in front of Budva's Old Town. The crumbling city walls and stony, red-hatted steeples behind us, we stared out at the Adriatic Sea from underneath our umbrella, glasses of lemonade in the pebbly sand next to us. Izzy had gone up for an afternoon nap, and Ben had just gone for a swim. He had made it past the wave line and was swimming laps. Liam had allowed these activities only with the promise that we go crazy that night and barely make our flight home in the morning.

I was trying to make notes on the manuscript I had finally finished ghostwriting. It was hard to be a ghost at the moment, though. I felt every inch of my body baking in the sun, and tingling under Liam's gaze.

"Why are you insisting on working right now, Franny?" he finally asked, giving me an excuse to look up at him.

"I'm behind. I was supposed to send my finished draft to the editor before we came. It still needs a final edit."

"Isn't that the editor's job?"

"I mean, *my* final edit."

He laughed and drained the last of his lemonade. "You've always been a little controlling."

"I'm not controlling. I just take pride in my work."

"Hm," he said. "Then why did you let yourself get behind?"

"Fuck you," I said, though I wasn't at all annoyed. Liam liked to throw barbs around. It was his way of snagging you, pulling you into him.

"Well, why?" he asked. "What on earth has Miss Perfect been doing lately that was so distracting that she blew through a deadline and ruined her vacation?" He was leaning closer to me now, and I could feel his breath on my cheek, hotter than the air around us.

"I know what you're doing," I said, setting down the printed pages of my draft. "If you want to know more about Celeste and Adam, you can just ask." Ben and I had told Izzy and Liam about our recent exploration of polyamory with another married couple a few nights ago. Izzy had been curious. Liam had been downright wolfish in his desire for details, but Izzy kept putting her hand on his forearm and telling him that he was making us uncomfortable.

"Well, I'm dying to know. How did you get straight old Ben out there—the elbow-patched philosophy professor who spends his vacation swimming laps, mind you—to fuck another couple?"

I bristled. "Who's to say it wasn't his idea?"

He laughed. "I know you. It was your idea. You've always been a little bit insatiable."

"Whatever do you mean?" I asked, putting on a fake, haughty good girl air that, despite myself, I hoped he would find a little sexy. I put my mouth around my straw and sucked.

"Oh, nothing. And anyway: I know the answer. Ben would do anything for you. It's part of his schoolboy charm. And you—you were a little bored, right? Feeling a little old, a little stuck? So you gave in to a desire, so slowly that you were able to convince Ben it was his idea, right? And then you became so obsessed with these new people that you couldn't think, couldn't concentrate, couldn't write. Right?" My face had gone red, hotter. I wanted to tell him he was wrong. But I was afraid he wasn't.

So I said, with a quiver in my voice, "That's a bit reductive."

He laughed a big-hearted laugh. "You sound like Ben."

"You know, when I said you could ask me about Adam and Celeste, I didn't say you could psychoanalyze me."

"Okay, okay. Truce. Can I still ask?"

"Yes."

"Was it just sex or was it something more?"

A small pang in my chest. "Something more."

"And was that the plan or was it an accident?"

"An accident."

"Oh, Franny," he said, shaking his head. "You always let the people you sleep with consume you."

Consumed by love. Torn apart and gnashed between its teeth. As Aunt Frances had been.

You're one to talk, I wanted to say. Liam had had plenty of casual sex, as far as I knew. Maybe some while we were dating, if my jealous teenage suspicions had been true. But—and the thought filled me with pride—our relationship had been intense. I had loved it at first, the way his arm fell heavily across my shoulders when we were at parties, as though he was keeping me all to himself. The way he would say to me, as we walked around campus, "You're prettier than her," and "He wants you; look how he's looking at you." The way he wanted to fuck me in public, in every academic building on campus, because I was the only girl cool enough to try it.

After a while, though, he became moody. He would disappear for days at a time, and when he showed up back in my dorm room, he would be irritated by my anger. "Don't you trust me?" he would say. "You expect me to trust you, right?" I began to feel that he was too domineering. Too possessive. By the time I summoned up the courage to dump him, I was almost embarrassed by him, finding his disaffection needy rather than alluring. I remembered, weirdly, that his mouth became disgusting to me. Strange how repulsive a mouth can be if you aren't interested in the person it's attached to, an open, watery, blistering thing.

Liam had moped; but a few weeks later, he asked if we could remain friends, and we had. In fact, he introduced me to Ben our senior year, his fellow philosophy major. "She was the smartest girl in our intro class," he had said as I shook Ben's hand. That might have been the moment I began to find him attractive again.

I thought about his mouth a lot. It was wide, maybe too wide. A tiny scar on his upper lip rendered it slightly lopsided. It was rakish, even a little obscene. How could I have ever seen it as disgusting? I turned to look at it now and wanted it to suck me dry.

"I like to be consumed," I answered, stuffing my manuscript into my beach bag.

"Sexy," he said.

I felt myself blush like a dumb little girl. "I mean...not like *that*."

"Between you and me, Franny"—and he leaned in again, his mouth close to my neck—"we both know you like it like that, too." He pulled back and winked.

I felt my eyes dart toward the water. Ben was still out there, far enough away that he couldn't hear us. I pulled a piece of ice from my glass and threw it at Liam. "Stop it," I said.

"Okay, okay. I'm being bad. Vacation does this to me, as Izzy has reminded me."

"She's right," I said, Izzy's name a welcome barrier between us.

"Just one more question and I'll let you get back to your pressing work. Will you allow it?"

"I'll allow it. Just for you."

"What do you want from it?"

"From what?"

"From seeing other people."

"What do I want?" I repeated, to give myself time.

"What do you want?"

What I wanted was to know how to answer that question.

At that moment, if I could have, I might have said: I want you to push me down on the sand and kiss me hard and slow. I want you to say to me, *I've never loved anyone the way I loved you*. I want you to spread my legs apart to feel how wet I am and then push your fingers inside me. I want to watch you pull down your swimsuit because you can't help yourself. I want to watch you touch yourself as you look at me. I want to hear you moan. I want to push myself onto you. I want to grab your hair. I want to feel you come. I want to make you finish me with your hand while you go soft, still inside me. I want you to whimper.

I wanted it. A part of me did want it.

I said, "I want to be adored."

He smirked. "Ben adores you."

"As you've said."

"So you already have that. What else do you want?"

Before I let myself think about it, I answered, "More."

We looked at each other for a long moment, enough time for me to take in a full breath. I let it out and said, "I'm going to get in the water, too. It's too hot out here." I got up and fussed with my bikini top, pulled my sunglasses off, and threw them into the chair. I walked toward the sea and tried not to think about what my ass looked like. I put my toes right on the water line, the edge of the earth, the edge of the sea. I stood for a moment right at the limit. Then I crossed it and swam out.

Liam had made us a reservation that night at what was supposed to be the best restaurant in town. It was shaded underneath masses of leafy lemon and pine trees in the old town, looking out over the sea. "We're going all out," he told us as he opened the menu. "No excuses. We're eating after we're too full and drinking after we're too drunk."

He ordered for the table, a mix of Balkan and Mediterranean dishes. To start, we had Njeguški *pršut*—a special Montenegrin prosciutto made from a pig's hind legs and hung for months in the mountain breeze—and mussels *buzara*, steamed in olive oil, wine, bread crumbs, and herbs and served with a garlicky loaf of bread. We had the same bottle of orange wine from Slovenia that we had tasted a week ago on a two-day wine tour of the Adriatic.

"It'll take a few days, but I'm going to miss the food," Ben said, using an empty mussel shell to pull the meat out from a second shell. "I can't believe I thought that all we'd be eating in Eastern Europe was borscht."

"I'm going to miss the wine," Izzy said after her first long sip.

"I can never find good orange wine in the US. It's thinner there or something."

We had learned on our tour that, once upon a time, all white wine was orange because it was less finicky to produce than white wine. It was made from white wine grapes that were kept wrapped in their skins during the fermentation process. As the world aged, and technology made it easier to remove the skins, wine became more austere, sapped of its color, drained of something vital. I thought about white wine grapes, peeled and naked and alone. The vintners hadn't called it "orange wine." They'd called it "skin contact wine." Izzy hadn't liked the term; she thought it sounded gross. Ben, on the other hand, had said that it sounded clinical. I liked it, though. All the little grapes, skin to skin. It was how you were supposed to bond with a newborn baby. Of course it was thicker, warmer. I took a hearty sip of the orange wine and said, to no one in particular, "This one eats well." I had heard that somewhere. The phrase left a hot taste in my mouth.

For our next course, Liam ordered the Njeguški *stek*, a pork steak stuffed with a local cream cheese called *kajmak* and *pršut*; marinated eggplant; sea bass cooked in a salt crust; and *hobotnica kao ispod peke*, octopus steamed under a metal lid with potatoes and onions. We drank a dry red wine called Vranac, a particular favorite in Russia, where, we learned, most of it was shipped. It was available to tourists only during August, so we counted ourselves lucky. We ordered two bottles, one slightly heavier than the other, which was, the sommelier told us, still produced in the old way, by crushing the grapes underfoot. I decided to prefer this bottle, on principle.

I said to the table, "It's mustier."

"That's the taste of the feet," Ben said.

"No!" Izzy yelped, her cheeks flushed. The sight made me smile. How often I had watched Izzy be a little drunker than me, a little more bashful than me. "You can't taste the *feet!*"

"Oh, but you can! And there's a special website for perverts where you can obtain pictures of the very feet which produced the wine you're drinking," Ben said.

Izzy appeared scandalized and Liam said, "Don't worry, dear. We've opted out on that one." And under his breath as he took a sip, "Of course."

For dessert, though no one was hungry, we ordered the *krempita,* a kind of Balkan custard slice, and a plate of *krofne,* airy doughnuts filled with marmalade, cream, and chocolate.

Ben raised his glass of red wine—we were still finishing the bottles—and said, "A toast! On the last night of our anniversary trip!" We all raised our glasses and he continued, "To Liam and Izzy, who have been married now for two years. Two of the best friends we've ever had. We love you. And you're welcome for introducing you."

We clinked glasses and drank. Then Liam said, "Actually, I believe it was I who introduced you two."

"That's true," I said, tilting my glass at Ben.

"Oh, whatever," he said. "We got married first."

"I can't believe how young we were," I said. "Our parents should have stopped us."

"Your wedding was *the best,*" Izzy said. "You have more fun at weddings when you're younger. You drink more and all of your best, oldest friends are there and everyone's in cheap dresses."

"I certainly don't regret it," Ben said. He smiled at me, so earnestly it embarrassed me.

"What is Meg up to now anyway? I don't think I've seen her since your wedding," Liam said. I saw Izzy stiffen. Meg had been his girlfriend at the time. She and Izzy had gotten along fine. There were no bad feelings, as far as I knew. But still: I wondered why he decided to bring her up, of all things. Liam never thought things through before he said them. He hurt people's feelings all the time because they didn't quite understand how his mind worked, how most of the time, he didn't mean things the way they came out.

"I don't know," I said quickly. "She got married, I think. I tried to find her on Facebook or something a few years ago. I know—*don't*. Anyway, I couldn't so she probably changed her name. That's the thing—everyone acts like we're more connected than ever, but that's not really true for women. Girls just disappear into their husbands' names and we never find each other again."

"Not us," Izzy said, and raised her glass to just me. As we clinked, Ben said, "Fuck the patriarchy!" and drained his own glass.

"I remember watching you walk down the aisle," Izzy said. She had been my maid of honor. I had walked down the aisle as much toward her as I had walked toward Ben. My heart felt full and then something twisted in it; I couldn't tell what. I wanted to hug Izzy suddenly. To be skin to skin. She continued, "I couldn't believe my friend was getting married. We *were* too young. But then I looked at Ben, and I watched him look at you, and I remember thinking: How does it feel to be loved like that?" She grabbed my hand underneath the table and looked Liam right in the eye sharply.

"I have a surprise," Liam said as we emerged into the street. He opened his hand to reveal four little gummy candies. "We are going to eat these and wander through that godawful fair."

"Liam, no!" Izzy said. The fair had been going on in the streets since last night. We had no idea what the occasion was—we just knew that the sounds of carnival games and the smell of fried food had kept us up all night.

"Where did you get these?" Ben asked.

"A magician never reveals his secrets," Liam said seriously. "But don't worry, they're just normal weed gummies, ten milligrams, totally safe. I can't fly home with them, so we have to eat them tonight. Now." We each grabbed one, bit into half, and saved the other half in our pockets for later. "Come on!"

We bought beers at a corner booth and watched children fight each other with Nerf guns. We played a Montenegrin version of Whac-a-Mole where you whacked a man with a mustache. We saw a child smoking a cigarette. We watched a man in a full Garfield costume breakdance on the corner for what might have been ten minutes or two hours. We threw all of our euro coins at his feet, cackling with delight. Ben won a T-shirt in a claw game, which, when he unfolded it, read: ORTHODOX BROTHERHOOD. RUSSIA SERBIA UNITE! We ran through the street, and Izzy's shoe fell off. We ate the other halves of our gummies.

We were walking along a windy stone street, vaguely in the direction of our apartment, when a man shouted, "Oi! My friends!" We turned and it was a night security guard who was posted outside the small art gallery that Izzy and I had briefly poked our heads into the day before.

"Ahoy!" Ben said, his voice weirdly booming. Izzy laughed.

"You're American?" the security guard asked, his face bright.

"We are," I said.

"I love Americans!" he said. "Please, would you like a private tour?"

"We would," Liam said, and we nodded behind him. Izzy could barely contain herself. Weed always made her laugh uncontrollably. Ben was catching it from her, letting out little breaths of delight every minute or two. My heart swelled with adventure.

As the guard unlocked the door, he told us his name was Yuri. He then pointed to his name tag and said, "See? Yuri." It did indeed read YURI.

"Hello, Yuri," Ben said.

"Welcome!"

"Are you sure it's okay for us to be in here after hours?" I asked.

"Oh yes, I'm the guard," he said. "You should see before you leave. Everything is so beautiful. Very authentic. I'll show you."

He began to walk around the gallery, which was quite small, and point at the various pieces. He led us to a large statue of a fish bursting forth from a frothy stone wave. A small sign beside the piece gave the name of the artist. A large sign behind it said, DO NOT TOUCH. Yuri said, "Please! Give it a feel! It's very smooth."

We all looked at each other. Izzy burst into another peel of laughter. I grabbed her hand, trying to keep from laughing myself. "It says 'no touching'!"

"This is no matter," Yuri said, shaking his head. "You can touch. Please, touch it."

I reached out and ran my fingers down the stone. It was, as Yuri had said, very smooth. I liked the feel of it on my skin, cold and glossy. I wanted to press into it. I felt a special, tingling thrill about the idea that I was touching something I was not supposed to touch. I wondered if I would feel this way if I weren't high. Then I wondered if I even was high.

"Why do you love Americans, Yuri?" Ben asked, sounding to me genuinely curious but unable to focus on Yuri's face.

"I have a beautiful American girlfriend," he said, reaching for his phone. "Would you like to see?"

"Definitely," Liam said. "Yes," Izzy giggled at the same time.

He opened up a dating app and began to show us picture after picture of what was, clearly, a series of different but similar-looking supermodels. He punctuated the slideshow with commentary like, "So sexy, yes?" and "So beautiful! Even with no makeup!" We all sneaked bewildered looks at each other at different moments. We had no idea if he was trying to fool us or if he, himself, was being fooled.

Izzy began to quietly shake so violently that she finally exclaimed, "I have to go to the bathroom!" She ran through the front door, out into the street.

"How do you know this woman?" Ben asked, his face a mask of confusion.

"We met online. One day, I hope we will meet in person," Yuri said fondly.

"Ah," said Ben, blinking confusedly. "I believe I'll join Izzy in the bathroom," he said. "Frances, Liam. We will see you after your visit of the gallery." I wondered if he really sounded this ridiculous or if my ears had filtered him to sound weirdly formal, a little British. He walked out after her, and as the door opened, we could hear Izzy exclaim something to him hysterically.

"Please, let's continue the tour," Yuri said, putting his phone away with a smile. "You two are the art lovers, yes?"

"Yes," Liam said with a stately nod.

Yuri took us to a stone urn with something like runes carved into it. DO NOT TOUCH, another sign warned us. My breath caught as the room spun around. I was suddenly certain that someone's ashes were inside the urn. It looked so solemn, sitting there, alone on its plinth.

"Please, touch," Yuri said, running his hand along the grooves.

"No, thank you," I croaked. As I spoke, the world righted itself, but I felt somehow outside it. Liam looked at me, worried. They had burned my mother and put her ashes in an urn. But first they had embalmed her and displayed her in an open casket. How funny she had looked, bloated and covered in makeup. How unlike my mother, nothing more than a plastic doll. I hadn't cried. I had almost laughed. Maybe I was laughing right now. I couldn't tell. I wanted to recoil, then and now. But I also wanted desperately to reach out and touch her, to see if it was really her skin. My mother. My mom. My mommy.

Don't touch, I said to myself at the very same moment that Yuri said again, "Please touch!" Liam reached out his hand, right next to my ear. I watched it stroke the urn, catching on the ravines in the clay. Behind me, my aunt Sandy was wailing through tears, "She was such a *beautiful woman!*" As if to highlight how dead my mom looked, they had surrounded the coffin with pictures of her from when I was little. All these pictures of a woman who didn't exist. At the time, I had whispered to Ben, "This is barbaric." I hadn't touched her. I had gone to the bathroom and looked at myself in the mirror.

The gallery around me felt like it was spinning again. I wanted to be sick. I didn't touch the urn. Instead, I grabbed Liam's hand.

"Thank you for the tour, Yuri!" Liam said, putting his arm around me, heavy, familiar, protective. "And best of luck with your American girlfriend!"

"You're welcome! We will see you soon in the States, I hope!" he said as Liam led me out through a side door that read NO EXIT.

"Are you okay?" Liam asked once we were outside.

"Yeah," I said. "Just high, I think."

"You three are such lightweights."

"Where are Ben and Izzy?" I asked, looking around.

"Probably went home. It's just over there." He pointed down a side street, which I realized, suddenly, was our street. I shook my head, disoriented.

"Sorry," I said. "Let me just breathe for a second."

"Okay."

We sat on the curb. I put my head between my knees. After a minute, I said, "Okay, that woman wasn't a real woman, right? That was, like, four fake women?"

Liam let out a loud laugh. "You're okay, then."

"Yeah, unless I was hallucinating that." It seemed possible. I wondered if the dancing Garfield had been real.

"You weren't, sad to say. Our poor Yuri is being catfished."

"Or was he just trying to show off for us? *Surely* he could tell that she wasn't real. It was so obvious!"

"I don't know," Liam said with a small shrug. "It happens all the time. He wants her to be real. He wants to believe that someone so beautiful would want *him*. Would be interested in *him*. Interested enough to choose him out of anyone in the whole world."

I nodded. "Sometimes what you want can take the place of what's really there."

"Exactly," he said. I realized, suddenly, how close he was

to me. His leg was pressed flush against mine. His arm was still heavy around my back. He reached his other hand up to my chin and tilted my face toward his. We looked at each other for a long time.

I said, "What do you want from me, Liam?"

"More," he said.

I moved away from him, and his arm slid off my back. "You can't quote me back at me."

"Okay, then tell me the truth. What did you get from your other lovers?"

"I got...I don't know. What do you want me to say?" He shrugged, but didn't look away. "I got...fullness. Affection. Intimacy. A feeling that I was...desirable. All that regular, boring stuff."

"What made it different?"

"Did I say it was different?" I snapped.

"No. But it was."

"It was ..." I sighed. I had no idea how to articulate what I felt, but I heard myself talking anyway. "It was different because it was useless. That's what I loved about all of it. It wasn't going anywhere. It wasn't productive. It wasn't necessary to me. What I mean is, we weren't on a path toward marriage or babies or whatever. It didn't have to lead somewhere. It was just...a little room I got to linger in. A cherry on top, just for me. Maybe I thought...maybe I thought I couldn't lose it, because it wasn't something that really mattered anyway. You know how you always seem to misplace the important things, and hold on to the useless ones."

Liam was looking at me seriously, taking in my words like they mattered. He said, "Everything beautiful is useless."

That took me a minute. Then I realized: "Are you quoting fucking Kant at me?"

"By way of the esteemed Professor Marsh, yes."

"The aesthetic is an object without purpose," I said in his gravelly, old man, academic voice. "It's good for nothing."

We laughed and it happened again: We turned nineteen. It was so easy to time-travel with Liam. What was about to happen had already happened hundreds of times before, so there was nothing we could do to stop it.

He scooted back into me and said quietly into my ear, "Nothing good can come of this." He grabbed my chin again and turned it toward his, and he kissed me. His mouth was warm and soft and big. I leaned in and let him consume me. He pulled me into his lap. I scraped my knee on the cobblestone curb but I didn't care, I didn't even feel it. My whole body was throbbing with want. I pressed my body into Liam's without a second thought. He breathed into my mouth, "Do you think about me when you're with Ben?" and I said, "Yes," and he said, "Does it make you come?" and I said, "Yes," and he said, "What about it?" and I said, "It makes me come imagining you doing whatever you want to me."

He grabbed my hair and yanked it, hard. The shock of it brought me back into myself. "Liam," I said, my neck still exposed to him.

"No," he said, and kissed my neck.

"Liam," I said, jerking my face forward, my hair out of his fist. "I don't . . ."

"You do," he said. "You've wanted to this whole trip."

"Have you?" I said, feeling a little sting.

"I've wanted to for years." I couldn't tell if he was serious; Liam blurred that line all the time. It was what I had wanted him to say. I tried to luxuriate in the words, to let them sit and warm in my mouth like I did with good wine. But their aftertaste was tinny and cold.

He sensed my hesitation, I could tell, so he moved closer to me and kept talking. "She took me from you." He put his hands on either side of my face. "Izzy took me from you. Don't you want to take me back? Prove that you can? That I'm yours?"

"What?" I said, pushing his hands down. This wasn't how I had imagined it.

"Don't you want that, Franny?" He leaned forward to kiss me again.

"What?" I said again, lost. "No, I don't want that at all. I... I love Izzy."

He laughed. "I love Izzy, too. Obviously."

"And I love Ben." I got out of his lap and stood up.

"God, Frances, what the fuck. This isn't a soap opera. We aren't running away together. You and Ben have an *open marriage*." He laughed again, and I felt silly. He had a way of doing that, of making me feel like I was overreacting.

"I know," I said, and tried to laugh, too. I ran my hand through my sweaty hair.

"It can just be like you said. Just a little cherry on top. At the end of the trip." He stood up and walked toward me. "Right?" The way he said it. It sounded so different coming out of his mouth. I realized: He hadn't understood what I had meant at all. He hadn't understood about any of it.

His face came into focus as he got closer to me, and I looked at his mouth. It was a gash in his face. As suddenly as it had happened when I was in college, he was repulsive to me. I was repulsive to myself. I couldn't conjure up the image I had had of him before, just fifteen minutes ago. It had died in my head. I shivered. "Don't touch me," I said. "Please don't." I turned to walk back to our apartment.

From behind me, Liam said, "Franny!" I didn't turn to look back. I walked faster. And then I heard his feet on the pavement, heavier than mine. A stupid, dramatic buzz of fear shot through me. That fear that makes you grip your car keys between your fingers when you walk through a parking garage at night. That fear that makes you share your Uber location with your friend's phone. That fear that must have gotten Aunt Frances in the end. That must have been the final thing she ever felt.

But then I heard him stop. I was so dramatic.

He yelled from behind me, "This never happened." In my head, I agreed. Maybe it hadn't. I could convince myself that it hadn't.

Good Girl

I CAN REMEMBER WITH astonishing accuracy the first day I felt real sexual desire, like the way some women report knowing the exact moment their child was conceived, even if they've been having consistent sex. I was nineteen and it was Valentine's Day, for fuck's sake.

By that point in my life, I had had six different dicks in my mouth, some short, some long, all circumcised. I had had two different dicks in my vagina, both medium, both circumcised. As far as I could tell, I had wanted all these dicks to be in each of these places; but once they were there, they invariably stopped making me feel any kind of want at all. I felt irritation. Boredom. These non-feelings, though, were obscured by how grateful I felt to be wanted, a pure, white, shining gratitude. I needed these boys to want me, even briefly. I wasn't good enough to survive feeling bad all the time. Those fleeting moments of feeling admired and cared for were sufficient, until I learned that they weren't.

Franny woke me up that morning. Wearing a robe and a towel wrapped around her head, she shook my shoulder with one hand and said, "Get up, Izzy. It's almost eight." Through bleary eyes, I saw she'd already made her bed.

"Happy Valentine's Day," she said as I sat up. She handed me a chocolate, melted slightly from the warmth of her hand. I asked if Liam had given it to her. "No," she said, rolling her eyes in an exasperated way, like something we had both seen in sitcoms. "I haven't even heard from him since Monday. He's doing his indie boy disappearing act. Trying to make me jealous maybe."

Her nonchalance never failed to surprise me. Franny expected people to like her. She mistrusted people who dismissed her. I wanted to be liked, but always became wary of the people who managed it. By finding me boring or useless, a person demonstrated to me that they understood me. There is a pleasure in being seen for what you are.

"This is from a Valentine's care package my mom sent me." She pointed to her desk, which was covered in hot pink miscellanea. A towel, I remember, printed with hearts. A heart-shaped wine bottle stopper. "In the card, she sent me a list of different ways my Valentine could make me feel loved on Valentine's Day. Very subtle."

She shot her eyes downward to her hand, which was still holding the chocolate. "Oh, thanks," I said, and took it as she guided me over to the pile of things.

"Look at this," she said. The card. It was white with a big, sparkling, hot pink heart on the front. Franny's mom had taken a Sharpie and added two capital M's, one on each side of the heart, so that it read M♥M. I let myself trace my finger down the side of the M, I remember. My hand where a mom's hand had been.

Almost like she had squeezed my palm, smiled at me. I'd never received a Valentine's gift from my parents. My father used to go through the shoebox of cards I would bring home every February fourteenth from elementary school and remove all the ones from boys, shaking his head silently. My mother hid the sweets and distributed them to me sparingly as rewards for good work. It hadn't occurred to me that parents might behave differently until I was in my late teens, too old and too unattached for Valentine's Day cards.

"According to my divorced mom, a noted expert, Liam could make me feel loved by, ahem, giving me a gift. Or planning a date. Or canceling his plans in order to spend extra time with me. Or cooking me a meal. Or telling me he loves me." She raised her eyebrows in irritation.

"Those all seem like good ways," I said, shrugging.

"They all seem like ways for her to tell me that she doesn't like Liam. It's very passive-aggressive."

"Cute nightgown, though." I pointed back to the desk at the lace-trimmed white nightie with red polka dots.

"Yeah. Well. I'm getting sick of Liam's shit anyway. And if he tried to cook for me, we'd probably both end up sick." She crammed another chocolate in her mouth. Her mom always sent her sweets, and she always ate them. She was the only girl I knew who didn't seem to worry about eating too much. "Eughh, mint," she said, spitting it back into her hand. "It tastes like toothpaste." Her back to me as she walked to the trashcan, she said, "Listen, since we're both flying solo, I think we should go to the SAE party tonight. What do you think?"

I thought of piles of red Solo cups, no toilet paper in the bathroom, no locks on the bathroom doors, the floors sticky beneath my feet with muddy, beery sludge. "We hate SAE," I said.

"I know, but ..." She gave me a sheepish smile and shrugged. "It just feels like the thing to do."

"Okay," I said. It never occurred to me that I could have said no. It never occurred to me that I might have wanted to say no.

Anyway, that was the day I learned to want, to really want. I think about it a lot now. Sometimes with nostalgia but mostly with regret, and with a desperate desire to reach out and cradle nineteen-year-old me in my hands. I want to hug her and kiss her, and then grab her by the chin, straighten her face, and say, *Fuck you for doing this to me. Fuck you for fucking me up like this.*

My nine o'clock class that day was Psychology of Personality. I remember because the material kind of messed me up later that day.

We were learning about attachment theory and the Harlow experiments on infant-caregiver relationships from the 1950s. Harlow had separated a bunch of infant rhesus monkeys from their mothers and had constructed for each of them two surrogate mothers: one made of metal that could provide milk for them through a robotic nipple and one covered in soft, fluffy material that couldn't provide them with anything. The monkeys that were caged with both surrogates turned out normal. They were both fed and comforted. When Harlow screamed at them (something I remember wishing I could see on video), they ran to the useless, cozy mother. The monkeys who had only the metal mother behaved the same way as the monkeys who had no mother at all: They didn't explore their cages; they just lay there, paralyzed, rocking back and forth.

My professor, who looked like Hugh Grant if he weren't British (uglier, sort of melty), had been hyperfocused on the unethical nature of these studies, as though any of us might try to secure our own batch of animal babies to torture. He barely delved into the actual findings but, instead, stuttered through the study's drawbacks in his disappointingly American accent. I guess the point was that comfort was as crucial to a child's development as food was. But all I remember feeling was a pang of recognition for the metal mothers. Imagine being the one who could provide actual sustenance to the baby and having to watch them choose the other mother, again and again. Imagine watching them sucking their tiny thumbs instead of your metal nipple.

"Of course, Harlow couldn't study actual human babies! Imagine the lawsuits that would happen nowadays!" the professor laugh-sputtered. "But in the seventies, a psychologist named Edward Tronick enacted a series of studies called the Still Face Experiments. Still borderline ethical, mind you! But, well, I'll let you take a look."

He took about three entire minutes to find the right cord to plug his laptop into the projector, and then another minute to realize he should turn off the lights. "It's just quick, just quick!" he prattled as all my classmates began closing their books and unzipping their bags. "Two minutes! I still have time!"

A video of a young mother and a baby sitting face-to-face began to play. The mother was doing that sort of annoying mom thing. Making her eyes all huge, laughing and clapping with the baby. "Yes!" she said in a high-pitched Disney voice. "What do you see?" The baby cooed and shouted happily in response.

"But look!" the professor said, standing protectively in front of the door lest a student try to slip out right on time.

The psychologist on-screen whispered something to the mother and her face went blank. Her eyes got smaller and her mouth turned down. She stared at the baby, totally expressionless. The baby looked around the room; she tried smiling, then pointing, then laughing. The mom stayed completely still for two full minutes, and so did the class. I couldn't stop watching her. No one could. The baby began to laugh maniacally, bigger and bigger, even as her eyes began to fill with tears, and the mom just blinked. She didn't even move when the baby started crying.

She looked so beautiful to me, that mother. I remember how her hair fell around her face, curling under her chin. Her straight brows. Her fluttering eyelashes. Her coolness. How much the baby wanted her and how little she seemed to care.

Then suddenly, she smiled and lunged toward the baby, petting her head and goo-ing. The baby smiled again, like nothing had happened at all, and I felt something strange, like maybe I hated that baby. The girl sitting next to me let out a sound that might have been a sob. To avoid looking at her, I packed up my books.

My next class, and my last class of the day, was Film and Culture, which was actually a class in the English Department. I had an English requirement on my pre-med track and figured I'd have more time to watch movies than read books alongside all my labs. It was supposed to be a blow-off, but it became my favorite class, for a lot of bad reasons. The biggest bad reason was the professor, Dr. Vachon, whom everyone just called Vachon. There was some debate about his age—boys seemed to think he was mid- to late forties, but most girls were convinced he was forty at most. He was balding—that was undeniable—but his baldness gave him an elusive, angular, almost thuggish quality at odds with his French accent. He was tall, at least six-two, and broad-shouldered, and leering. We saw him around campus, even on frat row at night sometimes, smoking cigarettes. He had a wife in the Environmental Studies Department, a small, mousy woman always in hiking boots. That they were divorcing was a fact; that it was because of his affairs with girl students was a rumor that turned out to be true.

Franny had had a class with him last semester and whispered to me one night that when you answered a question in class, he looked at you in a way that made you want to cover your throat with your hands. I never answered any questions in class and he never looked at me.

We were finishing our discussion of *Vertigo* that day. I hadn't liked it much when I watched it, but I liked hearing Vachon talk about it. He said things like, "Madeleine, possessed by the ghost of her great-grandmother. Judy, possessed by the figure of Madeleine, an unreal woman. Scotty, desperate to possess Madeleine even if it must be through the body of Judy. What does it mean for men to possess and women to be possessed?" He did things like validate the dumb responses that invariably came to these questions, even when what he wanted to get at was something like this: "Hitchcock is a filmmaker! The medium is his message. Susan Sontag writes that 'one can't possess reality, but one can possess (and be possessed by) images.' How are we violated, *feminized*, when we view a film? How does Hitchcock penetrate us with the camera?"

I could sit there and listen to things like this and stop breathing. *Look at me*, I would think. *Look at me.*

My sort-of-friend Shelley sat next to me in class, and Vachon looked at her all the time. She had a lot to say. She was nice, and easy to study or grab lunch with. But she wrote what I considered, at the time, to be a cringeworthy column in our school newspaper about Greek life and rape culture on campus. Franny and I weren't in sororities. We felt we weren't really like the sorority girls, and anyway, it was embarrassing to pay to have friends. But Shelley lived in the women's center and identified as a feminist, which was—back then—about ten times more embarrassing. "She's a hypocrite, too," Franny said. "She wears heels, like, all the time."

When Vachon explained that psychological thrillers like *Vertigo* were important precursors to a dying and understudied genre from the 1990s, the erotic thriller, Shelley sighed loudly and rolled her eyes. She turned to me and whispered, "It's such a joke that this class is cross-listed with women's studies. I can't believe I need this to complete my minor."

"Yeah," I said, and turned away, eager to listen to Vachon. We were slated to watch *Basic Instinct* for next week, and I had been looking forward to it. I had never seen an erotic thriller, but I had a vivid memory of walking through Blockbuster as a kid and picking up the VHS tape of *Eyes Wide Shut*, flipping it over, and seeing a woman undressing on the back cover. I remember my pulse racing as I slammed it back onto the shelf, terrified my dad would see what I had seen.

"Consider what we've been talking about—consider *possession*," Vachon was saying. "Particularly in the interrogation scene. You'll know which one I mean." A few of the students giggled. "We'll discuss how it relates, how Verhoeven allows his audience to possess Sharon Stone, if just for a moment, even as her character, Catherine, possesses the male characters. How the passive viewer is given a fleeting moment of power." Just then, I could swear, his eyes paused on mine, and he gave a small wink. It was true, my throat was raw and exposed. I looked down at my chipped fingernails and hoped my neck hadn't turned red.

"I'm not watching it," Shelley said to me as we walked out together. "*Basic Instinct* isn't even a *film.* It's a *movie.* Vachon's just a creep who wants to show us Sharon Stone's vagina."

"Yeah," I said. That's what I usually said to Shelley.

"She didn't consent to it, you know. I read about it when I saw it on our syllabus. The director tricked her into uncrossing her legs like that. She doesn't want me to see her vagina and so I don't have the right to. I don't care if I get in trouble for not watching it. I'd love to explain why to the dean if I have to. Want to get a coffee?"

"Oh," I said. "Um, no, I need to get to the library. Franny wants me to go to the SAE party with her tonight so I need to get some work done this afternoon." I was hoping I could check out the library copy of *Basic Instinct* that was on reserve for our class before anyone else did.

"Oh," she said, and grabbed my shoulder. "Okay. It's none of my business, but be careful."

"Totally," I said, and stepped away from her.

Franny had afternoon classes, so I had the dorm room to myself. I changed out of my jeans and into an old pair of flannel pajama pants with teddy bears on them. I grabbed my laptop and the DVD and slid into bed.

At first, I didn't really like it, either. I understood what Shelley meant about it being a movie, not a film. It reminded me of the airport thrillers my dad let himself read on special occasions, ones with the author's name on the front in red letters bigger than the title. Though my dad would never have read one with so much sex in it; I was sure of that.

But the longer I watched it, the more I felt like I wasn't ready for it to end. It wasn't that the movie made me think. It was more that it made me stop thinking entirely. A sense of tingling disgust washed over me and held me captive. When the police begin interrogating Catherine, I felt my pulse quicken. I knew what was going to happen but I didn't know when. Suddenly, she uncrosses her legs. I paused, rewound, watched again. I felt it, like Vachon had said I would: a sense of power. Of doing something bad and getting away with it. Catherine was so distant, cold, blond, controlling. The movie made it impossible to feel close to her—but suddenly, I could see into her, and she had no idea.

My disgust mixed with something like anticipation, a high. I had never watched something for a class that stimulated me viscerally but not intellectually. I wondered if that was the point. By the time the final scene came around, I felt hot and I had thrown off my covers. Unconsciously, I checked to see whether I had locked the door.

Nick and Catherine are standing close to each other. They start to dance and then they start to kiss and they have no idea that Roxy is watching them, violating their privacy. I reached down underneath the elastic waistband of my pajamas and put my middle finger on my clit. Catherine pushes Nick down onto the bed and begins to fuck him almost violently. I began to rub myself faster. She pulls out a white silk scarf and ties Nick's wrists to the headboard. *She's going to kill him*, I thought. And I kept going, harder, thinking about the softness of that scarf. The fabric is cool and buttery and comforting, but it's tied too tight, keeping him from moving, forcing him to do what Catherine wants. How good it must feel for him, to be told exactly what to do. How exciting it must be to know that she is strong enough to break his bones but is choosing not to, at least not yet. The relief he must feel when Catherine finally looks at him and loosens the ties. Knowing he did a good job and would be rewarded with his life. The cold mom with the still face popped into my head, and right as she looked at me, I came, long and hard.

Franny had secured a handle of Burnett's raspberry vodka from an upperclassman she had a seminar with and we were sitting on the floor of our dorm room, mixing it with various Crystal Light packets, trying to find the perfect combo.

"Raspberry Lemonade is the clear winner," I said, finishing a Solo cup full.

Franny wrinkled her nose. "Nah. Too matchy-matchy. Pink Lemonade is my favorite."

We always pregamed together while we got ready. It was smarter that way. We didn't trust any of the frat boys to make us mixed drinks, and they only ever had heavy beers on hand, which would bloat us. We had finished our makeup an hour ago and were just lingering at this point. I had the feeling Franny was hoping Liam might call our dorm phone, even though she wouldn't admit to it. It didn't bother me. We always had more fun during this part of the night than at the parties.

"Dare you to try Grape with it," she said, shaking the packet in my face.

"Nooo," I said. "It'll taste like medicine."

"Duh, that's why it's a dare."

In the end, we both tried it. And then one called Peach Mango Green Tea, which had WITH CAFFEINE emblazoned in calligraphy across the front. That made us crack up, for some reason. Franny decided, in a kind of frenzy, that we needed to try all of the WITH CAFFEINE flavors as part of a blind tasting, which she put together for us. I watched her, feeling warm and a little woozy, overwhelmed that she was my friend. She was smart and self-assured. But her intelligence didn't diminish her enthusiasm for things, which I discovered was a rare quality in a college student. She was the kind of person who could find something to love in anything. I wondered, sometimes, what that meant about her love for me.

We tried them all in quick, giggling succession before we collapsed into shouts of laughter. "My heart is beating so fast," I said, clutching it on the ground where we were sitting. "This isn't like a Red Bull Vodka situation, is it? Where my heart is going to explode?"

"Oh my god, what if your heart exploded on LITERAL Valentine's Day?!" she shrieked.

"Does Hallmark make a special get-well card for that, or do you just have to reuse the sparkly heart-shaped ones like your mom sent?!" I said, which sent us off again.

A half hour or so later, Franny said, "Okay, okay! If we're going to go to this dumb party, we need to go." She shut our music off and thrust the tube of red lipstick at me that had arrived with her care package that morning. I stood up, wobbled, and caught myself on the desk. We laughed and walked over to the full-length mirror that was mounted on the door leading to the bathroom we shared with our suitemates. I leaned in to put on the lipstick and then puckered my lips and glared at myself, unsmiling. I looked sophisticated, I thought. Like a real woman.

"What the fuck is that?" Franny whispered to me as she pressed her ear against the door.

"What?" I whispered back.

"Oh my fucking god, Alexa's listening to that John Mayer song from middle school, what's it called... 'Daughters'!" She rolled her eyes and widened her mouth at me like, *Can you even?*

"Oh my god!" I said. "Ewwww!"

"How *sad*," Franny said. "Should we make her come with us?"

"Nah," I said. "She's clearly going through something and needs to be alone."

As we walked down our dorm stairs, Franny chanted, "'Girls become lovers who turn into mothers, so mothers, be good to your daughters.' Fucking gag! It's, like, you don't even get to turn into a *person!* You're just, like, someone else's lover and then someone else's mother, like totally erased inside."

"Yeah," I said, even though I didn't want to talk about that. I had always thought becoming a woman was how you became a person. I was looking forward to it happening to me one day. But then I thought about the still-faced mother, how easily she had gone blank looking at that baby. That had been inside her the whole time. Like how the soft mothers were just metal mothers covered in cloth and robbed of their actual source of life, the milk. I felt really down then, which meant I was either sober or way too drunk. "God, fuck, it's freezing out here," I said as we walked outside.

"It's not too far and I am *not* bringing my coat again," Franny said, shivering. She had hidden one behind a tree outside a party a few weeks ago so it wouldn't get stolen, and someone had peed on it. She stumbled off the curb and caught herself and laughed, but it didn't really seem funny to me.

I grabbed on to her arm and walked next to her. I said, "Franny. It's cold. This is going to suck. Let's just go back and finish the vodka. We can pair it with the peeps."

"Ugh, Izzy. You always do this!" She wrenched her arm out of my hand and started moving faster. She was glaring at me, but trying not to sound too mad, I could tell. "We got all ready and everything and it's Valentine's Day! We're not staying in our dorm just the two of us!"

I felt stung by that, even though she sort of laughed her way through saying it. Franny always liked hanging out, just the two of us, until suddenly she didn't. I never knew when I was about to stop being enough for her. I felt drunk and miserable and angry and sick of *her* all of a sudden.

But I just sulked and kept walking. It never occurred to me that I could go back without her.

After a minute, she sighed and said, "Okay, that's it, it's too cold." She stopped and faced me and grabbed my hand. She got a big determined look on her face and then started sprinting. I almost fell as she pulled on my fingers, hard, dragging me through the empty street toward the blare of music. "Let's go, Izzy! Come on!" Like a switch had flipped, I felt myself lightening as the cold air slapped my face. We were running like little kids, our limbs going everywhere. I screamed, too, like she had done. And suddenly, we were there, mixing in with a big crowd of people smoking or peeing or throwing up outside the party.

I stopped to catch my breath, and my face broke into a huge, wild smile. "Oh my god," I panted. "Franny. We made it!" She wrapped me into a hug, and we both cracked up. As our breathing slowed, I looked up to smile at her, but she was looking away from me. "Franny?"

I followed her gaze and saw that Liam was there, standing in the doorway and holding a twelve-pack of High Lifes. He looked at us sheepishly and ran his fingers through his dark hair the way he always did. "I can*not* believe he's here. He has *so* much explaining to do," Franny said. "Sorry, Izzy, I'll see you in a bit. Go inside without me!"

And she walked away from me. I watched as she grabbed Liam and laughed in an *I don't care* way and pulled him to the backyard. She took one of his beers as they rounded the corner.

So I was alone. And I was cold. And I was sweating now, because she'd made me run with her. I hated her again. I could imagine her telling people about how we ran across campus to this party, making it into a funny anecdote. She always did that, and she always made herself the main character. She took up a lot of space, even in other people's stories. I thought about going home. I thought about going inside. I thought about how sad I must look to people, standing alone with no one to talk to at a Valentine's Day party. But I didn't think anyone was looking at me anyway. And besides, what had I expected to happen? This was familiar. I kicked the ground and noticed someone had left a Solo cup full of some kind of red punch on the front porch near me. A lot of the frats made that stuff, and it was lethal. *Fuck it*, I thought, and picked it up and drained it.

I heard a low, growling laugh at my right shoulder, which made me jump.

My vision blurred as I turned to look for the source of the sound. I refocused my eyes, but I still wasn't sure I was actually seeing what I thought I was seeing. It was him, leaning against the stone wall in, I swear to god, a leather jacket and smoking a cigarette. "Vachon?" I said. It had come out girly, breathy.

"Don't you mean Professor Vachon?" he said through a smoky exhale in his French accent. As fake as it sounds, that's really how he was. And he really was there. I wish he hadn't been.

"I—" I said, looking down at my feet.

"Relax," he said, putting out his cigarette on the wall and tossing the butt on the ground. "I'm teasing you."

"Oh." I was still looking down, but I became aware of his gaze on me, grazing my cheeks, my collarbone, my outfit, down to my feet. I forced myself to look up and lock eyes with him. I breathed out. I felt the sugar and Everclear roll down my veins into the tips of my fingers and toes. I smiled.

"Did you just pick up an abandoned cup at a party and drink from it?" he asked, pointing at my hand.

"Oh," I said again, and then shook my head. "Yeah. You saw that?" I tried to stand up straighter. Maybe it would seem cool, that I had done that. "Finders keepers," I said, and felt like an idiot.

"I saw it," he said. "You know that's very dangerous, right?"

"I don't know," I said, trying to imitate the higher, breathier voice that Franny sometimes put on for boys. "People can get really worked up about stuff that doesn't actually happen that much."

"It happens," he said. "I should keep my eye on you."

I flushed all over. I didn't think it was the drink this time.

He took a step toward me and said, "That was very bad." Suddenly, I realized I wasn't sure exactly what was happening. Was I in trouble? Would he be able to punish me, in some way, as my teacher? "I'm surprised at you."

"Well . . ." My heart began to beat with anxiety.

He came nearer to me. I tried to keep my eyes on him, but

it was like bringing my fingertips closer and closer to a candle flame. Abruptly, he was right in front of me, towering over me, his sharp jawline cutting into the air above my head. If I touched it, I thought, it would slice open my finger. He grabbed my chin and tilted my head upward so that I was looking him directly in the eye, my throat bent back at a slight angle. His hand was bony but warm. I stopped shivering in his shadow.

"You're usually such a good girl," he said quietly. "I see you in class, taking your notes. Doing your homework. So good. So quiet."

"I—" I said.

"You won't do it again, will you? Put yourself in danger like that?" His eyes darted back and forth between my own. His hand tightened on my chin. My whole body was throbbing, just as it had been earlier, when I watched Catherine tie Nick to her bedpost. I thought of Catherine, her cool, sharp lines. The ice pick underneath her bed. *This was what it feels like*, I realized, *to desire someone*. To want to be at their mercy. To want to lose yourself in them. Not to know if you will survive them or if you deserve to. This was what I had been missing with those other boys, who kissed me and cradled me after. This was what I would spend the next ten years trying to replicate.

Without flinching, I said, "No. I'll be your good girl from now on. I promise."

"Good," he said, and ran his thumb down the line of my throat.

The Rules

"YOU LOOK SO PRECIOUS when you sleep," Frances said one morning. She brushed his hair out of his face and pressed her nose into his hairline. "You smell like a baby."

"Like a baby?" Ben repeated groggily, pulling the sheets up to his chin.

"Mm. Baby smell." She kissed his forehead.

Precious like a baby, but also like a jewel. Something to clutch tight. To hoard. How he wanted to be hoarded by her, especially in moments like this. He rolled to his side so that she would cradle him in her arms, and she did until her phone buzzed on her nightstand. The scent of grapefruit and mint—her shampoo—and of her warm skin drifted away from him.

"Mmm," he groaned, repositioning.

"Sorry, it's this same woman."

"With the huge boobs?"

"I was going to say 'with the Renaissance Faire outfits,' but yeah, that's the one."

"I know why you're still messaging with her, and it's not the gowns."

Frances grabbed him again and wrestled him over to her side of the bed. "Shut up," she said. He bit her lightly on the wrist. "It's too early for all this." He kissed her where he bit her, and they lay in silence for a moment, in the heat of their bed, before she asked, "Are you starting to feel a little exhausted with it all?"

"With dating?"

"Yeah."

"Mm...I don't know," Ben said. He feared he had been led into a trap. He *was* beginning to feel exhausted with it all, the first dates, the small talk, the surprisingly closemouthed kisses some people gave, feeling self-conscious about his body, watching Frances walk out their front door. There was so much important television the two of them were behind on. That felt weighty to him now.

What he wasn't tired of was the way Franny looked at him sometimes, like there was no one else like him. No other man as understanding and open and supportive and (well) feminist and (well) queer-affirming as he was. He loved who he was under that gaze, and he didn't want to blow it. He shrugged and said, "You're dating more than me." Letting her lead the way.

"I guess so," she said. "I'm not connecting with anyone the way I used to. I feel...I don't know. I don't love feeling..." She looked down and wrinkled her eyebrows. "So on display. For sale?" She shrugged. "Well, anyway. Wasn't the point finding a real connection?"

He thought about that and said, "For you, I think it was. Maybe I was more excited when it just felt easy, fun."

"Mm. Yeah."

"But it's easy and fun with us. And connective." He thought he had hidden the plea in his voice. She smiled at him, as he hoped she would, and she kissed his forehead again. "It was nice, just being the two of us again, for the anniversary trip." They'd gone with their oldest friends, Liam and Izzy. How cozy it had been to fall into coupledom, into those mundanities men and women always boxed themselves into. *She's like a furnace, but god forbid we remove the comforter in the summer! Ah, it's the same with Izzy!* When Liam wasn't being moody, that was. And looking at Frances in that way he always did.

She pulled back from him, something like a wince on her face. He had said something wrong. Maybe he had seemed too eager, too pushy. "Want me to make some coffee?" he asked quickly, sitting up.

"Obviously," she said, smiling again now, stretching out that way she did. As he opened their bedroom door, she added, "I might take a break soon. Delete the app, I don't know. We could maybe talk more seriously about the whole baby thing."

Framed in the doorway, Ben asked, "Really?"

"Yeah. I think so. Maybe it's time."

He felt his face break into a smile. He wanted this, but it surprised him, the way the muscles in his cheeks seemed to know it before his brain did. "Okay," he said. "You know I'm on your timeline with pregnancy. Whatever you want, really."

"Okay," she said, and curled back up.

* * *

That afternoon, instead of meeting his friend Max for a drink as he often did after their concurrent classes, he stayed in his office, waiting for a former student.

"Do you mind if I shut the door?" Cassie asked when she arrived, something of a grimace playing across her mouth. Perhaps she detected his momentary hesitation, because she added, "Sorry, it's just... well, it's a bit private ..."

"Of course not," Ben said. Very quietly, he pushed her chair slightly farther away with his foot.

As she returned to her seat, she blurted out, "I was hoping you might step in as my dissertation advisor."

"Oh!" Cassie was one of their more talented graduate students, in his opinion, and had passed her prospectus defense the previous academic year. When she had requested the meeting, he had assumed that she was filling out her full committee. He'd like to sit on it; it would bolster the tenure package he was actively building. "Well, I hope you know how much I respect your work. I still think about the final paper you submitted for our seminar—I'm thrilled there's a version of it under contract already, if I haven't already said. But, well, I thought you were working with Agnes?"

At her name, Cassie seemed to wilt. "I guess I'm not sure we're really clicking." She said this to her bag, which sat at the foot of her chair. It was a canvas tote that read I KANT EVEN.

"Great bag," Ben said. He cleared his throat and tried to blaze on. "Um, well, is it her feedback? Because I know that Agnes has high expectations. I guess you know that I was one of her first students after she was tenured."

"Yeah, that's part of it," Cassie said. "She supported my prospectus—at least she seemed to. But ..."

"You can say it. Really."

It came out in a gush. "She's made me rewrite my introduction now six times. It's all I've done for the past year. *Six.* And in each revision, she takes out more of my ideas and tells me to do more research into her own areas of interest. I'm ready to go on the market. And... well! My CV is already twice as strong as people in the cohort above mine!" Cassie's pale face had turned red. She took a deep breath.

Ben tried to remain calm. He thought he understood what was happening here; unfortunately, sentiments like this were all too common. It tended to rub people the wrong way when a woman held a position of authority, even girls! *Other women*, he corrected himself. Cassie was a woman.

He said, "She's definitely hands-on. She had strong ideas about my arguments, too, which could feel overwhelming. But I found that she generally turned out to be right ..."

The ghost of an eye roll flitted across her face. "That's what Aaron said. He's her other advisee. But ..."

Ben nodded encouragement. "You can—"

"I don't think Agnes likes working with women."

There was a brief silence, one in which Ben held back the obvious statement that was reverberating in his brain: "Agnes *is* a woman." When they both began to speak at the same time, Ben said, "Please," and motioned for Cassie to continue.

"Look, I hope you can keep this between us, because I don't want to be branded as a problem student or anything. But... I've met with her twice in a group with Aaron, and both times she barely gave him a note. She had nothing but praise for his work, which... well, it's an Aristotelian perspective on ethical knowledge and practical reasoning," she finished, suppressing an eye roll.

"I'll agree that it's less edgy than your work."

"Right. And besides that, she's asked me to babysit for her three times, and I keep doing it. It feels . . . well, it kind of feels like I can't say no." She let out another long breath. "She's a really big name in the department; I don't need to tell you that."

"She is." She had worked hard for that big name, Ben knew.

"What do you think? Would you . . . well, would you want to step in? I think you . . . Well, I know you like my work."

"I . . ." Ben shifted in his chair, a sudden pain in his back. "Well, I don't have tenure yet. It's kind of against the rules. You'd have to petition the GPC—ah, graduate program coordinators. It's happened before, certainly, that non-tenured professors guide dissertations. But . . ." But poor Agnes, he thought. He didn't want to be yet another man who overstepped her. "Let me look into it," he said. "I'll figure out if this could work logistically."

"Okay," she said, and she seemed to intuit some of his hesitation. "We can keep it between us for now."

"I'll be in touch soon," Ben said, standing. Perhaps a few days would give Cassie the time to rethink her decision. If not, he'd surely be able to walk it back with her.

She got up to leave but turned to look at him as she opened the door. Something in her expression had changed, had become both probing and accusatory.

"Did she ever ask you to babysit?" The question hit him like a barb.

"I—" Ben thought for a moment. "Well, no."

"What are you going to do?" Frances asked him as they wandered through the produce section that evening.

"I really don't know if I'd even be allowed. But, well . . ."

"What?"

"I'm not sure she's really seeing the big picture here. It's different for this generation of students. Women students. The barrier to success is much thinner now. I'm not sure Cassie understands how difficult it's been for Agnes to prove *herself* to be 'rigorous' enough to be promoted to full professor. It sounds to me like she might have higher expectations for Cassie because she's determined to see her succeed. Whether or not that's misguided these days, I don't know . . ." Ben grabbed a bag of Yukon gold potatoes.

"No, no," Frances said, taking them out of his hands. "We need red potatoes. Also, add sour cream to the list. That's how my mom makes them."

He placed his hand on her back, rubbed his thumb up and down. "Right," he said. And then, "You're very bossy."

She reached for his phone and added sour cream to the list herself. "Not as bossy as Agnes." She winked at him and then added, "Babysitting! That *is* fucked up, if it's true."

"Yeah."

"And you don't have kids, so you're a safe bet." Frances smirked.

"Right," Ben said, and tried to laugh with her. "No kids."

To love someone is such a private experience. It's impossible to communicate what is lovable about the other person. If pressed, you find yourself listing off silly things they do, reducing them to a series of oddities or compulsions, little fragments. Little gems.

The way Frances smirked when she bossed him. The way she stretched out like a cat in the mornings when she wanted him to tell her she was cute. The way she still used the present tense, sometimes, when she spoke about her mother, who was almost three years dead.

My mom hates carpet downstairs, except in bedrooms. My mom puts lilies out in the spring and sunflowers out in the summer. No, no, no, Mom says you shouldn't stir the sugar while it's melting or the caramel will seize.

He wondered about it, how her mom's ghost was always housekeeping. Whether Frances ever noticed how often she put her to work.

Agnes had taken one woman graduate student, Allison, while Ben was working with her. He didn't know what had happened to her, but he was pretty sure she had left ABD for personal reasons. He decided to reach out to her, to find out whether she had had problems working with Agnes. It wasn't that he didn't believe Cassie—he had repeated this to himself several times over the last few days, each time with more insistence. It was just that he wanted the bigger picture before he made any other moves.

Ben knew a bit of departmental gossip, but not much. Rumors seemed the purview of graduate students still in coursework and the oldest, most senior professors only. As a cog in the not-yet-tenured middle, Ben tried to remain uncontroversial—and to seem too busy and inspired for idle talk.

Of course, everyone knew about the white-haired male professor—a former chair, in fact—who had been quietly let go a few years previously after several undergraduate women had made accusations against him to the Title IX committee. Nothing "heinous," the department had been told; "all consensual encounters," as far as could be proven. But still, the power dynamic. The age difference. Best to retire him early, in the current climate. Plus, he'd had a habit of grabbing you just after a too-long department meeting to tell you a joke about academia—a knock-knock joke, a chicken crossing the road joke, once a yo mama joke. You'd have to laugh, in order to escape. Good riddance, the department widely agreed.

But Agnes was a woman herself. And there had been less than nothing whispered about her, as far as he knew. No preferential treatment. No boundaries breached.

The jokes were things like this:

Question: How many professors does it take to screw in a light bulb?
Answer: None. That's what their graduate students are for.

After some more digging, he found Allison. She still lived in town and worked in fundraising for a theater company loosely affiliated with the university. He sent her an email explaining Cassie's concerns (without names, of course) and asking about her experience.

Most likely, she would report having had a perfectly normal one, as he had. He'd meet with Cassie, offer to join her committee, and encourage her to push forward with Agnes. He would stay in Agnes's good books, bolster his packet, and achieve tenure before becoming a father, as he had always planned.

* * *

Hi Ben,

Yes, of course I remember you! Sorry for my delayed response; end of quarter madness over here.

I'm really sorry to hear about your student, and I understand your distress about it. I'd be happy to talk about my experience with Agnes before I left the program, but it feels like a bit much to type. My office is right by campus; I'm in three days a week. If you're teaching today or Monday, I'm free after 5:30 to talk over a drink, maybe? My ex has my daughter for the long weekend.

Let me know—

Allison

Ben read the email and sat in silence for a long time. *Fuck*, he thought. *Fuck*.

He stared out his office window. Two boys were outside, kissing, one sitting on a short brick wall, his legs spread, and the other pressing his pelvis into the sitting boy's thigh. It was sunny, around three o'clock. The sitting boy held tightly on to the arm of the standing boy's jean jacket, like he wanted to pull the patches off, or pull the boy's skin off and get inside it. Ben had had a jacket like that in college. He had worn it mostly indoors, at night, to gigs where he was surrounded by jumping, sweating, pretty boys like the kissing ones. Sometimes, they bumped him and said, *Oh, sorry*. Once, a boy bumped him and smiled at him. Ben had smiled back, and then had retreated to get another drink.

His phone buzzed. It was Franny. Ren Faire wants to meet for a drink tonight. What do you think?

He read it twice. He felt irritated, maybe angry. She had told him she was deleting the app.

But he was angrier than he had a right to feel about that. Maybe it was the dread that had dropped into his stomach when he read Allison's email. What was "a bit much" to have to type? Fuck! But still, Frances making a big deal about deleting her app and then scheduling a date? And then asking, *What do you think?* She knew he wouldn't tell her not to go. She just wanted to be absolved.

Cassie's voice floated through his mind: *It kind of feels like I can't say no.*

Franny texted again. Just to tell her in person that I'm going to take a break. Seems like the right thing to do, since we've been texting for a while?

The right thing. Not just the thing she wants to do.

He texted, Sure—without punctuation. Whatever you want—again no punctuation.

He watched the boys outside for a while. He wondered if they wanted to be seen. Or if they didn't even think about the fact that they might be seen. Was it true, that the world was different now? Or was it just that he'd spent his own student years insulated by the cloak of his anxieties, terrified of asserting himself. Both options made him feel lonely. In any case, it didn't matter what they thought about their visibility. His third-floor office was high enough that he wouldn't register to them.

He hit "Reply" on Allison's email and asked if she wanted to meet after work that evening. Since he didn't have any other plans.

* * *

They decided to meet at the grad student pub across from campus. When Ben arrived, he found Allison waiting for him at a high top near the bar. He hadn't seen her in years. Was it seven or eight? Either way, the number astonished him, and he tried to shake it out of his head. But she looked very much the same: untamed, dirty-blond curls hovering around her shoulders, pushed back behind an ear stacked with cartilage piercings; a sleeve of fine-line floral tattoos up one arm; wide green eyes and a heart-shaped face. She stood as the door closed behind him, losing a few inches in height.

"Allison, hi," Ben said, hanging his bag on the chair opposite hers. He leaned down and they hugged. One arm only. Extricating themselves, they began to say, at the same moment, something along the lines of "Long time." Realizing it, they laughed, and Allison shook her head in a sort of zany way. "Sorry," Ben said as he sat down, "I guess this is a little weird."

"Nah," she said, hopping up into her chair. "It's nice to see you again. I'm happy I can help with your student." She looked around. "I haven't been here in forever, maybe not since I was studying for exams."

"Me neither," Ben said, and then flushed. "Sorry, I don't know why I said that. I come here all the time."

Allison laughed.

"Is that sad, do you think? For a professor to still come to a grad student bar?"

"Only if you come alone. Do you?"

"No, I usually come with my friend Max. He teaches English."

"We'll call it fine, then," she said, and grinned widely at him.

They ordered beers and loaded fries to share. ("Do you mind?" Allison had asked. "I'm always starving after work.") Allison told him about her daughter, Lou, who was in the first grade and who had yet to shake an obsession with construction equipment. Ben told her that he and Frances had gotten married—had they ever met, in grad school?—and then heard himself say, "I'd like to have a daughter. We've been talking about kids for a long time, but Frances hasn't felt ready. We were about to start, actually, but then her mom . . ." He shook his head. "Sorry. That was probably too personal." Something about the warmth of her open face had pulled it from him; he had a feeling people often overshared with her. Or dumped their problems on her. He finished his first beer.

"Just to warn you, my shit is about to get pretty personal, too. I'm glad you broke the seal." She took her final sip and said, "Should we have another round before we get into it?"

Once, the joke was:

Question: How many graduate students does it take to screw in a light bulb?
Answer: Just one, but it takes him nine years.

"I told you I left ABD when I got pregnant, but it was more than that, to be honest. I was married at the time—did you ever meet Zach? My ex?"

Ben tried to conjure an image of him and failed; he shook his head.

"I didn't think so. He didn't socialize much—so I didn't, either, back then. Anyway, our marriage was . . . well, we got married while we were still in college, only twenty years old. It was his idea. He told me he never wanted to lose me. It felt very romantic at the time. It's easy for me to see, now, that he wanted to own me. I learned later that he'd proposed to his high school girlfriend, too. She was smarter than me—or maybe her parents were. She said no." She ate the last fry and then said, "Sorry, I promise this is going somewhere relevant."

"No," Ben said quickly. "I'm—" *What? I'm curious? About you and your traumas?* "I asked."

She smiled. "It's all to say that he was possessive. Really possessive. My therapist would want me to tell you that he was controlling and emotionally abusive, which he was but which still feels melodramatic to me when I say it. I hadn't dated a lot; I didn't realize it wasn't normal. Anyway, I was supposed to get through the program as quickly as possible so we could start a family. I asked Agnes to be my advisor, thinking both that her guidance would ensure I passed my defense and that she might be sympathetic to my situation, as a woman. But then—I was working my ass off, but nothing I produced was ever good enough. My writing was 'very pretty,' I remember her saying." She rolled her eyes. "I took comments like that as compliments at first. But Zach got more and more restless, so I tried to work harder and harder, and Agnes wanted more and more revision—anyway. Eventually, I thought, why am I so far behind other people in my cohort? So I asked Dr. Turner for notes on my chapter—she was on my committee, too. And she had them, for sure; but she was also really enthusiastic and helpful, and told me my work was solid, that a dissertation was expected to be a bit messy. When I told Agnes, she got... well, angry. It surprised me. She told me that it was too early to be 'muddling my research with outside influence.' Her words. And on top of that, I had just found out I was pregnant, a good year before

I wanted to be. Well, something about being trapped made me realize how angry I was at her. How possessive she was of her students. And after a while I realized... why wasn't I this angry when Zach wouldn't allow me to go out for drinks with friends, or go to conferences in other cities? It's amazing what you can accept when you love someone."

She took a deep breath in and then added, "That's the personal version."

"What happened? After that?"

"Oh, I took the summer off and never came back. I asked Zach for a divorce and full custody. I got partial custody, which my lawyer told me was a win since I had no evidence of abuse. I had a baby. I got a job that pays as well as any academic one and that I like perfectly fine. I learned that no one owns me but me. I dated around, men and women. I decided to never tie myself exclusively to anyone I'm dating ever again. It's just me and Lou." She shrugged and laughed. "You know, easy breezy summer stuff."

"So you practice non-monogamy?" *Practice!* Why had he asked that? Of all the things he could have taken away from what she had just shared with him. He wanted to take it back instantly.

She laughed. "*Practice.*" Ben wanted to die. "Yeah. I guess that's what people say. Someone I'm seeing calls it solo poly. I don't really call it anything."

"Cool," Ben said lamely. "Us, too. Frances and I. Non-monogamy." He shook his head. "Sorry, I just never meet anyone else in real life—like, off the apps, I mean—who... It's beside the point. And none of my business. I'm just feeling... surprised, I guess. I think I was hoping you'd tell me something different. About Agnes."

"Sorry."

"No, don't say that. So you're saying you think Agnes abuses her power?"

"Yeah, I think so. And your student would be right to stop working with her, if she wants to. She might even consider reporting it."

"Why didn't you?" Ben asked. "Sorry, I didn't mean—" He was making an ass of himself, and he wasn't sure why. He often left social situations anxiously, deeming at least one or two things he'd said embarrassing or corny. He felt jealous, sometimes, of Frances's perpetual confidence that she had both been herself and said the right things. But mostly, he felt validated by it. If she had chosen him, she had done it with certainty. And that meant that he must be better than he thought he was. But tonight, he felt unmoored. He wasn't sure if it was the topic or something else—Frances's absence maybe. Or Allison's presence.

"No, it's okay. With all my other personal shit going on, I didn't think anyone would take me seriously. I didn't even take myself seriously; I figured I was transferring my anger at Zach onto her. But really it was just easier for me to recognize manipulation tactics in a powerful woman than in a man. Go figure."

"Right," Ben said.

"What about you? Did she get upset if you took feedback from your other committee members?"

Shame coursed through him. "I never even tried to. She… well, she mostly liked my work. And I let her pick my whole committee."

"That sounds about right."

"I feel …" He downed the rest of his second beer. "I feel like an asshole. I had no idea. I never thought …"

To his surprise, Allison reached across the table and grabbed his hand. Hers was warm and soft. He clutched it tightly, certain he didn't deserve comforting but grateful for it nevertheless. He looked up at her. She said, "If it makes you feel any better, you can come and babysit for *me* sometime. I promise I won't try to pay you."

In the bar bathroom, Ben looked at himself in the mirror. Was it possible that he had been like what's-his-name? Aaron? Blind to the fact that other members of his dissertation group were being belittled because he was being praised? Was it possible that he had been able to complete his dissertation in two years—just in time for that tenure-track opening, a little voice in his head reminded him—because he'd been given preferential treatment? He wasn't sure he could handle it, discovering this about himself. He wasn't that guy. He was this guy, looking out of the mirror. This guy who worked hard, and advocated for his students, and loved strong women, and loved his wife. One of the good ones.

He remembered how many undergraduate women had reported the ex–department head to the Title IX committee. At the time, he had thought the sheer number of them was merely reflective of the level of abuse. But now, he realized, you *have* to have that many. There's no case otherwise. *How many women does it take to convince me that a professor in my department is sexist?* he mocked himself.

More than one.

His phone buzzed in his pocket, and he opened it to find a text from Frances: The dresses are not Ren Faire. They're fantasy cosplay!

He replied, Is that better or worse?

Unclear, she said. And then she kept typing.

He waited, his eyes on the three little dots blinking in and out. She would say, "This was a bad idea." She would say, "She's sort of weird." She would say, "I've told her I'm taking a break from dating, that we're going to refocus our energy on having a baby."

The text came through. Boobs as advertised though, and then the smiling purple devil emoji.

He clenched his phone tightly in his hand, flooded with heat. Have fun—no punctuation.

Once, Ben had asked, "Do you love me? Or do you love getting what you want from me?"

"Why not both?" Frances answered, trying on a tentative, sly smile.

"So greedy," he said, and grabbed at her. They had cracked up, then, and sublimated whatever seriousness had originally colored the question.

Outside, saying good night to Allison, Ben heard himself say, "Do you . . . would you want to get another drink sometime? Not as . . . not as colleagues or whatever this just was. Just as . . ."

"As friends?" she asked.

"I—not as friends, either?"

The next morning, he and Frances went out for breakfast. She told him about her date, and he filled her in on what he had learned.

"This is a big deal," he said a bit shakily. "I'm starting to feel like . . . fuck, I don't know. I thought . . . I think I thought I was *actually* smarter and more accomplished than other people in my cohort, and that's why we got to stay here. Why I graduated so quickly and got the job, I mean. I thought *I* had done that. But I think maybe she did it. Because I was so pliable. And I just... took the job. Did what she wanted me to do."

"Ben," Frances said, and grabbed his face. "You wanted the job. You applied for it. You're smart, you're accomplished... and all of your anxiety around this just shows you were the right person to hire! Okay?" He nodded. "And anyway, if you had an easier path... well, you can make up for it, right? Help Cassie? It's the right thing."

The right thing. It was, he knew it. But anxiety still coursed through him. What would Agnes think?

"And I will. But it's also... there's tenure." *And I want it*, he thought. *I need it.* He ran a hand through his hair. "I don't want to make any enemies in the department anytime soon."

"God, does Agnes really hold that kind of power?"

"I can't tell, but maybe."

"You work hard for them. You get great student evaluations. You're published. You've got some pull, too, you know. You'll get tenure, I'm positive. And it'll be just the right timing." She smiled at him and ran a hand across her belly. "Right? Soon?"

Soon. But when was soon for her? She was looking at him with such honest concern that his insides began to squirm. Because what he hadn't yet told her was that he had set a date with Allison and felt a little jump in his chest every time he thought about it.

It had been Frances's idea, after all. She was the one who had wanted to try polyamory. Sure, their first threesome, he had suggested it.

They had both wanted to. They'd talked about it before. They'd left their number for that woman together, their server at that restaurant. It would be fun, he thought. Make-believe. They'd seen her only once. He'd have been perfectly happy if that had been the only time they'd done anything. Perfectly happy! With just Frances! She was the one who wanted more. And he'd let her have it, hadn't he? He'd watched her go on second and third and fourth dates. He'd never said a word about it. He'd been happy for her. Genuinely! People fell in love with her left and right. She had her pick of them, while he sat at home waiting for her to choose which ones she wanted to share with him.

His paltry number of first dates had only reminded him how much he liked being with Frances. Pathetic. It occurred to him that maybe that's what Franny had wanted. He felt, suddenly, that she had engineered it this way somehow. Had she encouraged him to go on those specific dates? He couldn't totally remember now. That could have happened, that she had chosen for him only people who couldn't hold a candle to her, who just proved to him how perfect she was. While it had been easy for her, to meet people who were better than him.

Sometimes the righteousness of his anger burned hot through his skin. He tried to hold on to the heat, to protect and keep it like a ward.

"I think," she had said to him, maybe last year, "I think I might not be done falling in love yet. Is that okay?"

It had sounded sad to him at the time. Sweet.

But he was tired of being cool, dowsed out, pathetic. He tended the kindling inside him, saying, *I am not done yet, either. It's my turn to be unfinished.*

* * *

He got lucky the first time. The cosplay woman invited Frances over for dinner for the very night that he and Allison had planned to meet. When she told him that she thought she'd go, he said—as though he'd only just thought of it, as though he hadn't been glued to his phone, texting with Allison all week—"Maybe I'll go out, too. You remember Allison? The one who I met with to talk about Agnes? She's divorced and, well, she asked. I said no, but maybe I'll see if she's still free?"

He felt himself wilt in her gaze. He was ashamed of himself, a worm.

"Just since I'll be home alone otherwise," he said, sinking farther into the dirt.

"Sure," she said, shaking her head a bit. "Of course you should go if you want to. I just didn't realize."

He saw her once. And then he saw her again. And by the third time, he couldn't imagine not seeing her.

He wanted to understand her, to learn her things. He found her old dissertation drafts in his Dropbox and spent a full workday reading them. Inspired, he added Kristeva to his spring syllabus. He began to listen to the soundtracks of her favorite musicals. He checked out *Beach Read* from the library because she told him that when she'd finished it, she started it over again right away.

He remembered how he had once learned Frances's things. How they had become his things. The perfect cheese plate. *The Lives of Others*. Black Forest gummy bears. *School of Rock*. Babies wearing hats. *Persuasion*, not *Pride and Prejudice*. Multicolored Christmas lights. Not stacking the dirty dishes. Strawberry and cream cheese sandwiches, made by her mother, which the other kindergarteners thought were weird. All of it had become his own backstory, his own landscape.

Dear Ben,

I've just had a troubling meeting with a current student and felt it was my duty to reach out to you about it, as an advisor as well as your friend and supporter... The student in question... who has no reason to lie to me... tells me that an advisee of mine—Cassie Carlton, I think you once taught her?—intends to approach you about directing her thesis. She's a bright girl, but has hit a roadblock and seems to be making a bit of trouble about it... I wanted to just send a quick warning... She may not understand that department hierarchy makes it quite difficult for a nontenured faculty member to direct a diss. Not a smart move to jump rank, and I know you're a team player. She seems to be at loose ends... perhaps personal problems—it wouldn't be the first time a student let private matters affect their work. I intend to do all I can to ensure she sticks with the program, and graduates when she's able... I'd appreciate you giving her a bit of encouragement, if she does indeed reach out. Do let her down gracefully...

Quite a compliment, of course. You remain a student favorite! Unlike me, it seems!... Well... Something which I will of course bring up on the tenure committee next year.

Thanks...

AG

* * *

They stayed home for their fourth date. They ordered takeout and ate in Allison's unmade bed. Sitting next to her, Ben thought: *She is so beautiful.* It felt generic, but he couldn't phrase it any other way, even in his own head. He wondered, briefly, what was wrong with him.

But he stopped thinking when he reached out and put his fingers into her hair, which was thick and coarse and curly. Frances's hair was dark and glossy, and his fingers swam through it with ease. He had felt every inch of every one of Frances's hairs, even the ones long ago sucked down the shower drain or swept up at the salon. He had felt every new hair as it sprouted from her scalp and had loved each one for its softness. But now, he felt a thrill as his fingers caught in Allison's curls. They seemed to tangle up on purpose, to reject him, like thorny plants in a labyrinth. It was exciting, to know that he had not and perhaps would never run his fingers down every inch of this woman's hair. That some strands would remain hidden from him. He let himself pull downward, just slightly, and felt Allison's head tilt backward with the force of his hand. Her chin rose. The light on her face shifted. He liked it, the feeling that he had controlled this change of the light, of her body. His stomach squirmed, and he couldn't tell whether he was turned on or disgusted with himself. He clenched his hand into something like a fist around the clump of her hair, and she said—was it a whimper?—"Mm." He pulled downward again, and she gasped. Her whole neck was exposed to him, and before he realized that he had done it, he had licked her upward, from collarbone to chin.

"Does that hurt?" Ben asked, his grip still firm, her neck still taut and at an angle.

"Yes," she said, and he clamped his jaws around her.

* * *

"And you never saw her like that before? When you were in group together?" Max asked him over lunch.

Ben shook his head. "Not at all. If you'd asked me a month ago, I'd have barely been able to describe her to you."

"Weird."

"I know." He took a long, ruminative sip of his iced coffee. "Maybe because I knew she was married. Some part of my brain shut her out."

"Isn't that what women are afraid of? That they stop existing when they get married?"

Ben laughed. "Yeah. Fuck."

"I'm telling Franny," Max said, singsong. His face changed then. "What have *you* told Franny?"

"The truth," Ben said as he picked up his glass again, looking down at his hand. He had told her last night, knew that he couldn't talk to Max until he had. "That I like her, that we've slept together."

"And she's okay with—"

"*Yes.*" Ben set his glass down hard. "Sorry. But I'm getting kind of tired of having to explain myself to you." He *was* tired. He hadn't slept.

"What do you *mean*, you want to keep seeing her?" Frances had practically screamed the night before. They were in their dining room, a room they were never in. "I thought... I thought we were going to stop seeing other people!"

"No, *I* thought we were going to stop seeing other people! You were the one who decided that, and you were the one who *still kept doing it!* What am I supposed to do, just sit around and wait for you to keep your promise?"

Frances's eyes welled with angry tears. "I'm *ending it.* I don't even care about—"

Ben let out a gust of breath. "Really? Are you?"

"I—yes! I told you. This isn't fun for me anymore."

"For you! Sorry, I forgot this was all about you."

Ben said to Max, "This *works* for us. And it works because we're not keeping secrets about it."

Max raised his hands and widened his eyes, a gesture of innocence.

In the dining room, Ben had asked again, "Do you love me? Or do you love getting what you want from me?"

She said, "I love you. And this—" She gestured around the room, indicating that she meant their fight, the anger between them, their current situation. "This wasn't what I wanted when we decided to open our marriage."

He steeled his resolve. "*This* being me enjoying our open marriage, you mean?" Her lip quivered but he pushed forward. "Then what did you want, Frances? Do you even know?"

The tears began to roll down her cheeks, and she said, "I want...I wanted...to feel...something."

The vagueness of her answer set his blood boiling again. "Something. Something what?" he demanded, his shoulders tensing and his hand clenching into a fist. "To feel wanted? To feel in charge? Don't make me figure it out for you. This is exactly what I mean. You went in without knowing what you wanted, and you dragged me along and made me feel like I wanted it, too, and now you're telling me I'm bad for it."

"No!" she snapped, and her eyes flashed. But then she shivered and got quiet again and said, "You're misunderstanding me. That is what I wanted."

"What is?"

"To feel something." She looked taken aback, like she hadn't meant to say it. Or like she hadn't meant for it to be true.

Ben unclenched his hand. He felt his shoulders slump again, like he had lost the will to keep arguing. "Just something," he said. He knew, of course, that they had opened their marriage so that Franny could try to fill the black hole in her life left behind by her mother. He had tried for almost two years to fill it on his own but hadn't seemed to be able to. She had faded, with just him; so how could he have denied her these other sparks of connection that had, little by little, seemed to bring her back to vivid color? But hearing her say it out loud was something else entirely.

"How do you think that makes me feel?" he asked, quieter. "Do you even care about that?"

"I'm not trying to—" She coughed, and then began to sob. "I do care, I—"

Ben softened. "I know," he said. He let her cry for a minute. He watched her scrub at her face with the back of her hand and worried that she was hurting herself.

Finally, she said, "I don't know how that makes you feel."

It could have ended then, if Frances had said, *I wasn't thinking about your feelings, only my own. I'm sorry.* But instead, she said, "I just know that you seeing Allison makes me feel bad."

"I didn't do anything wrong!" He pushed away from her again, and threw his arms out wide. "I didn't...I didn't break... I mean—"

"You didn't break any of *the rules?*" Frances mocked him. "Are you a child?"

He was acting like a child; he knew it. And fuck her for noticing. "Don't condescend to me, Frances. You always...We *agreed* on rules for a reason. The rules are important. Our...*hierarchy*..." He floundered, ran his hand through his hair. *Don't jump rank*, he thought. *Not a smart move.*

"Okay, if 'the rules are important'"—she lowered her voice to mimic his, and made air quotes—"then how about the *no friends* rule?"

It was too much. "The no friends rule! You want to litigate the no friends rule?" He stood up straighter. He felt himself take the high ground.

"You have a *history* with All—"

"*A history!* Like the history you have with Liam?"

Her face drained of color. He had read about that happening to people, but had never really seen it until this moment. She looked sick. It bolstered him.

"What does—"

"Because you *dated* Liam. For a long time. You wanted to *marry* Liam."

"I was ninet—"

"And now he's our *friend*. Our *very good friend*. Who we go on *anniversary trips* with."

"Liam was *your* friend—"

"Do you think I don't see how you act around him?"

"What is that supposed to—"

"How you look at him, and flirt with him, and pose for him—"

"Pose!"

"And Izzy sees it, too. His wife. Your *best friend?* So if you want to talk about the *no friends rule*—"

"*He* kissed *me!* I didn't—"

Frances's face, which had been white, turned bright red and blotchy. There was a very long silence. Her hands were shaking. She said, finally, "I—"

But he cut her off. "You kissed?"

"I didn't... I didn't mean ..." She was sobbing.

"You didn't mean to tell me—is that it?"

"I didn't mean for it to happen. I didn't kiss him back. I didn't. And nothing else... He—"

"What the *fuck*, Frances! What the FUCK!" Loud again, too loud. But he couldn't seem to stop. "Who do you think you are? Making *me* feel like *I*...! I barely knew Allison in graduate school. She's not a friend of mine, and you know it!"

"You're right. I know, I ..."

"But you never do anything wrong, do you? You just waltz around, smiling and flirting and taking up all the air in every room, sucking down attention, filling up on other people's love, just so you can *feel something*, and who cares how that makes anyone else feel! Who cares how that makes ME feel! Or how it makes IZZY feel! And if some kind of consequence comes from your actions, then, oh poor you! You didn't *mean it!*"

"My actions!" she said, raising her voice to match his. "I didn't kiss him, he kissed me! What was I supposed to do? I haven't spoken to him since! I've *actively avoided*—"

"You can't '*actively*'"—air quotes—"'*avoid*'"—air quotes—"things! It doesn't make sense. You do or you don't."

"Oh, *sorry*, Professor."

"Good one."

"If you'd just listen to me, you'd—"

"If I'd just listen? To something you've been hiding from me for months?"

She blushed. "I'm sorry. I didn't—"

"But I should have known, shouldn't I. I saw you. I watched you two together. Stupid Ben. So *trusting*. And right after Celeste."

"Hey! That's not fair."

"Whatever, Frances. You wanted him, it was obvious."

"Are you telling me I *asked for it?!*"

"Oh, don't do that. Don't try to get out of the bad thing you did by twisting my words into some narrative about men."

"A *narrative about men*." She had lowered her voice again, to sound like his. "Wow. Maybe you are that guy, after all."

He laughed mirthlessly. "That guy." He thought about his job. He thought about how much he liked the look of Allison's exposed neck. He thought, *Maybe I am. Maybe we all are*. He said, "What I know, what I *know*, is that you broke the rules. And you hid it from me. And still, you're perfectly happy to stand there, and make me feel like an asshole."

Frances turned away and didn't say anything for a long time. Finally, she said, "Okay, well," and left the room. Upstairs, Ben heard the shower begin to run. He stood there, not moving, until he heard the water stop. Until it became too late to expect Frances to come back down.

"Sorry," Ben said to Max again. "Sorry." He rubbed his forehead, irritated with himself. He was so tired.

“Hey. It’s okay. I shouldn’t have—”

“No, it’s me. I’m being defensive.”

Max looked at him. Searched him. Ben could feel his eyes on his skin. “I know it works for you. I’m glad. I’m…trying to understand.”

“I know.”

“I’m proud of you. I don’t think I could do it. You two are… really solid.”

Ben opened his mouth, as if to say something, and then finished his coffee instead.

“Allison, though!” Max said, to end the awkward pause. “You like her?”

Ben squirmed. “I’m afraid I’m—fuck.” He scratched at his face and then barreled into it: “Allison seems like someone I could love.”

There was another long pause and then Max said, “Shit.”

“I know.” Ben ran a hand through his hair. It was greasy; he had left the house early that morning, before Frances awoke, to think things through in his office. He’d sent a few emails, and then had set a meeting with Cassie for that afternoon. His body went cold and clammy, thinking about it all, and his eyes filled with tears.

Question: How many women does it take to screw up Ben’s marriage?

Answer: Only one. One extra one.

* * *

It had slipped out, the last time he saw Allison. He was saying goodbye to her at her front door, whispering so as not to wake Lou. She was in a green cotton robe. Her eyes looked tired, without makeup. His fingers pushed an unruly strand of hair behind her ear. "You are precious to me," he heard himself say.

Franny's word.

"Thanks for coming in," Ben said as Cassie sat down. She was wearing a T-shirt that said, SERVING KANT. "Great sh—Oh!" he said, and blushed. "Sorry. Um, good... shirt ..."

"My undergrads liked it."

"I bet." This wasn't how Ben had wanted to begin the meeting, on the wrong foot. A fool. But here he was, unshowered and unslept and unsure. "I, um, well. I wanted to follow up with you about your request."

"Great," she said.

"I, um, I looked into the handbook, and I emailed someone on the GPC, and I'm not sure I'll be able to function as your advisor. I'd be more than happy to join your committee, if you want me to. You're an excellent student, I hope you know—"

"You mean, if Agnes wants you to," she said. Her expression had gone cold.

He took a breath. "If you keep working with Agnes, it would be good if you both had a say in the full committee."

"I'm not going to keep working with Agnes. I told you, she doesn't support my ideas."

"Right, well, I—"

"Did she tell you not to work with me?"

"Not in so many words."

"This is bullshit," she said, and stood up. "Look, sorry, but it is."

"I..." Ben slumped. "It is. I'm sorry. For what it's worth, I happen to know that other women students have complained about Agnes, too. I believe you that—"

"You believe *them*," Cassie said.

Ben bristled, but he couldn't argue. He didn't want to argue. He had made peace with his decision, with the fact that he was ceding the moral high ground. He knew that he would tell Allison, and anyone else who asked, that the GPC had disallowed it, but that wasn't entirely true. They'd made it clear to him that it would be unusual, but not unheard of. But when it came down to it, he wasn't willing to petition, publicly, against Agnes. He liked his job, loved it even. He wanted the security. He wanted a higher salary. Would need it soon. He didn't want to have to find a new job, to pack up, leave town. *Not now*, he thought; but even in his head, he couldn't finish the sentence. He wanted tenure, and he could learn not to care how he got it.

"I'm sorry, Cassie. If I can support you another way, I will. I think your work is really—"

"Right. Okay."

"Look, I understand why you're frustrated. It's... well, in my position... The truth is, I'm not very good at breaking the rules."

She laughed. "Especially not when they benefit you."

Ben closed his eyes, then opened them, and said, "I'm sorry."

His hand shook when he pushed the key into the lock that evening. He felt like an intruder, the bad guy coming to take whatever he wanted from inside. He tried to tell himself, *That's not me*. But he wasn't sure. Not really.

Frances was sitting on their sectional, wrapped in a blanket. She looked tiny, scrunched in the corner. Her hair was wet. The TV wasn't on. He had no idea what she'd been doing before he entered. For a second, he just stood there, disoriented. She usually filled the room.

"Please don't be mad at me," she said, and the words sounded so pathetic, so childish, to him that the sound of them made him begin to cry.

He put his bag down and then sank to the floor next to it. He looked at his knees, pointy and akimbo, and couldn't believe it was he who suddenly held the power. He who was being pleaded with. He searched himself, trying to find out whether it felt good. But his insides were too vacant. He was a pile of clothes being held up by two iced coffees and some sticks. "I'm not mad at you," he said, and suddenly meant it.

She sniffed and asked, in a squeak, "Are you going to leave me?"

"Leave you?" He almost laughed. The idea was preposterous to him. Something from a domestic drama, a show Franny would like. Not from their real life. But there she was, small, in their living room, on their couch, asking him. "Franny," he said. "I would never, ever, ever, ever, *ever* leave you. I—I love you." It felt too small, not enough like evidence. But it was all he had.

Her mouth trembled. "Do you?"

"Yes, so much." He swallowed, and continued, "I went into our relationship knowing I was second best, that I would never be the first person you called when you needed advice, or when something good happened. I—I didn't mind that, not really. She was your mom."

Frances furrowed her brow, surprised. "My mom? Ben, you were never—"

"Stop. It's okay, that's what I'm saying. The way you were close with your mom—it was one of the things I fell in love with. If I was jealous, it was only because I wished I had had that, too." He hadn't said this out loud before, had barely verbalized it to himself. But it came out fully formed, having grown and matured inside him over the years. "I grieved her, too, you know. I loved your mom." He felt it catch in his throat, that grief. "But I also felt really anxious when she died. It was a lot of pressure, to try to fill that space. I didn't know how, or if I could, so I thought..." He ran his hands through his hair roughly. "I don't know. But I was sure that, eventually, it would work, and I would be enough for you."

"Ben, you're enough for me. You're—"

He shook his head. "But I don't like that way of thinking now. There's not a finite space in us that needs to be filled. That space grows and changes and expands. It'll get as big as we let it. And that's...that's a good thing." He looked up at her from his place on the floor.

She scooted off the couch, pressed her knees into his so that they interlocked. "Do you love Allison?"

His heart began to beat, fast. He felt it big and oppressive in his chest, almost in his throat. He said, "I don't know."

She shut her eyes, and nodded. "You still want more."

He swallowed. "I think you do, too."

She paused for a long moment and then said, "Maybe more is a baby."

"Maybe it is," Ben said quietly. "But I don't think we...should expect that from a baby."

She nodded. She sniffed. "I'm really...I'm really sorry...about Celeste. I know—"

"No," Ben said, and looked her firmly in the eye. "Don't be sorry about Celeste. I'm not sorry that that happened for you."

"How did you…?" she began, and then stopped. She nodded. "I'm sorry that I didn't tell you about Liam. I should have. I didn't—"

"It's okay," he said. "I'm sorry I called you selfish."

"I am selfish."

"I like that about you, though."

She laughed, a small laugh. Then she asked, "What do you want to do?"

He thought about saying, *I want to do whatever you want to do*. He was this close. He could keep being a team player. But he was tired of doing what other people wanted him to do. He wanted to be in control of his own life, make his own choices, live with his own consequences.

So, instead, he said, "I want to be a dad. Not because I want to save our marriage. It doesn't need to be saved. I want to be married to you forever. I love you. I'm just ready. I've been ready. I'm going to be tenured soon, I think. And I…" He knew she knew what he was going to say, but that didn't make it any easier to say it. "I want to keep seeing Allison. I want to see what happens."

He looked at her, waiting for her to yell at him, or maybe to get up and walk out, or maybe (worse) to crumble before his eyes. Nothing happened. He waited. He opened his mouth and began to say, "But if—"

"Okay," she said. She took his hand and shook her head to keep him from finishing his sentence. "Yes."

The Best Boy

THE BEST BOY DIED on a Monday, the worst day to die.

The notification came in as Gina was arriving home from day care, the high-pitched *ding!* cutting through the white noise of *All Things Considered* and Sophie's intermittent bursts of "Happy know it! Happy know it!" She parked and took out her phone, clicked the little envelope at the bottom of her home screen (Sophie, two years old, holding a cupcake in their kitchen window, Bernard's hand on her shoulder, his face obscured by the Instagram button).

She felt the corner of her mouth twitch upward. It was from the gaffer (the gaffer!) to the whole group. She clicked out, put her phone in her pocket. She would save the email as a treat.

She thought about it as she tried to settle a thrashing Sophie into her booster seat before giving up, letting her sit in her lap at the dinner table. She thought about it when Sophie refused to eat the very meatballs and sweet potatoes that she'd happily devoured when Bernard had been home for dinner the previous evening. She thought about it when Sophie began to cry in the bathtub for her stuffed bunny. She thought about it as she squeezed Sophie's tiny, fat arms through the sleeves of her pajamas.

With the ghost of Sophie's body still on her chest and shoulders, the baby smell of her curls still in her nose, Gina wiped tears from her eyes as she closed the nursery door silently behind her.

Settled on the couch in her pajamas, she reached for her phone.

All the usual people were cc'd: the cinematographer, the key grip, the other best boy (the second-best boy, as she thought of him), several more grips. She'd googled all of them before. There wasn't much to be found online about these people, but she'd found their names in a few credits—nothing big, unfortunately. But one day, she knew they'd land a blockbuster. She wondered where they'd be traveling to this week, what complications they'd need to be prepared for on set.

But the email looked different than usual. It was short, with no bolded headings. There was no schedule laid out. No mention of that week's location, or any special modifications. No estimated work hours or equipment questions.

The email began, By now, I'm sure you've all heard the devastating news about Gina.

She felt her breath catch in her throat. She clicked out of the email, and opened her browser. She typed in her own name. Four results down was an article in the *Hollywood Reporter*: "Crew Deaths Turn the Spotlight on Studio Safety, Again." She let her eyes wander over the words, a series of names, until she found the one she was looking for.

"Gina Coggeshall died—"

She felt her breath catch, seeing her own name like that.

"Gina Coggeshall died in a car accident shortly after leaving set at 5 a.m., after a 14-hour production day for ..."

"You look like you've seen a ghost," came a voice. She looked up, startled. It was Bernard, still in the tie and tennis shoes he wore under his white coat.

"How was the lab?" she asked.

"Fine," he said, sitting down to untie his laces. "Long. Did Sophie go down okay?"

Gina nodded. "She cried again. She kept holding on to my hair when I laid her down."

He laughed. "I think Frances is right. She's trying to get back inside you." Sophie had refused to leave Gina's arms at their friends Ben and Frances's house last weekend. When Frances had said it, she'd looked on with tenderness, maybe longing, and so Gina had smiled and kissed the side of Sophie's face. Tried to conjure how it had felt, before, to have her daughter's body pressed into her own. It had felt good, once. Now it felt heavy and oppressive, like gravity. She couldn't remember what bodies other than Sophie's felt like.

"It'll pass," he said. "All of the Covid babies seem to have more separation anxiety." He patted the back of her hair tenderly.

"Mm," she said.

"What are you reading?"

"Oh, it's stupid. You know—I mean, do you remember how I sometimes used to get those emails for that other Gina Coggeshall? The movie crew person?"

"Oh yeah," he said, his brow furrowing as he sank down next to her. "I thought that stopped."

She shrugged. She hadn't shared with Bernard—with anyone—

her attachment to the other Gina. He wouldn't have understood. He'd have figured out a way to make the emails stop.

It was a weird name, Gina Coggeshall. Because Gina had been alive and emailing when Gmail was invented, her email address was her name, ginacoggeshall. By now, the incoming freshmen who she had to email about insurance or financial aid had addresses like michaelhiggens6789x. Once, she'd admitted a student whose email address was amberNOTTHATONEheard.

She'd never encountered anyone outside of her family who shared her last name. And so, when she first received an email from something called a key grip, she thought it was a joke. When she got a second one, this one with a set of what felt like important directives, she responded to the sender, who apologized and told her about one of his grips, who shared her name. She'd thought that would be the end of it—but then another email rolled in. Again, she'd responded. The fourth time, she took matters into her own hands. She spent her workday emailing all the likeliest Gina Coggeshall email combinations, from A to Z. GinaAcoggeshall. GinaBcoggeshall, etc.

Nothing.

Sometimes months would pass between emails, but they always found her. Eventually, they felt less like a joke and more like a sign. Bernard had told her about the many-worlds theory (many times), and though it had initially sounded like bullshit to her, she found herself wondering about it with every additional email. They were waves across worlds, from one version of herself to another. When she'd watched *Everything Everywhere All at Once*, she'd cried, and not for the reasons Bernard had. Laundry, taxes. She had enough of those in this universe.

She wanted to understand the other Gina. She googled what

all the words meant. A gaffer was the head electrician on a movie set—not just the name of Samwise Gamgee's dad. A key grip led a camera crew, made up of all the other grips. A best boy was the right-hand man of the gaffer and the key grip, supervising all the other grips, and he was called a best boy even if he was a girl, which she thought Gina Coggeshall probably was. Also, he was called the best boy even if there were two best boys on set, which there almost always were. The name came from seafaring, referring to the captain's right-hand man. Considering all the nineteenth-century ship movies she'd had to see with Bernard, Gina thought the title probably had a pretty gay legacy.

The emails became special to her, privileged glimpses into another kind of life. She liked seeing where movies were filmed, learning about new, strange-looking places. She liked the sense of these people, wandering the country, finding the perfect backgrounds. She began to watch movie credits from start to finish, looking for names she recognized, grips who began to feel something like friends to her. She wondered what it would be like, to be that Gina Coggeshall, building and lighting worlds.

When she'd received an email addressed not to Gina Coggeshall the grip, but to Gina Coggeshall the best boy, she'd felt her heart expand with pride. She thought, *We did it!* Soon she'd be the gaffer, and then the cinematographer, and then she'd win an Oscar, and Gina would get to see her face, and see if she looked like herself, Gina, and watch as the music started to play almost immediately into her speech because no one cared about cinematographers except Gina, but she wouldn't mind; she was just honored to have been nominated, and shocked to have won!

Gina Coggeshall had nowhere to go but up.

She said to Bernard, "Yeah, it's just... I got one today, and it said that the other Gina's dead."

"Oh wow," he said, and to her surprise, he put his arm around her and pulled her in. It felt good, to be the smaller body. "Did she have kids?"

"No," Gina said. She was sure of that.

"Well." He squeezed her shoulder. "If you ask me, it couldn't have happened to a better Gina Coggeshall." He smiled. He'd used his dry, rom-com voice, the one that had first attracted her to him. His English accent masking, for the first months they knew each other, the substance of almost everything he'd said. She forced herself to linger in the sound alone, as she once had, and smile back.

He leaned in, and for a wild moment, she thought he was going to kiss her, here on their couch, in their living room. To run his hand through her hair and pull her mouth into his. To pick her up and carry her, her legs around his waist, her hands in the back of his hair, to bed.

She felt her body spark, and she leaned forward to meet him.

He kissed her cheek and then looked into her eyes and said, "What would we do without you? You're such a wonderful mum."

She woke up in a funk, even though Wednesdays were usually the best mornings. Bernard worked from home on Wednesdays, which meant that it was he who woke Sophie, dressed her, fed her breakfast, while Gina had a shower and drank her coffee in peace.

If you die on a Monday, you either have to schedule a Wednesday funeral and no one's able to come because it's only hump day, or you have to wait until Saturday and by then your choice is made for you: no open casket, even if you want one. Even if you're beautiful and young and your skin is still where it's supposed to be when you die, your body lets you down after a few days dead. Even if they preserve you right, which Gina imagined they would for a best boy. Especially one who was a girl. They really know what they're doing in LA. Cosmetically, that is.

There were so few choices you got to make in life. Gina's heart hardened on the best boy's behalf, knowing a path had shut for her in her death. Hopefully she'd already chosen to be cremated. Then she could throw her funeral whenever, and all her friends could be there.

When Bernard leaned in to kiss her in the driveway, Sophie loaded into his car already, she turned her face, and felt the relief of shutting her car door, of looking forward, of driving away from them.

As she turned onto the main road, out of her neighborhood, a horn blared on her right side and she jolted into her body. A white Volvo slammed on his brakes as she cut him off, blazing through the stop sign. "Sorry!" she mouthed, frantically. "Sorry!"

Her body went cold and she heard herself say aloud, "What the fuck. What the fuck."

"Where are you slinking off to so early?" Robbie had snuck up on her, as usual. She wondered if he walked extra quietly on purpose around her, as she did around him. It never worked; he always noticed her, and asked her things. It surprised her, even flattered her, but in a way that ultimately left her embarrassed.

"Oh," she said, shaking her head slightly. Was she slinking? The word felt obscene somehow, though she was sure he hadn't meant it that way. "I'm meeting my friend Frances for lunch."

She mock-grimaced as she stood up, holding her bag. "Don't tell on me?"

"Who would I tell?" he asked, pressing his hand to his heart, leaning against her doorframe in a casual, cool way. He smirked at her. Or maybe it was more accurate to say, he smirked. He always had a smile on, sometimes underneath another expression. Like everything was amusing. "You're the boss."

"Barely," she said. It was true that she was his senior, an assistant director of admissions where he was an admissions officer. Pre-pandemic, they'd held the same job, traveling to high schools across the country, putting on recruiting events, staying in shitty hotels and drinking in shitty hotel bars. Calling home to their partners (Bernard, then her fiancé, and a short series of different girlfriends for him), pretending to be less drunk than they were.

She had liked it. The traveling, the job fairs, meeting new people, the excitement on all the high schoolers' faces, knowing that they were becoming adults. It had energized her, made her feel, too, that something new was ahead for her. Made her reckless, even.

Because she'd kissed him once. Robbie. In some nothing town, in some nothing hotel. He was slightly younger than her, two or three years maybe, and had had more shots than she had. She could still taste the lime on his mouth, the few times she let herself think about it. He'd walked her to her hotel room, had watched as she fumbled the key card, took it from her shaking hand and slid it in and out, smooth. She could still hear the swish and mechanical click, the few times she'd let herself. When he handed it back to her, she'd grabbed his wrist instead. Pulled it into her waist, under the button-down shirt she'd untucked an hour previously. She could still feel the calluses on his fingers, the width of his palm, on the small of her back, those few times.

They'd never talked about it. She wasn't sure he even remembered it. The world shut down soon afterward, and he became a pixelated image on her computer screen.

When she'd told Bernard, she'd recast Robbie as an admissions officer from another school, someone she'd never see again. He forgave her so quickly that she could almost forget she'd ever told him. The silence of the thing made it feel that it had happened in yet another universe, one where she had the kind of hands that reached out for others when they wanted to.

In this one, she became pregnant with Sophie not three months later. She applied for the assistant director job, so she wouldn't have to travel so frequently. She grew up.

Robbie shrugged. "Whatever you say, boss lady." He doffed an imaginary hat and stood aside as she approached the door. To her surprise, he walked down the hall with her instead of turning back to his desk. "I can't help but notice, though, that you haven't been coming to Wine Wednesdays. We may be lowly admissions officers, but we know how to have a good time."

She laughed. "I know, I'm sorry. It's hard for me to do things after work."

"The little one," he said.

"The little one," she confirmed. It wasn't true, though. On Wednesdays, Bernard picked Sophie up, hung out at home with her. At first, she hadn't wanted to spend the time away from Sophie. Sophie had been her horizon, her new, strange, perfect location, ready to be lit and made perfect. Now she said no mostly because she felt guilty not saying no, worried that Bernard, too, would begin to feel the weight and monotony of their life if he took on too much alone. She could spare him the devastation of that feeling. She owed that to him.

"Well, if you change your mind, we're going to Harry's after work."

"Harry's!" She wrinkled her nose. "That place is the worst."

"Not posh enough for you?"

"I'm not posh."

"You're so posh. I bet you're meeting your friend somewhere without lunch specials, with small plates only."

"Fuck you," she said, surprising herself. She clapped a hand to her mouth, and smiled behind it.

"You are, aren't you!"

She nodded.

"Come to Harry's."

"Maybe," she said as she walked out the door.

She found herself walking quickly. The run-in with Robbie had pepped her up, even though she'd been dreading the lunch. Frances was on her nerves, and she'd been afraid her general bad mood would make this obvious. She'd considered canceling, but then she'd have to deal with the usual rescheduling back-and-forth and she didn't think she could face admitting how little free time she had now. Better Frances think that she had the kind of clout at her job that she could take a long lunch when she wanted, rather than that she was so often stuck at home watching *Vanderpump Rules*, half-heartedly reading admissions essays next to a baby monitor.

She looked at her watch. One o'clock, Sophie would be napping. Her face squished into her cot on the floor, her body on top of her bunny, her blanket half on, half off. Gina's guilt pressed into the backs of her eyes so forcefully, they felt they would burst.

* * *

"It was wild!" Frances was saying, spooning the rest of the couscous onto her plate. "I don't think it's really my thing, you know, but I felt like...really in my body. I could feel where the ropes were pressing into my thighs, but it didn't hurt, it just made me aware, like, that I *had* thighs, you know?"

"Mm," Gina said, putting a piece of prosciutto into her mouth so that she could avoid answering. She wanted to roll her eyes. She didn't want to hear about Frances's thighs, or whether or not she had them. It annoyed her, Frances and her open marriage. It was embarrassing to be in your thirties, talking about being ghosted, getting your heart broken, having great sex, having terrible sex, the "queer experience," blah blah blah.

Frances had gotten married before Gina. She'd found her path, hopped on it, and reached out a hand saying, *This way is fine.* You couldn't just turn around and branch off with no consequences.

Today, Frances was using Gina to process her feelings about having gone on a first date to a rope-tying workshop at a lesbian bar that weekend. It was called *shibari* and it was a *Japanese tradition* and it wasn't *scary*, it was *interesting* and *sensual*, and *cool to learn about.*

"I don't think I'll do it again, and I probably won't see Mia again, either, but I'm so glad I went. On top of just learning something new, I was describing it to Ben the next morning, and it was so hot, he was ten minutes late to his first class!" She raised her brow at me.

"Morning sex," I said, trying to smile.

"Morning sex. I didn't used to like it, but . . ." She shrugged and smiled. Then added, tentatively, "Fingers crossed. I'm ovulating."

"Ha, then don't get too into it. You'll never do it again once you have a baby." She'd meant it to sound lighthearted and maybe a little wise, but there was an edge to her voice. She watched Frances notice it.

"No, yeah, I know things change."

She took a sip of her iced tea. "I mean, not totally. Bernard and I have great sex, it's just hard to fit it in, in the mornings. After bedtime's a whole different story." She copied Frances's brow raise, feeling the ghost of that kiss on her cheek. "It's just about priorities, you know."

"Totally. I think it's amazing, how much you guys, I don't know, put Sophie first. She's so lucky."

"I mean, you just have to."

She heard the bitterness in her voice, and it made her want to shudder. She didn't like herself when she was around Frances lately. When they went out with other friends, she watched them listen to Frances and Ben with curiosity. There was an occasional eye roll maybe, but overall, their friends seemed happy to have something new to talk about. New people to gossip about. Hazel and Christine had even been talking about having a threesome, and they were on their second course of IVF. Gina wasn't sure she could handle it, having to hear about more threesomes, like they were life-changing and not just something else to do to distract yourself from the fact that you'd already made all the big decisions you were ever going to make in your whole life and now you were just watching them roll over you.

"I don't think you have to," Frances said. "I think you chose to."

"Oh my god," Gina said, and then it happened. She rolled her eyes.

"Okay, sorry," Frances said, clacking her fork down on her empty plate. "I guess I have no idea, right?"

"No, you don't." Gina felt her chin tremble. She wiped her hand across it, pretending she was brushing something off. But she saw Frances see, and saw her anger melt.

"Is everything okay?" she asked.

"I—"

She could tell Frances. Frances was her friend. She'd told Frances how hard it had been to be pregnant, and how scared she had been that Sophie would get Covid, and how confusing it felt to breastfeed. But those things were difficult for everyone. You were supposed to be used to being a parent by the time your child was almost two and a half. You were supposed to feel your freedom coming back. You were not supposed to read stories about women leaving their children and understand why they did it. You were not supposed to read the private emails of a woman who shared your name and imagine that, instead of being yourself, you were her, and now you were dead.

"I'm fine. Sorry. I'm really sorry."

Frances reached across the table and squeezed her hand. "It's okay," she said, "it's okay." She pulled her hand back, and they sat like that for a while.

On her way back to the office, she texted Bernard.

Go! We'll have a blast! he responded. He meant it, she knew. He hated his long hours, hated missing time with Sophie, had endless energy to throw her in the air, dangle her by her feet, roll her onto the bed and tickle her underneath her arms, to laugh as genuinely as she did.

She scrolled down to Robbie's name, which she hadn't done in years. She clicked it, and typed, Hey, actually I think I can come today.

Harry's had been practically empty at six, but by eight thirty, it was filling up rapidly with what Gina could only assume were college students using fake IDs. Gina was sitting in a booth with the other stragglers: Robbie, two other admissions officers who looked almost as young as the students, and to her surprise, Joan, the assistant director of financial aid, who had recently sent her son off to college. Gina was on her third gin and tonic, having been dissuaded from ordering a glass of Harry's wine by Joan, who'd made that mistake before.

Gina felt animated, almost feverish. The too-loud music, the buzz of conversations, the flushed, giddy looks on the kids' faces, like they'd never been anywhere as cool as this. She was sure that the women's bathroom would be full of crying girls in a few hours, but for now, everyone was happy, without anything or anyone else to worry about. She found that she, too, wasn't worried about anything anymore, aware that Sophie was safely in her bed and that Bernard was safely watching some kind of war show on TV. Nobody would need her again until morning.

After the two admissions officers raced off to claim the newly free dart board, Joan leaned forward and asked, "So, Robbie, still seeing the same woman?"

He beamed. "As a matter of fact, I am."

She nodded her head and widened her eyes, to indicate that she was impressed. "What's that, a first for you? How long has it been?"

"Old dogs can learn new tricks," he said, taking a glug of his beer.

"Who is she?" Gina asked.

"She's *married*," Joan mock-whispered.

"*What?*" Gina asked, sounding so earnest that she wanted to kick herself. "Like, really married?"

"It's no big deal," Robbie said. "Joan's just trying to shock you."

Joan shrugged, with a smile on her face. "Someone's got to keep things interesting around here."

"What do you mean?"

"I mean, she's married, but her husband knows about it. She has another boyfriend, too, some guy with a name like Chas or something."

"Doesn't that bother you?" Gina asked.

"What, Chas? He's a gym rat, probably an idiot."

"No, I mean, the whole thing. That she's married, that you're not, like, I don't know, the only person."

"Okay, kids," Joan said, finishing her drink and sliding out of her side. "Sounds like my work here is done. I'm going to go try to turn Aidan and Kyle against one another. Aidan's better at darts—look." She made her way over to the dart board, leaving Robbie and Gina sitting next to each other.

Robbie laughed. "She's a fucking riot. Even more so since what's-his-name left home."

Gina didn't laugh. The pearly sheen of the night had gone dull.

"What?" he asked.

"What do you mean, what?"

"I mean, why are you looking at me like that?"

"I'm not looking at you like anything."

He scoffed. "What, you're mad because of the sanctity of marriage or something?"

She scoffed louder. "I—no, it's not like that."

"Okay, good, because she's the one who's married, not me."

"And that means it's fine for you to see her, I guess."

"You know, Gina, it actually *does*. Mostly because she says it's fine, and it's up to her, not me, and definitely not you."

"I'm so fucking sick of this," Gina said. "Like, half my friends are married and dating other people."

Robbie raised his eyebrows. "Oh. Okay, so you get it."

"No, I don't get it! Can no one just, like, pick a life and be happy anymore?"

He shrugged. "I think it's nice to have options."

"God, you sound like my friend. You can't just have options forever."

"Why not?"

"Because at some point, you're going to have a family, and you're going to have to have a routine, and it's going to be organized into morning wake windows and afternoon naps and afternoon wake windows, and three meals, and two snacks, and you have to be home every night because your kid needs you, and might get sick, and probably will get sick, and you have to be there to sleep in their bed and not in your own bed and definitely not in some random other person's bed." She heard her voice becoming higher pitched, and felt beads of sweat building on her hairline. But to her surprise, the stupider she sounded, the bigger Robbie's smile became. "Stop looking at me like that," she finally finished.

He shrugged. "What's a wake window?"

"Oh my god." She shook her head, and finished her drink.

"You've just never thought about this. You have no idea what I'm talking about."

"Nope."

"Don't you want to get married?"

"I don't know."

"How can you not know?"

He shrugged again. "I like not knowing things."

"You're describing being dumb."

He smiled.

"Aren't you mad that I'm being such a bitch to you?"

"Honestly? I kind of like it."

She sighed, let out a defeated laugh. "This is the second time today I've gone insane about open relationships."

"When—"

"Don't ask. I'm sorry. I'm really sorry," she said. "I think I'm just on edge because..." She shook her head, grabbed a glass, and felt the ice clink against her teeth. "My friend—" *My friend, how sad.* "Someone I know died this week."

"Oh my god, Gina." Robbie picked up his hand, put it on Gina's forearm, ran his thumb across it. The hairs on the back of her arm stood up, so surprised to be touched by an adult's hand. "I'm so sorry. Who was it?"

"Just...just someone. She was a best boy." She could feel the heat of him on her right side.

"Is that like wake window? Should I know what that means?"

"It's a camera crew person. For movies."

"Oh shit!" he said. "That's awesome."

"Yeah, it is awesome," and she felt her face light up with it. She turned her face toward his, and pulled in slightly closer. "You get to travel all around, with location scouts, and find the perfect places to set scenes, and make sure the angles and the lighting are all good, and meet new people all the time, like actors and directors and things. A lot of people probably think it sucks, never to be home for very long, and to drive a ton, and to sleep in hotels and probably worse sometimes, but it's really exciting."

"Sorry, Gina." His hand was still on her arm. "I didn't realize that's what you did. Before you moved here."

"What?" She thought back on what she had said. *It's really exciting!* As if she knew. She felt her face grow warm. She couldn't think of a way to backpedal that wouldn't feel even more embarrassing, so she said, "It was another lifetime."

"Why'd you quit?"

"Oh, you know. It was long hours. And a lot of traveling, like, all the time. You can't do that and be a mom, too."

"And you knew you wanted to be a mom?"

She thought about that, and then said, "I think so. But sometimes I . . ."

"What?"

"Sorry, we don't have to talk about this." She pulled her hand out from under his, but he grabbed it back and said, "I asked."

She let out a heavy sigh. "Sometimes I'm not sure if I chose it or if it was just out there, waiting for me. You grow up, you get married, you have a baby, you know?" She laughed, "Well, I guess you don't know. But I bet Joan would know." She nodded her head across the bar, toward Aidan demonstrating to Joan the right way to hold a dart.

"And your friend?"

"Oh, her? She was more like you, I guess. She could go anywhere she wanted." And before she could stop herself, she said,

"But she's just stuck in one place forever now. I didn't think that would happen to her."

"I'm really sorry, Gina," he said again. He turned his face toward hers. She became suddenly aware of how they must look, sitting next to each other, their arms touching, their legs pressed against one another. If someone were to walk into the bar and see them, they'd think they were a couple. Maybe, in some universe, they were.

Maybe in some universe, she'd pulled him through the door that night, pulled him into her bed, and then into the shower the next morning. Told Bernard the truth, watched him leave. Had to put her life together again from scratch. Building it from her own ideas about what she liked, what she wanted. Kissed Robbie again, if she wanted to. Fucked him again, if she wanted to. Kissed other people, new people, any people she felt like. Some here, some in other cities, other countries.

And where was Sophie in that universe? Just an egg inside of her, back where Sophie wanted to be? No—Gina had to believe she would still come to her, as her full self, would find her in any world. Gina had Sophie now, and all the worlds would end if she lost her.

"Do you think about wanting to travel with us again, ever?" Robbie was saying, in this world, next to her. "It's not as glamorous, but—"

"Yes," she said. "I liked it."

"Then maybe," he began, and he looked down at their hands on the table. And suddenly his other hand was on her leg. She felt her mind come back and settle into her body, felt her skin prickle, and she thought, I have thighs.

"Maybe," he continued, "if you miss it, you could find a reason to come to the next fair."

Her heart beat fast in her chest. What this Gina was supposed to do was to smile, pretend she didn't understand what he meant. To pull her hand away and turn her legs, so that they were out from under his palm. To pull out her phone and say, "Gosh, it's late. I've got to get home." And then get into bed, set her alarm for six, get up and make a pot of coffee, pour milk into a sippy cup, pull her sleepy child out of bed, bring her down to the kitchen, set a bowl of oatmeal in front of her, begin the first wake window.

Instead, she stayed where she was and said, "I guess anything's possible."

A Survey of Modern Art

WALT AND ROSE WERE playing with the dog in the garden, and I was on the porch swing, when that word he had been saying found me through the buzzing white noise. "Barbaric," he said. "We're sorry, ma'am, it was a barbaric thing someone did." I was conscious of the hairs on my arm and tried to smooth them down. *Barbaric*, I thought. Wordlessness is a kind of barbarism.

"Ma'am?" the man said, and I looked up. "Do you understand what I'm saying?" I wondered if he thought I was stupid. Then I wondered if I was stupid.

"I'm sorry," I said, and smiled. I almost stood, but then I remembered that I hadn't been able to dress properly for the day—stupid dog, always riffling through my drawers. I didn't want this man to see how the front of my blouse sagged on one side where my breast should be. So instead of standing, I jerked in place and pulled my textbook into my belly. "You're right. I don't understand." I shook my head and smiled *silly me*.

"Your brother-in-law"—he glanced down at his pad of paper—"Mr. Cary Michaels, he called us round this morning. She was in the bathtub. I can spare you the details, ma'am." He hesitated and looked over at the children, who were busy digging.

"It was barbaric," I repeated. A barbarism is a poorly formed word. Hadn't I just learned that? "So it was an error?" Now I felt like I was looking at him too intently. His eyes were a dopey brown. One drooped slightly like he hadn't had enough sleep. They reminded me of the dog's. The dog, who had been so bad this morning, I had swatted him on the behind. Where had he hidden that damn thing anyway?

I only realized that my eyes had started darting around the yard when I saw that the man was trying to catch them. A flush came to my cheeks as he continued, "Well, no, ma'am, not an error. We have every reason to believe it was intentional." I noticed he had slowed down for my benefit. "Frances Michaels—that is, your sister—she seems to have been stabbed. Several times. Mr. Michaels, he found her in the bathtub."

"Naked?" I asked. My hand shot back up to the hole in my chest and pulled compulsively at my top.

"I—like I said, I—we covered her. The boys—we didn't like to see. Someone did a . . . well, a truly barbaric thing."

The picture tried to flower in my head. I couldn't remember what color her bathroom was. Peach? Was the tub full? Had she used bubble bath? Had she had her hair done? Where had she been stabbed? I tried not to notice her breasts, but there they were anyway. Both of them and fuller than mine. Then my mind ripped them to shreds. I swallowed. "Who did it?"

"I'm not at liberty to say, ma'am. But we have our ideas. We found some . . . well, I shouldn't . . . well, we think we have some leads." He gave me a probing look, like he expected me to understand something from his expression.

"Cary didn't do it," I said. He was a good husband to Frances, despite everything. Always there. Dependable.

"No, ma'am. That's nothing for you to worry about. We've got a good handle on this thing already, and we don't suspect your brother-in-law. But...well, if you have anything you want to tell me, you could. Now." I stayed quiet, but my brain started whirring. Although I suspected that Frances might have been seeing a man outside of her marriage, I didn't want to tell this to a stranger unless I had to. What would he think of her?

After a long moment, he shut his little notebook and nodded at me so slowly, I found myself mirroring him. "Okay? You okay now?" He tilted his head kindly. He felt sorry for me, I realized. Not just because of Frances, but for some other reason, like I was sick. I hunched over to hide my chest, trying to block out Mother's voice in my head. When I didn't answer, he continued, a little too carefully, "And what's that you're reading?"

I sat up straight like a lady, as Mother would have said. But when I flipped the book over, I made sure to keep it pressed to my front. *A Survey of Modern Art.* On the cover was a black-and-white woman who looked like she got flattened by something. Her face was the shape of a wrench. She was screaming at a bull and dropping the baby she was supposed to breastfeed. She was surrounded by a pile of arms. *Guernica.* "I'm taking some classes, just part time. I drive to Vanderbilt on Tuesdays and Thursdays when my sister can sit for the children." As I heard myself say it, I knew that sentence didn't mean anything anymore. A barbarism is the destruction of a world.

He winced. "Your sister was here this Thursday?" I didn't

answer. His eyes darted to the sitting room window and tried to pry it open. To my horror, he reached into his pocket and pulled out the tiny notebook again and jotted down what I had said. I fidgeted. *Sit still, silly girl*, a voice like Mother's said to me. "Listen," he said, looking up with something like dread in his eyes, "You are home alone, right?"

"Me and the two youngest. Sam's with a friend."

He looked over at the garden again. I used the moment to re-adjust my top.

"Your husband, Mr. Autry? He's not here?" This time his eyes x-rayed the front door. He was standing rigid and tall.

"No. Don had to go into work today."

"Saturday work, too, huh? Just our luck." He patted his badge and then softened, looking more at ease. He turned toward the dog. "That's a good pooch, though. No need to be afraid. Listen, it's important. We'd really like to talk to Mr. Autry. If he comes back by, let us know by ringing the station. That okay?"

"Yes, okay. I—when should I start planning the funeral?" That felt stupid as soon as I said it, and it got a little laugh in return.

"Reckon that's up to your family." He gave me that look again, and I hunched. "You take care now. And let us know if Mr. Autry gets off early today." He turned and walked down the driveway. As soon as he pulled out, I threw my book across the porch—the children barely looked up. I began to pace.

My sister was dead. It seemed important to start thinking of her that way. Dead sister. But my head was full of Frances as a baby in her carriage, Francie, crying my ears off, my own hand loosening to let her roll down the rocky hill by our house. I shuddered. Then little Francie, when she had her first fit in church, Mother holding her arms down on the pew. "You did this," she had hissed. I had looked down. I could still see my patent leather shoes under their crown of lacey sock, a size too small. Had I done that? Had her carriage crash as a baby given her the shakes she would have all through childhood? Her eyes open, her mouth gaping, her head jerked back. I shut my eyes. Had I been so violent? Well, children all are, aren't they. Anyhow, if it was my fault, I had surely been punished. Poisoned and cut apart, not so long ago, and all for my own good. My own health. I stood and looked out into the street. The line of houses and the men pruning the bushes or reading the paper. All of them trying not to look at me. Some men stayed home on Saturdays. The women were walking back and forth, decorating their lines with laundry.

A woman across the way caught my eye, so I bent down quickly and picked up my book. I waved behind my back and returned to the swing. As I looked down at the cover, I wanted to cry. It was such a beautiful book—even with the piles of arms and legs. I had thought the way they were layered was lovely, but the boy who sat next to me in class had asked, "Have you ever seen something so ugly? I bet your kid could do a better drawing than this!" How had he known I had children?

"After World War Two," our professor had said on Thursday, "there was a movement of philosophers who believed that making art had become unethical. The aesthetic object, they said, could not represent a violence so total." He flipped to a slide showing a pile of uniformed bodies next to a trench. Then to a slide showing a pile of naked bodies next to nothing. Had Father seen things like that? Had Don? I thought of the images we had seen on television last year when Lieutenant Calley was on trial for murder. The accumulation of those poor villagers and their children in the road. Don had said it was uncivilized. I didn't know if he meant the war or the photograph or Vietnam. They had looked like the collage on the front of my textbook. The television had flattened them into cartoons.

"'To write poetry after Auschwitz is barbaric,' as you know." Our professor paused. "That's Adorno." The boy next to me nodded vigorously and copied down the quote. I leaned over to see how he had spelled "Adorno." The professor and the boy and what seemed like the rest of the class happily moved on, but I wanted to pause. That hadn't seemed right to me. My own private devastations had made art feel more immediate and necessary to me. I had wondered if maybe I didn't know what "barbaric" meant, and had looked it up in the library after. Strange how you hear words back-to-back like that.

Would I have to see Frances's body?

She was the first person to see mine after I got better. I reached my hand up to where my prosthetic breast usually was, and remembered it was lost, stupid dog. "You've got a hole where your heart should be," Frances had said to me in the hospital. She was joking but I had cried. I might have still been tired from the surgery. My punishment. She had patted my hair then, *shh shh*.

"What will Don think?" I had croaked out through sobs. I had read in a women's magazine that I could try a biopsy first, before having the radical mastectomy. Shirley Temple had had it done, and she hadn't had to have surgery after that. But when I asked about it, the doctor had scoffed. I wished I hadn't mentioned Shirley Temple. It felt too stupid to say that I didn't want to lose my breast, so I said I thought my husband and I might try for a fourth, and wouldn't I need to breastfeed? "You silly, stubborn woman," the doctor had said. "You could be dead in weeks."

Frances was dead.

"Don't worry about Don," she had said to me in the hospital room, speeding through her words. She always steered the subject away from him. "Didn't President Nixon say we're in a war on cancer? You're nothing but another veteran who lost a limb. Don't think another thing about it."

But Frances didn't understand marriage. She didn't know that to have a good one, you had to know that your body belonged to that other person, just as much as it belonged to you. Even after she got married, she hadn't learned. I sometimes thought maybe I shouldn't have listened to her when she encouraged me to start taking classes again. Maybe she had wanted me to do something bad because she was doing something bad.

I didn't like to think it, but I wondered, sometimes, if the man she was seeing was also married. It was a feeling I had in my neck and chest, more than a real idea. She never spoke to me about him. I had only asked for his name once, and her whole face had gone white. It was her guilt, I thought. She didn't mind that she was cheating, I knew her well enough to know that. But that she might be the other woman, harming someone's wife without their knowledge. Maybe even a woman she knew. Someone she liked. I thought that must be the real source of her unease. But when I told my suspicions to Don, he got big and red and told me I was being a gossip and to mind my own business. It was just a silly feeling.

How might I feel, if I were that woman, putting her children to bed alone, eating dinner alone, never knowing my husband was seeing Frances? I supposed I might not feel much different than how I did already. Don was gone all the time. I had even wondered, a time or two and in my silliest moments, whether he might be seeing another woman. But no. I didn't think he really even knew any other women. None but me and Frances anyway.

I wondered if the police had discovered her infidelity. Maybe they had found proof. That worried me. I was afraid that the knowledge might make them feel like it was okay to take a good long look at her naked body in the morgue, or wherever she was right now. I stopped looking at her body in my mind. I wasn't sure how many stab wounds it had.

Would we be able to have an open casket? We had for Mother. That's what was done. Would we stand in church in our nice clothes and sing while Frances's body sat like it had been hole-punched in the corner? Would we squeeze past the box she was in as we walked up to the altar? What if I bumped it and knocked her out onto the ground in front of everyone? The carriage, her little body shaking, our Francie. Any act of civilization is also an act of barbarism.

There was a shriek, and I jolted upward, my book flying once again. I ran to the sound. Had the murderer come for me, too? Had he come for the children? In my mind there was a bloody man in the garden waiting for me. Little Walt ran up to me, and grabbed my legs. "Mommy!" he said. "We found something!"

I looked over at the pile of dirt and saw a squashy skin-colored mound. Rose was poking at it. My stomach seized. It was human. A breast. I put my hand over my mouth as my mind told me, wildly, that it was Frances's. That the faceless, murdering man had cut it off and left it here for me, a warning or a joke. I felt a thunderous urge to run. Bouquets of questions bloomed in the corners of my mind. How had he known where I lived? Where the children lived? Where was Don? Why was he never here? Don, who had promised to love and protect me and who, instead, went to work and went to the club and played golf. Who couldn't even be bothered to stay home and watch the children while I took my class, who insisted that I ask Frances to do it, since the whole ridiculous idea had been hers in the first place. But who I sometimes found at home, on those evenings after I returned home tired and made aware of my own intellectual inadequacies, sitting in our den, sharing a drink with Frances, his face flushed. Where was he now, when we needed him? Why hadn't I seen him all day, and today a Saturday? The day my sister was found dead in her home, a piece of her found buried in our garden?

Why did the police want to see him?

A horrible thought gushed down from my mind into my chest, ran along my veins and into my tingling fingertips, and settled in my boiling stomach. I turned my head away from the kids, from the thing in the dirt, and was sick right into my new rosebushes. Hot waves of vomit that made my forehead go cold and sweaty. *Please let the neighbors have gone inside*, I thought. *Please.*

"Mommy threw up!" Rose shrieked, waving her shovel in the air. Walt started to giggle. "*Shh*," I whispered. "*Shh*, babies. It's going to be okay." I moved toward them, pulled them both into me with one practiced sweep of my arm. I looked down at the horrible thing, braced to run, to take the children with me. Something rose in my throat again, and I was surprised to hear that it was a choked laugh. The sound got louder and more insistent. My body started to convulse with it. The kids were laughing, too. We were all laughing at silly mommy. Oh.

I put my hand on my flattened chest to slow my heart. I had walked over it a dozen times this morning and not even realized. It was just me, after all. Not Frances, just me, that new, plastic part of me. The dog had buried it. It had been partially shredded by his teeth and claws. I pulled Walt closer into my legs, wanting to sigh with relief, wanting to tell Frances what had happened. What a funny story it would be! But instead, I felt a tear roll down my left cheek, and I lifted my hand to it and wiped it away, feeling my face, still cold. My mind, not yet resettled, still snagging on something. I said, "Get away, kids. Come inside. Mommy wants to go inside."

Third Space

I WOKE UP THAT morning, tucked in and cozy, to the familiar sounds of my house being kept. The suction cup squish of the dishwasher opening, the wooden whine of a hinge, and then the rhythmic clink, clink, clink of the plates being stacked neatly back in the right cabinet. That my mother was downstairs was a comfortable sensation more than a thought. But as I tried to articulate it to myself, the feeling faded, never fully captured. She was gone so quickly, and I was an adult in a messy house. Just like that.

It turned out I was hearing the fucking bats in our chimney, clacking and swishing and clawing. We weren't sure how long they'd been there—maybe since winter. But they'd been getting rowdy over the spring; the babies had become hormonal and loud, all cooped up. It was driving me out of my mind. We saw them swoop around the side of our house at twilight, giving it an ominous, haunted look. The area around our mantel smelled horrendous, a meaty, rancid smell that made me want to be sick. I was embarrassed to have friends over, but Ben told me it was barely noticeable. My sense of smell had gone berserk since I had become pregnant eight weeks ago.

Worst of all, they scratched the walls and rustled against one another behind the bricks. During the day, it was a little eerie. At night, it was alarming, indistinguishable from the sounds an intruder might make as he jimmied open the door, sneaked up our stairs, and pressed softly against our bedroom door. It had woken me up more than once. Panicked, I had waited quietly—almost demurely—to be raped and murdered. Ben always seemed to sleep through it, unafraid.

I wanted them out. These bats were not my dead mom and fuck them for pretending.

But Ben had done some research. Bats mated in the fall, hibernated in the winter, then gave birth in the spring. Bat pups weren't able to fly for the first months of their lives, so if we started the "exclusion process" (as Ben called it, per our local wildlife professionals) before late summer, we ran the risk of stranding the babies inside our chimney to die of starvation, abandoned by their parents.

"I am pregnant!" I had shouted at Ben more than once. "I don't care about *bat babies!* I care about *our baby*, and I don't want them in my house!" I had done my own research, too, and had learned that they could give us rabies or histoplasmosis or ebola. Diseases that seemed to be very bad for pregnant women and, so, good fodder for my argument.

Ben said I was more irritable than usual. Maybe I was.

When it came down to it, though, I didn't want the little motherless pups to die. And so instead of calling wildlife expert services, we had merely made sure the flue was sealed tight against them. Ben and I agreed that this boundary was an acceptable compromise, but I took out my anger on the invisible bats nevertheless, playing loud music into the chimney to annoy them when Ben wasn't home and, sometimes, knocking on the mantel like a cranky downstairs neighbor with a broom handle.

I rolled out of bed, and the motion made me feel nauseous. I ran to the bathroom and got down on my knees, ready to throw up. But nothing happened. The nausea transformed into a kind of low ache at the bottom of my stomach. I got up and peed. I was lucky. I hadn't experienced much morning sickness so far. When my friend Gina was pregnant, she was so sick, she could barely function during her first trimester. She subsisted on a diet of plain, untoasted bagels.

I got up, pulled my hair back, and washed my face. I applied my eye cream. I applied my sunscreen. I applied my moisturizer. I pinched my cheeks. I widened my eyes at myself in the mirror. Not drinking had helped my skin. I thought I looked a bit younger, my eyes a little less lidded and puffy. I smiled at myself in the mirror.

It was important to me to look young today. Ben was at a conference and his girlfriend, Allison, was coming for dinner. She was a few years older than we were, a fact that I held on to desperately to mitigate the fact that Ben had fallen in love with her and wanted me to love her, too. Another home invasion.

In addition to being full of bats, the house was also covered in papers. I was usually very tidy. More than one person had accused me of being compulsive about it. I typically made our bed first thing because the image of an unmade bed could stick in my brain all day, nagging at me until I returned home and made it. Which

I would, even if I were going to bed within the hour. After leaving the bedroom, I'd take my cup of coffee—Ben made the coffee—and walk through the house, making sure everything was in the right place. Throw pillows in their proper configuration on the couch. Seltzer cans removed from the coffee table and placed in the recycling bin. Coasters returned to their neat stack.

A month or so ago, when I took on a new ghostwriting project, I abruptly realized that I had stopped doing these things. I had been contacted by a historian who was attempting to produce a pop history book about how technological changes transformed the midcentury kitchen and, with it, the figure of the housewife. Her editor had, twice, returned drafts to her with the feedback that they were too academic for a general audience. She was hoping I could soften her research into living, breathing prose, readable and easy, like "eating a chocolate chip cookie," she had said to me.

But I'd found it more difficult to complete than I'd expected. All of the reading about kitchens had focused my attention on my own kitchen, on the plates that newly remained in the sink overnight. When had they gotten there? How long would they stay there?

In the preface to *Portrait of a Lady*, which was my mom's favorite book and so was, for a time, also my favorite book, Henry James describes the novel as a house with a thousand windows through which the reader peers in and spies on the inhabitants. The idea made me squirm. If the reader is a Peeping Tom, then the author is a housekeeper—a woman, a mother, a compulsive tidier—who keeps the story neat and ordered and contained. A ghostwriter is a poltergeist, coming in and moving things around and hoping someone notices their presence, so that they can feel alive again.

I found myself as reluctant to clean up the manuscript as I was to clean up my living room. I had no idea exactly when I had become so lax, if it was gradual or immediate. It just didn't seem to matter anymore where the pillows lay. It didn't seem to matter whether the sheet was folded down over the top of the comforter, pulled one quarter of the way down the bed.

I had a number of theories as to why this had happened to me. My therapist didn't like to hear my theories, laid out on bulleted lists. She thought I intellectualized my thoughts and actions as a way to distance myself from them—and so, from myself. She was more interested in how I felt about the change. But what could I say to that? I felt nothing at all. I still felt at home—just as though I were in a different kind of home.

But I had always liked to make lists. My mom had liked to make lists. Sometimes, growing up, I would wake and find them taped to my bathroom mirror, things like "Ten Reasons to Skip School Today and Go to the Movies with Mom" or "All the Ways You're Going to Rock Your Math Test." So I had made a list and stashed it in my bedside table. I pulled it out every now and then to add notes to it before bed. This helped me.

Reasons Why You've Become Untidy

1. You're finally a feminist. Congratulations!
2. All of your organizational energy has gone from managing the home to managing your body.

Monitoring calcium intake, getting enough sleep, limiting strenuous activity, etc.

3. You queered your marriage when you became polyamorous so it follows that you queered your home.

3.5. Book idea: Queer nesting.

4. You are depressed because you are going to be a mother without a mother.
5. You are depressed because your husband fell in love with another woman and you did not.
6. You are depressed because you are more jealous and less open-minded than you thought you were.
7. You are depressed because (per 4 and 5) any control you thought you could exert over the world was an illusion, so why stack the coasters anyway?
8. You believe that if you seem less uptight and less rigid, you will be more lovable to Ben.
9. You are afraid of being a mother so you are not behaving like a good mother.

That morning, when I went into the living room with my laptop to start my work, I thought I saw scratches on the edge of the fireplace, perhaps from before we effectively sealed the bats off and did nothing about them except shout up at the flue. I sat down on the couch and picked up a stack of Ben's loose papers from the coffee table.

Even at my tidiest, Ben's papers had found their way into the nooks and crannies of our home at the beginnings of the semester. He was currently co-teaching a course called The Philosophy of Horror with our friend Max, who was in the English Department.

I found myself regularly sitting down among them, picking them up and reading them. Actually, I couldn't seem to keep myself from reading them. They all seemed to relate to me in a profound way, and I found myself thinking about them throughout the day. The fact was, becoming pregnant had made me weirder. I was crabbier, but also maybe paranoid, sometimes wondering if Ben had me in mind specifically when he wrote his notes about monstrous women and uncanny houses. Some of the ideas unsettled me; and for whatever reason, the most unsettling ones seemed to have lodged themselves into my brain permanently. They had sneaked their way into the midcentury housewife book, their presence like teacups I had knocked over between the pages. One chapter, for instance, was about how midcentury novels like *The Stepford Wives* and *The Body Snatchers* depicted technological changes as horrifically altering suburban women. I was supposed to be making it more accessible, less academic. But I couldn't help myself from adding that the gothic, as a genre, bonds domestic space to the woman who inhabits it and uses household rooms to represent undiscovered territories within the self. Ben had written that down on a little slip of scrap paper.

What territories of my mind were undiscovered? Did Ben find me unknowable? The thought terrified me. But the fact was, I sometimes felt unknowable to myself. And I had been confronted, recently, with the fact that there was something inside Ben that I hadn't seen before. Some need that I hadn't discovered and so hadn't been able to fulfill—at least not to the extent that Allison could.

I had fallen in love with another woman once. Celeste. I wasn't sure at the time, but now, I knew that it must have been love. Before I became pregnant, I dated a few other women, together with Ben and on my own. I could find something I should have loved in each of them. One who had recently lost her grandmother and who cooked me dinner from a recipe written in looping cursive on a yellowing index card. One who had read *A Song of Ice and Fire* hundreds of times and collected beautiful brocade fabrics from which to make cosplay gowns. She had let me run my hands down them both on and off her body. In each case, I left these women not really caring whether I saw them again. They never felt right, or tasted right, or smelled right to me. It took me an embarrassingly long time to realize that this was because they didn't feel, or taste, or smell like Celeste. Neither did Ben. But Ben felt, and tasted, and smelled like Ben. Which is to say, like home.

But then Ben fell in love with Allison.

I didn't believe in vetoes. I didn't have a scarcity mindset. Ben's love for Allison did not diminish his love for me. He had told me that. And I had reminded myself that my love for Celeste hadn't diminished my love for Ben.

But still. Being in love was a horror.

Today's loose papers seemed to be notes from a lecture Ben was preparing. I read them for clues about me and our marriage and how he felt about it. He had typed:

> In *In the Dust of This Planet*, Eugene Thacker proposes a new terminology for thinking about the blurring of the human and nonhuman worlds. The world-for-us is "the world that we, as human beings, interpret and give meaning to, a world that we relate to or feel alienated from." It is a fabricated thing, established through organization. It must be continually produced and taken care of. It exists alongside

> another world, a "world-without-us." That world "bites back, resists, or ignores our attempts to mold it." Thacker argues that horror as a genre makes visible and grapples with the world-without-us by expressing it "in a whole bestiary of impossible life-forms—mists, ooze, blobs, slime, clouds, and much more. Or as Plato once put it, 'hair, mud, and dirt.'" The world-without-us is expressed, then, by what Julia Kristeva has called "abjection"—the "me that is not me"; the breakdown between what is self and what is other.

Fuck me, I thought. I heard a little bat swoop down, hit the barrier, and fly back up again.

I did clean up later that afternoon. I would establish my world through organization, I told myself. I talked to Ben on FaceTime as I wandered around, picking things up off the floor. I had the sense that watching me clean made him happy, which made me mad, and I got a little short with him.

He was appropriately abashed, though, when he realized I was tidying his papers. "You don't have to clean my stuff," he said. "I should have done that before I left."

I said, "The household must be continually produced and taken care of."

He said, "Yes, but not by you. If you don't want to." Then he asked how I was feeling and made me hold the phone up to my stomach so he could kiss the baby that wasn't a baby yet. When I tried to hang up, he said, "Wait!" Then his face got all serious and tender and he said, "Frances, thank you. I know this isn't your ideal night, but it really, really means a lot to me that you want to get to know Allison a little better." His earnestness made me feel like I had been bad.

So I put my heart into it. I Febrezed around the fireplace. I put the dishes in the dishwasher. I made a tray of crudités, with regret. Crudité trays were always a disappointment, the cheese tray's dumb CrossFit boyfriend. But still. I wanted Allison to feel welcomed. A part of me did anyway. I even got out a bottle of wine I wouldn't drink. Soft cheeses. Cured meats. Wine. All the little restrictions.

I changed into jeans and a V-neck top. I wanted to look casual, like I had forgotten she was coming, but also sexy. I wasn't sure if that was because I wanted to be attractive to her or intimidating to her. I looked at my butt in the mirror before I left the bedroom. It still looked pretty good. I wondered if the baby would destroy it.

I found myself pacing around the house, as though this were a first date. My stomach felt like a pit of anxiety. A cramping, churning pit. Allison and I had never been alone together. Not that she hadn't asked. I'd always made excuses and watched as Ben's smile faltered. Still, I'd spent plenty of time with Allison before, so I wasn't sure why I was having such an intense reaction. We'd had dinner, the three of us, a few times.

She'd even come to the party we'd thrown when Izzy moved to town, after she left Liam. I'd watched as Ben introduced her to people with his hand on the small of her back. My friends had given me supportive looks, reminding me that they still didn't understand why we were doing "this whole thing," as one of them had said to me, a bottle of wine later. I had had to be so friendly to Allison that night because of them.

Izzy had been good, though. She'd been warm to Allison, had mirrored my friendliness. Had said to me—not to Ben, to me—that I was lucky to have someone as kind as Allison in my life. And she'd squeezed my hand as she'd done it, a special touch just for me to say, *Don't blow it.*

I didn't deserve her. Izzy. Maybe not Allison, either.

Because here was the thing: I liked Allison. And that sort of made me hate her.

She was pretty. She was smart. She read romance novels and spouted off against people who called them trashy. She would shoot me conspiratorial eyes when Ben said something pompous or corny. She loved her daughter. She did things like let her eat dessert for dinner if she wanted so that her daughter wouldn't grow up to categorize some foods as bad. She canceled on Ben if her daughter wanted her to stay home. She smiled at me. She wanted to be my friend. She wanted to be maybe more than my friend, if I wanted her to be.

Maybe I did want her to be. I didn't know. I had thought about her once, when I was with the cosplay woman. I imagined that I was Ben and that she was Allison. I tried to guess what he liked to do to her. I liked it. But afterward, the woman transformed into both not-Allison and not-Celeste, and I tried to forget about it.

Was she so different from me? Different enough that Ben needed her? The fact of her made me doubt that I was pretty, that I was smart, that I had sweet, interesting opinions about books, that I could love my daughter. In my most unhinged moments, I wondered if he was keeping Allison around in case I proved to be a bad mom, so that our kid could have her instead. How could I ever ask Ben if that was true? I could barely allow myself to wonder about it. The thought was making my stomach cramp again.

A knock at the door. The bats went wild.

* * *

"So how are you feeling? Is it hell?" Allison asked, holding a celery stick in her hand and still chewing on the part that she'd dipped into the hummus. I was about to answer when she swallowed and said, "Ugh, sorry. People are going to start asking you that all the time. I told myself I wouldn't be that person when I was pregnant. That person who only asks about the baby or the pregnancy or whatever."

"No," I said. "It's okay. It didn't seem like that was what you were doing."

"Okay, thanks," she said, and dipped the rest of her celery into the hummus.

"I feel fine, actually? I haven't really had any morning sickness. Mostly, I feel distracted, I guess. And like I wish I were serving you disgusting, moldy, unpasteurized cheese instead of a plate of vegetables."

She laughed. "Hey, at least there's wine." She took a sip. With her other hand, she pushed a piece of hair behind her ear, which was pierced all up the side. Ben sometimes licked my ear when we had sex. I wondered if he did it to her, too. What that was like. Maybe he didn't. Maybe he was too afraid one of the earrings would rip out. I think I must have been staring at her because she cleared her throat and said, "But no, I get that. About being distracted. I had that, too. I couldn't concentrate on my work at all. And I was supposed to be writing a dissertation prospectus at the time."

"Oh shit," I said. "Yeah. Ben told me that."

"Yeah. Man, to be honest, I found it bizarre to be pregnant. I stopped doing my research and wrote a paper on pregnancy. My advisor was, like... what the fuck?"

"She's such an asshole, though," I said, without thinking.

She looked at me. I wondered if it had been insensitive to say that. Ben and Allison had had a fight about her, Agnes, who was a particular champion of Ben's in his department.

"Yeah," she said, taking a long drink of wine. "She really is."

I barreled forward. "Weren't you mad at him? Ben? When he kept working with her, after you told him about how horrible she was to you?"

I wasn't sure why I asked her that. I was afraid that I had done it to gain her allegiance in some way. To make her like me more, at Ben's expense. Because I wanted her? I didn't think so. Because I wanted her to like Ben less? Maybe. I hoped not.

She let out a heavy breath. "Yeah, I was. Actually, I almost ended things. But when it came down to it, I didn't want anything that happened to me during that time to keep dictating my life. She made enough of my decisions for me."

Had Ben known how close he'd been to losing Allison? If he had, he had chosen me and our future over their relationship.

"Aside from that, though," she said, refilling, "the pregnancy paper was sort of ridiculous. But it was all I could think about at the time."

"What was the argument?"

"I actually looked at it recently; it's still saved in my Dropbox. It was...obtuse and obvious at the same time." She blushed and took another sip of wine. It occurred to me, then, that she might be worried about what I thought of her, too.

"Try me," I said, leaning closer toward her. "It can't be that bad. Or any more ridiculous than the shit I've been thinking about." I told her how I'd become obsessed with the notes Ben had left around, feeling like they were deeply personal to me and my pregnancy.

She laughed at me, but in a nice way. "No, no, I get it! Being pregnant makes everything feel personal. I was reading Freud and Kristeva and Plato and being, like, *This is about me!*"

"What had they said about you?"

"Oh, things like . . ." She trailed off and then shrugged. "Okay, so you know Plato's cave?" I nodded. I was pretty sure I remembered that from college. "It's this kind of third space outside of fantasy and reality. If you're born and raised in a cave, and all you've ever seen are shadows moving on a wall, you believe that's reality. I became really obsessed with the maternal overtones of the cave, as an enclosed space that's both part of the world and outside it. That when a person becomes pregnant, they become the receptacle for a possible reality that's both real and fictional. Two different realities, existing at once."

"There's both a baby and there isn't. And a me that is not me," I said. "That's Kristeva, right? A breakdown between self and other?" My stomach lurched again as I said it. I felt queasy suddenly, maybe because I had read that in Ben's notes just that morning. I wondered if she had told him that, had helped him write that lecture. Her thoughts melding into his thoughts, and me only finding out later when I snooped through his trash.

"Right," she said. "I hadn't planned on becoming pregnant when I did, so I think I experienced pregnancy as a kind of invasion by a foreign body. There's something inherently queer about pregnancy, isn't there? It's your normal state, radically transformed."

I had felt that way. I did feel that way. But I wanted very badly to disagree with her suddenly. So I said, without thinking about how revealing the admission would be: "Sure. But it's also incredibly mundane. Like, my most basic, everyday desire made real. That desire to pull the people I love into me, to hold them as a part of me, to consume them." I let out a nervous laugh, but found myself barreling forward. "It's how I feel when I love Ben most fully, when he's kind and sweet and little-boy-ish. When it isn't making me sick and angry, I feel like my pregnancy is a fulfillment of that desire. To feel another, lovable person as myself."

She reached forward and grabbed my hand and squeezed it. For just a second, something warmed the air between us, something like intimacy. But then my stomach cramped again. I stood up quickly and said, "Sorry. I'll be right back." She looked hurt and confused, but I didn't have time to worry about it.

I shut my bathroom door behind me and breathed hard. Another fast, hot pain. I unzipped my jeans and pulled them down and sat on the toilet for a full thirty seconds before I realized what was happening.

It wasn't even that much blood. When I had imagined this—which, of course, I had hundreds of times, as I was sure every pregnant person did—I had imagined a devastation of blood. An apocalyptic amount of blood, rushing out of me and draining me of color. This wasn't really so different than my period. A little heavier. A little thicker. The clots, too, were something of a disappointment. Small clumps of tissue or old blood. I wasn't even sure. They were dark red, almost brown. They looked like nothing. I had imagined something gruesome. Recognizable human tissue issuing from me, like I myself was being regurgitated, inside out. Abjection. Ooze. Hair, mud, and dirt. *Poor baby*, I thought. *You just weren't anything at all yet*. I thought this without wanting to. I had started to cry, I realized. Not because a baby had been lost, but because something was happening to me that I hadn't wanted to happen. The special, indulgent kind of crying reserved for feeling let down.

I had lost my favorite sparkling jelly sandal in the lake. I had left my snuggle bunny at my grandma's and would have to sleep alone tonight. I had said something mean about my best friend and she had heard about it and hadn't come to school today. All my own fault. All, somehow, still unfair. All my own losses that I knew would never be satisfactorily understood by anyone else.

I must have been up there for a long time. Long enough for Allison to follow me upstairs and into our bedroom to knock on the bathroom door. Even though I knew I had closed the bedroom door.

"Frances?" she asked, her voice shaky and high. "Are you okay?"

Fuck her for being here. A presence in my house, and not the right one. Not at all the right one.

"Will you just leave, Allison?" My voice sounded pathetic, hoarse and full of snot.

"I... are you... I can help if..."

"If I'm having a miscarriage?" I said, hot and sharp. I blew my nose loudly into my hand and then wiped it on my ruined jeans.

"I... I've had one before. I can help."

"Well, this one isn't *yours*, Allison. It's mine! It's only mine!" I stamped my foot. It was involuntary. Then I realized what I had said, and I started to cry again.

When I visited Gina in the hospital after she gave birth to her daughter, she confessed to me a deep feeling of anger at her husband that she couldn't shake. I thought, at first, that she was referring to the tritely humorous reaction often depicted in sitcom birth scenes: a feral anger toward the man who got you into this whole fucking situation. But that wasn't it. Once the baby was born, the doctor had placed her on her mother's chest. The most confusing feeling in the world, Gina said. Wholeness and separation at once. The doctor asked her husband, Bernard, to cut the cord. He had, with tears in his eyes, clutching Gina's hand as he did it. Then they picked the baby up. They wiped her off. They handed her to Bernard, who held her so tenderly, so preciously. He thought she was so fragile. It had made Gina want to throw up. It had felt to her that Bernard was holding her own organ in his hands: her stomach, her liver, her heart. It had taken everything in her not to shout, *Don't touch me like that!* She began to cry as she said to me, "I can't shake it. I can't shake it." I kissed her forehead through my mask and said, "Don't worry, it's just that you're on a fuck ton of drugs right now."

As I looked down at my hands, which were covered in thick blood, I almost laughed. It was my blood and it was someone else's, like I was a killer.

"Frances," Allison said again through the door. "Frances, I'm coming in, okay?"

I didn't say anything this time. I let her in.

I was still sitting on the toilet, my bloody cotton underwear pulled down around my ankles, snot webbing my fingers. She knelt down in front of me, her face across from my vagina, which she had never seen before. It had to be the grossest vagina she had ever seen or would ever see. Well. She had sat at miscarriage level. She placed one hand on my knee and lifted my chin slightly upward with her other one, so that I was looking forward. I kept my gaze firmly to the right of her head. She didn't say anything to me. Out of my peripheral vision, I saw that the corners of her mouth pulled out slightly into a kind of knowing smile that seemed to say, *Well, that's that.* She wiped the tears off my cheek and behind my ear as she ran her hand through a wisp of hair that was stuck to my face. I looked at her then and saw that her eyes were filled with tears. I wanted to be mad about that. I wanted to yell at her again. But instead, I slid myself forward without deciding to. My knees crunched up around me as I oozed into her lap. I slid my left foot out of my underwear and wrapped my arms and legs around her totally. I put my face into her hair, which smelled like something I had smelled a hundred times before in my life, some drugstore shampoo. I breathed her in. She let out a sound like an animal, but quiet, and pressed her palm into the back of my head, holding me in tight. With her other hand, she rubbed my back. She said quietly, "It's okay, baby. It's okay."

I realized I was talking then. Whispering into her ear. "I can't keep anything for myself. I can't keep anything . . ." I hiccupped into her hair.

"Frances, *shh*," she said. "This isn't your—"

"Don't say it isn't my fault," I snapped at her. "I know it isn't. It's stupid that women always think it's their fault."

"It's not stupid," she said. "And it's also not your fault."

"I'm almost thirty-four." Thirty-four. How had it happened? Saying it out loud felt like another grief. "Now, if I ever have a baby, I'll be a geriatric mother."

Allison laughed a little, which surprised me. She said, "Nothing queerer than an old lady who's pregnant. I actually think Freud said that."

I let out a breath that was almost a laugh. I leaned back and wiped my nose and looked around. My jeans and underwear were in a heap. The toilet seat was covered in blood. "I can't keep my house clean," I said, and began to cry again.

"It's okay," Allison said, and pulled me back into her. I bled my miscarriage into her lap.

After a while, my face still in her hair, I asked, "What should I do?"

She leaned back from me and put her hands on the side of my face. She let me stay where I was, my legs wrapped tightly around her. "Right now?"

I nodded.

"Right." Her voice became firm and confident. "First, we're going to get up and wash off. Do you have a maxi pad you can wear? You're going to keep bleeding. It probably won't get much worse. But if you wear a tampon, you might get an infection."

I sniffed. "Okay. Yes, I have one." What then? I wanted her to give me a full list of things to do, easy tasks I could achieve. I wanted her to be in charge of me.

Before I could ask, she said, "Later tonight, after you've calmed down a little, you're going to call Ben."

"I . . ." I felt physically sick at the idea. "I can't tell Ben, I can't tell him."

"You have to," she said, her voice low and melodic in its sternness. "Ben loves you. It'll be okay."

"He'll be so disappointed."

"I think he'll mostly be worried about you," she said. "Ben loves you so much. You're going to get through it together." How did it make her feel, to say that, I wondered. I couldn't detect any secret feelings from her tone. Maybe she loved that he loved me, the way I loved that she loved her daughter. The idea flooded me with shame and with warmth, for Ben and for her and for myself. I leaned into her again, back into the hug.

Into her neck, I asked, "And then what?"

"Then, you're going to make an appointment to see your ob-gyn for tomorrow."

"Okay."

"But first, right after you get dressed, we're going to have a glass of wine together. And we're going to do one really fun thing, anything you want. What do you think?"

"I want . . ." I couldn't think of anything, nothing achievable. My body felt runny. Grimy. I wanted to seal myself up, to stop feeling so formless. I wanted to eat whatever I decided to eat. I wanted to drink whatever I wanted. I wanted to have the kind of body that stayed safe under its skin. I wanted to feel like I was secure, and that the things that were mine were mine. "I want to get the bats out of my chimney," I said.

She laughed. "Perfect."

Allison went downstairs while I got dressed. I put on a pad and sweatpants and an enormous T-shirt of Ben's. When I went into the kitchen, she handed me a glass of wine and said, "I've been doing some googling." Bats were nocturnal, she told me, so one way to frighten them was with bright, flashing lights. "Fluorescent, if you have them." The sound and light together would send them flying out. They wouldn't be gone for good. They'd come back. And then we'd wait a few more weeks like we were supposed to. But they wouldn't scratch around in the walls and bother me tonight, at least.

Together, Allison and I went into Ben's office and got his desk lamp, an enormous, horrible light from the eighties. "This is so ugly," Allison said as we carried it over to the fireplace.

"Bat signal," I said.

We plugged it in and positioned it so that the light was aimed upward, into the cave of the chimney. Allison counted down, and on one, I flipped the light switch and she pushed the lever to open the flue. There was a mad scrabbling in the chimney, and without meaning to, I let out a scream, a feral, uncontained, final girl scream of a kind I didn't know I had in me. My throat felt stretched and raw.

The bats began to screech along with me. We heard them go wild, emitting high-pitched, mousy wails. They began to flutter, louder and louder.

"I think they're flying out!" Allison said, her face flushed with conspiracy.

"Come on," I said. I grabbed her hand and pulled her up. We ran outside, each with our glass of wine, sloshing them as we went. In our side yard, we could see a cloud of bats rising out of our chimney.

Our neighbor, who seemed to be trying to enjoy a nice meal al fresco, shouted over, "What in the hell is going on with you girls?"

I ignored him and kept looking up at the bats. "Fuck you!" I shouted.

"Fuck. You!" Allison screamed. I began to laugh. I looked at Allison, who was laughing, too. The front of her jeans was smeared in my blood. My laugh turned into a weird, uncontrollable cackle. I couldn't stop. Allison wrapped her arms around my body and we stood there, together, while the bats circled around us.

Scraps

March 1, 2002

FIRST DAY TOMORROW. NOT sure what to wear, or who to ask, since most of the other staff are in veils and some even in the full habit. Would think I'm silly probably, or vain. Well.

Something conservative, I guess. Franny said not to wear black because the other women would think I was a nun, and they wouldn't confide in me about their husbands or boyfriends or whoever had put them there. Seem relatable, but professional. Surprised me that she thought of that. So smart!

Miss wearing jeans to school. Won't miss the drive to campus three days a week, seeing Franny for an hour or so at most before her bedtime. Trying to undo whatever Ma told her. She's finally eating ice cream again, but meant I had to every night for almost two weeks.

Nervous. Feel like an imposter. What do I know about the

lives these women are leaving? With little children, some of them. I left with one, I guess. But not like that. Didn't have to hide in a tiny, half-furnished apartment. Wasn't afraid. Had Ma to help me.

I should be more grateful, but the women make me ashamed of her. They're stronger than she was.

March 2, 2002

I think it went well! Mostly got acquainted with everyone and the house rules, etc. Only one other person who doesn't live there, social worker like me. An older woman, there since they opened the house. I think she helped get the grant, along with Sister Anita.

Surprised by my guide—Sister Dorothy. Looked like she was my age and pretty, too. Everyone I met in interviews was about a hundred. Nice, sort of funny. Didn't say anything about God.

I wonder what her real name is. Could be a Jessica or a Britney for all I know—imagine a Sister Jessica. Who's that other one, Mandy Moore? Sister Mandy. No wonder you change it.

I'd change mine if I could. One of the most boring flowers, not sure what Ma was thinking. Franny very impressed by it, after *Titanic*, though.

Possible nun names:

1. Sister Helen
2. Sister Elena
3. Sister Elaine
4. Sister Eleanor
5. Sister Claire
6. Sister Emily

Just realized those are all the same. Maybe more will come to me. Wonder how long they think about it. Always a saint, or sometimes someone from a book you love, or a friend, or an aunt?

March 10, 2002

Woman came in today with a toddler with a cut down his cheek. Husband hadn't meant to, she said. The drinking makes his aim bad. He wasn't a bad guy; it was just the alcohol.

Where had he been aiming, I asked, and she didn't say anything, just wrinkled her forehead.

March 15, 2002

Franny and I watched *Moonstruck* last night. Maybe she was a little young for it, but she loved it. Saw she had the soundtrack from *La Bohème* downloading on Kazaa this morning. Found Ronny very romantic, missing his hand. Liked the idea of marrying someone with a missing limb (?) Think she felt that she could fix him, comfort him. Be his other hand. Weirdo, I thought for a minute. And scary. But then thought, there's a long tradition of smart women who only marry broken men. It helps them to be equals. Jane Eyre, for instance. Rochester had to go blind.

Men without hands can hit you all the same, though. I found Ronny scary, the way he yelled. Didn't remember that about him. Maybe work getting in my head. When he said, love ruins everything. We're on earth to break our hearts and love the wrong people and die. I guess plenty of people live that way and probably it's very exciting, until you get to the dying part. Aunt Frances loved the wrong person and she died. I don't want to die.

Even if you marry the Jonny, the safe brother, you still get your heart broken. Bounce back quicker though.

March 26, 2002

Was eating my lunch on the bench outside when Sister Dorothy came over, asked if I wanted to get a coffee, maybe something sweet. I hesitated, I don't know why. Maybe the idea of walking down the street with her, in her veil and her rosary. Not really a great time to be Catholic, if there ever was one. Walt asked me about that, if I really wanted to take the job right now. Honestly surprised he was keeping up with the news. Pretty insular, usually—if it doesn't affect his wife and kids, etc., then why worry. Maybe because you don't usually see it about men. Boys. Feels more personal. Wonder if Sam has been keeping up. He knows better than anyone boys can be—not sexual, but still.

Said no matter what was happening with the priests, the women needed the help. Wonder if the nuns think about it that way or if they're ashamed. Shame has to be part of it no matter what, I guess. Hiding their bodies, hair.

Anyway, I think she saw me hesitate because she said, "If you don't want to—" really fast, and I felt terrible, so I said, "No!" and we went to the bakery a few blocks down. Not her fault.

I got a croissant and she got something called a religieuse, which is two cream puffs stacked on top of each other. Apparently it's supposed to look like a nun. She said she always gets them, just thinks it's funny, a nun eating a nun.

I said, "I thought you guys only ate human flesh on Sundays."

She didn't laugh and I felt bad again for a second, but it turns out she's just not the kind of person who laughs when they think something is funny, because she said, "Even nuns have cheat days."

She took two big mouthfuls, then dipped the last piece into her coffee and said, "God, I love these things." Surprised me! Joy she took in eating.

April 1, 2002

Took Franny to Ma's this weekend, Walt and Sandy brought the kids, too. We did a little pool party, so warm out. Walt grilled. Jason brought a girlfriend, couldn't believe it. Fifteen. Looked so much like Sam when he was that age. Wiry build, tall, hair that I still think is blond, even though it turned brown years ago.

The girl seemed so much older than Franny and Haillie. Wore a bikini. Mostly sat by the pool to tan. F and H acted like they had since they were kids, tea parties at the bottom of the pool, Martha Washington hair. Big difference, between fifteen and twelve. Maybe Franny wouldn't have acted like that, with her own friends there. Something about being with her cousins, allowed to be a little childish. Sweet to see. Still in a one-piece.

Sandy asked me who I was dating after her second white wine and hot dog, though, and I spent the rest of the night defending myself. So tired of it. Walt has some divorced colleague something or other who would be perfect for me, blah blah. Do I want his number? Could we all four go out together?

I don't want to get married again, I said, for the 900th time. It's just a date, no pressure. Lots of pressure!! I said.

Sam showed up still in his scrubs. Notice he never gets bullied about not being married, not having kids. Men are allowed. His career more important than mine, I guess. He dates, though.

Maybe just to get Walt and Sandy to shut up about it. Never asked.

Worst part is, Franny heard. Was he cute? she asked. Was he nice? Why did he get a divorce? Does he have kids?

On the way home, she said, "Dad's dating. You know that, right?" and I said yes, and she said, "Doesn't that make you mad?" and I said, no I'm glad he's dating, and yes, I hope he's happy.

"How come you never date? Uncle Walt is right, there are lots of men who would want to date you! You're pretty and smart and you have a cool job and you're still pretty young, for a mom."

When I was twelve, I thought Ma was quiet, and lonely, and old, and had no interests. I'm so proud that Franny doesn't think that about me. I'm so scared that she will start to.

Things That Are True

1. 29% of women report experiencing domestic violence.
2. My mom never reported anything so that number should probably be way higher.
3. If you love someone, you will forgive them when they hurt you. Or maybe not even realize that they hurt you.
4. 93% of domestic violence offenders are men.
5. The best way to ensure that you and your kid aren't hit or kicked or screamed at or raped is to not have a man in your house.
6. Most women let men into their houses anyway

because they trust them. They are their husbands or boyfriends or fathers or priests.

7. You can break cycles. You can have a better life than your mom, and you can make sure that your daughter has a better life than you.
8. It means that you might be lonely sometimes.

April 4, 2002

Found myself telling all of that to Sister Dorothy today. Fourth time we've gone for pastries and coffee at lunch, and today I realized how much I've started to look forward to it. I was thinking ahead, about things I wanted to say, questions I had about some of the residents—but it just kind of slipped out.

I told her the truth, or most of it. I don't want to date, I'm sick of it all. Putting my interests on the back burner for some guy's benefit. Pretending to give a shit about all the shit he gives shits about! Sports and Philip Roth and whatever else! I did that already, and it didn't work out. What was I supposed to miss—sex? It was one fat disappointment, every time.

She asked me, "What about your friends, what do they think?"

That sucked. I've been thinking about it. I used to have friends, right? Peter and I with Jake and Amanda, and Arn and Jen in New York. Couples, though. And then I left. What would we talk about now? My life's too different. Think Peter still sees them. Wonder if they have dinner with him and Sarah. More fun than with me?

Before Peter, I had lots of friends! Alice, Nancy, Tammy. Came over to swim, spend the night. We went on double dates together.

Went to the football games and hayrides and dances together. I used to tell them everything.

That's not true. I don't know why I wrote that. Came to swim, but when we did slumber parties, it was at one of their houses. I never wanted them to see how Dad was.

How sorry they were when Dad died. All had nice things to say about him, and I remember thinking, *You didn't know him at all.* I didn't tell you anything about him. Makes sense, actually, why Nancy was so surprised I reached out. We didn't have much of a foundation to draw on, I guess.

It's not like I don't have anyone to talk to. There's Walt and Sandy and Sam. And I like some of Franny's friends' moms.

And Franny!!! There's no one I'd rather talk to. Pizza and movies on Friday nights. Still read out loud to her, fantasy books. Hasn't outgrown them yet. I don't miss the dinners, the wine, the plays, the launch parties, whatever. Peter doesn't have what I have. I'd trade ten thousand Jakes and Amandas and Arns and Jens for Franny. Ten billion.

To SD, I think I said something vague like, "They don't really get it."

She shrugged and said, "Yeah. My people didn't really understand, either." Then she got all embarrassed and said, "I'm not calling you a nun." I laughed.

April 15, 2002

Franny spending the night at Walt and Sandy's tonight, going to watch movies with Haillie. I miss her, miss her, miss her, miss her miss her miss her miss her

April 15, 2002, later

Is that what I am, a nun? They live such small lives. You should see the nuns' apartments, so cramped. Worse than the ones for the women. Little spare twin bed next to a window. SD shares hers with two others. One is Sister Mary, whose name choice shows you exactly how boring she is.

Wonder if she gets lonely, with only those old women to talk to. I guess she talks to God. Feels that someone is there to listen to her, help her, understand her. Still. Not known for being very responsive. Talking into a void.

Who am I to judge, writing into a diary. Scraps of thoughts jumbled together.

April 20, 2002

Phone call from Ma today, more of the same. Am I safe at work? What if one of the husbands figures out the location, finds us, brings a gun, etc., etc. Wouldn't I feel safer working somewhere else? Wouldn't I feel safer if there were a man at home?

All I could do not to say, a man in the home is what makes you unsafe!!

Know why she is scared. Trying to be patient. But need her to understand my work and why it's important that I do it, why I have to be there. If someone could have helped her. If someone could have helped Aunt Frances. She won't look at that, but it shapes how she sees everything and everyone around her. Always waiting for me to be killed by someone's husband.

Things That Are True

1. 34% of murdered women are killed by an intimate partner.
2. More than ⅓ of those domestic killers have a reported history of domestic abuse.
3. My aunt was stabbed 18 times in her bathtub.
4. She had a husband, but he was proved not to have done it.
5. My dad avoided us when he could and was mean to us when he couldn't.
6. He came home from work early on the days Aunt Frances babysat us.
7. He was nice to us on those days, and made sure we went to bed on time, before Ma got home.

April 27, 2002

Franny and I went to the mall today—summer clothes. I'd rather go to hell than step back into a Hollister. I think the smell is still in my hair.

But guess what F found! In one of those dumb stands in the middle, someone was selling calendars, and Franny flipped through and saw one called *Nuns Having Fun!* She thought it was hilarious. Bought two—one for our fridge, and one for SD. Think she'll get a kick out of it.

Things Nuns Do to Have Fun

1. Share a milkshake from three different straws like the cast of *Friends!*

2. Jump in the waves! In their habits!
3. Paddleboard!
4. Pretend to be the Beatles crossing the road!
5. Bowl!
6. Shoot guns (?) Suspect this picture staged.
7. Ride the log ride at Disney World! In their habits!

May 3, 2002

Horrible night, Frances came into my room maybe 3 a.m., terrible stomach pains. Crying. Haven't seen her cry from pain in years, scraped knees, etc. My sweet girl, we didn't know what was happening. She lay down next to me, I pressed on her tummy, asked where it hurt. Thought maybe appendix, but wasn't localized there. Almost rushed her to the hospital anyway, just in case, but then we saw the blood. Thought we would both pass out, it scared us so much. If I lost her—I can't even think about it. I realized, finally, her period.

So young. I didn't think she would be so young. Not 'til fourteen, like me.

Cleaned her up, she slept with her back pressed into my stomach, cried for another hour, doubling over every few. I stayed awake all night, afraid, holding on to her like when she was a newborn.

Always knew some women had unbearable pain. I never did. Hope just because it's the first time. My sweet girl.

Kept thinking about Sam, his appendix. He was fourteen or fifteen, before he had a driver's license, but old enough to understand how. In the middle of the night, too, woke up Ma and Dad. Pissed Dad off. Stop whining and go back to bed. Stole the car, drove himself to the emergency room. If he hadn't, his appendix would have burst. Told it like it was funny now. Always had the makings of a doctor, knew something was up.

Not funny at the time. Never forgave Dad.

God, only just now wondered for the first time. How could Ma have stayed in bed? Saw him in pain. Had to have known. Had to have heard the engine start. Had to have wanted to hold him, how I held Franny. Right?

Ten Reasons It's Awesome to Have a Period!

1. You're a grown-up now!
2. You can be mean and demanding to me once a month and I won't be mad!
3. You have an excuse not to go to those end-of-year class pool parties!
4. You can eat as much chocolate as you want!
5. Your other friends will be jealous of you until they get theirs (and realize)!
6. When that happens, they will think you are wise and knowledgeable and they will come to you for advice!
7. You'll know you're not pregnant! JK YOU SHOULD ALREADY BE CONFIDENT ABOUT THIS.
8. You're connected to the moon or oceans or something!
9. I don't know, there are not really that many reasons it's awesome!
10. Ten!!!

May 10, 2002

The woman who came in with the toddler didn't show up for our session today, and when Dorothy went to check her apartment, all her stuff was gone.

May 18, 2002

Frances at a birthday party. Feeling low.

Want to believe that what we do adds up to something. All the scraps of advice can eventually add up to a new life. That every time you leave, you become stronger, even if you go back. And it makes it that much easier to leave the next time, for real. Not sure.

Bright side: Saw that D had been marking off the *Nuns Having Fun!* calendar. Makes me feel better, seeing it on her fridge just like on our fridge.

May 30, 2002

Everyone upset at work today. Sister Mary heard a rumor that we were going to lose some funding. Lots of donations being pulled from churches right now. But we're such a small organization. Came as a surprise to everyone.

Heard Sister Anita whispering to Sister Mary. Never heard her so angry. Hadn't been sure whether the nuns were following all the news coming out, but it became clear they had been. Were horrified by everything. Even in a safe house, the abuses of men still seep in, Sister Anita said.

D seemed most upset of all. Face was red and puffy all day, and every time I saw her, her hands were clenched at her side. Tried to find her for pastries, but like she'd disappeared.

May 31, 2002

Still nothing—hopefully just a rumor. Feel I'm only now getting to do real work here.

Didn't see D at all today. Sick? F says I should check on her tomorrow. "She's your friend," she said with big, wide eyes. "Is she?" I asked. Franny rolled them at me and said, "Duh."

Felt so stupid for a second. Of course she's my friend. Why didn't I know that? Easier for kids, until it isn't.

June 1, 2002

Asked Sisters if D was starting to feel any better, and Sister Mary gave a kind of side eye to Sister Angela. Asked again. Said she's not sick, just harder on her, because of where she comes from.

"Didn't you know?" Sister Angela said. Nuns are just women in the end, I guess. Gossiping.

Having a harder time thinking about closing, because she used to be one of the women, they said. (!!!) Not here, but somewhere like here. Got married when she was really young, some boy she knew from church. From a good family. You know the story, they said, and I did. It was the same as all the women's stories—except that she got out. The nuns helped her to get a divorce, to find a place to live. She became a sister after that, after a while.

Felt shocked—still feel shocked. I guess I just imagined her as always having been a nun. Born fully formed. Stupid of me. Should have seen the compassion she has toward the women. The understanding. More than the others.

After work, went to D's apartment. Didn't answer, but I knocked and knocked again. She finally let me in.

She has blond hair, short. Maybe cuts it herself. Very striking to see her like that. Like someone I'd just see on the street, notice they were pretty. Maybe wish I had their cheekbones. But her eyes, so puffy, like she'd been crying since I last saw her. I didn't even think about it, just hugged her. She seemed stiff at first, like it had been a while. But then she hugged me back.

We sat on the couch, just like normal friends.

June 6, 2002

Sam thinks it's good, donations being pulled. Fuck the Catholic Church, he said. I wanted to hit him, thinking of the sisters. They hadn't done anything wrong, I said.

Seeing something, and doing nothing, that's just as bad, he said. Could have sworn his eyes shot over, lingered on Ma for a little too long.

June 10, 2002

Staff meeting at the end of the day, and it's true. Losing some money, not as much as we thought. Will have to try to stretch budget, keep afloat. Everyone brainstormed ideas, but D left.

I followed her. So angry, I couldn't have imagined her like that. Had to leave, she said, and she was walking back and forth on the sidewalk. Told her to get in my car. I started driving, I understood how she felt, I said. I was angry, too.

Turned on me, her face so sharp. Did I? she asked. Had they told me about her?

Yes, I said. Felt guilty, saying it. She hadn't wanted to share that with me. How I'd feel, if someone had told her about Peter before I had.

And she said, "So you think you know. You think you know what it's like to be so lonely, and so hurt, and so ashamed, and so afraid, and then to finally leave, to think you could be part of a force of good, and peace, and love, and now to find out that you didn't escape, you only swapped roles, became a hand on the arm of the abuser."

I didn't say anything, just let her keep going. Because you don't understand, she kept saying. You don't, you don't. Finally, "Peter never hit you," she said. "You have Frances. You still have your family. Your brothers, your mom, you're a big happy family. I thought I had sisters, but I have no one."

I stopped the car. Realized I had started crying.

What kind of daughter wonders if her dad stabbed someone 18 times? A bad one, a really, really bad one. Here's a thing that's true: I'm going to die and never know, because I've never asked and I never will, because if I know for sure, then Franny will have to know, and I never, ever want her to know that about her own family. It's better for me to feel it alone than to force her to carry it with us.

To D, I said, "Everything is so fucked up. I am still so fucked up."

"I'm sorry," she said. "I'm sorry."

I want to do some good in this life. Even if we get shut down, I think I can, even if it's only small, only for Frances. That could be enough for me, I think.

I said that to D, and she just smiled kind of sadly. "I don't know if anything will ever be enough for me. Which is something that sisters aren't supposed to feel. I'm afraid I'll never be satisfied until I've fixed everything, which is impossible."

"At least you have an afterlife. You can keep working and working, forever and ever."

"Amen," she said. And then she laughed. We sat there in my car for a long time after. Quiet, together.

Pump and Dump

"I WANT THEM TO look real," she said. Izzy, the bride. "I have tons of pictures from my first wedding and I hate all of them. They're all me and Liam standing up straight, looking right at the camera, mouths closed, eyes open, doing that Tyra Banks eyeball thing. You know, *America's Next Top Model.*"

"Yes!" Lily said, and sipped her cappuccino. A little before her time, but she'd seen an episode here and there, watching over a babysitter's shoulder. "We can do real. I like to get onto the dance floor, right in on the action, capture the real laughter, the bad dance moves, the wine spilled down the dress, all that."

Izzy laughed. "That's perfect. Totally the vibe. I want it to all be different this time . . ." She trailed off, then cleared her throat, took a dainty sip of her matcha, and said, "I can see why Miranda recommended you."

"I've assisted her with dozens of weddings. From a technical perspective, I've got it down, and it sounds like we're a good fit in terms of aesthetic goals. I really think you'll be glad you gave me a shot."

Lily knew she sounded painfully eager. But she'd been trying to land a wedding contract of her own for a year now—that was where the real money was, and she was sick of *still* picking up the odd restaurant shift after officially quitting to photograph full time. She had a big portfolio of her own work—headshots, new baby photos, even a few boudoir sessions—but clients weren't willing to risk a first-timer when it came to their weddings. Izzy hadn't been, either; she'd hired Miranda. But Lily's years of assisting seemed to have finally paid off: When Miranda broke her ankle hiking the week before, she'd sent Izzy directly to Lily.

Izzy smiled and said, "Me too. I was really panicked when Miranda called me. Apart from anything else, I'm relieved you can fit me into your schedule last minute."

Lily gave a wave of her hand like, *Oh, I made it work*. But she didn't have a job on the books for another two weeks and had spent the last weekend at the movies alone. She had seen *Challengers*. Twice. The first time, she'd been stood up by her best friend, Annie, whose husband, in the end, "couldn't babysit." The second time, she'd reserved the open seat next to a couple, just to see what would happen.

They pulled out their devices—Izzy, a smartphone, and Lily, a laptop—and went through Lily's portfolio and the email correspondence Izzy had shared with Miranda. After they'd gone over the style, schedule, and pricing, Lily asked Izzy to send her a list of who she particularly wanted to feature in the candid pictures. "I don't want to give you a wedding album full of your second cousins and plus-ones," she explained.

"Can do," she said, and stood up to leave. "I'll get that to you tonight. Off the top of my head, though, I know Jess will say his brother Daniel and Daniel's husband, Max. And my best friends are the most important to me. Ben and Frances. I moved here to be close to them after my divorce. They'll be with their—well, their friend, Allison. I'll point them out to you; don't let me forget. They'll all be hanging around together.

"Mmm," Lily said, trying not to look like she'd been spooked. Surely it wasn't *her* Ben and Frances. Not that they were hers, even the real ones. Not that whoever these ones were weren't real. She took a deep breath. "Can do!" she parroted Izzy.

But their ages fit. And something about the way Izzy said "friend." Lily felt a frisson of jealousy rise up her arms. She had had a threesome with a Ben and a Frances four years ago, and she had masturbated about it just that week. Pathetic.

"So she's, like, thirty-five, right, and I found her on Facebook and her profile is private, but her picture is her with, like, three other women at a winery or something, and I'm almost positive one of the women is Frances."

"Stop bouncing your leg like that; you're making me anxious," Annie said. They were sitting on her couch, two empty take-out containers and a buzzing baby monitor on the coffee table in front of them. Annie was in a robe, her hair unbrushed, with a three-month-old baby latched on to her.

"Sorry," they said at the same time.

"No, I'm sorry," Annie said. "She woke up three times last night to eat, and then Jace got up at five a.m., ready to party. He's about to figure out how to climb out of his crib. I'm exhausted."

"It's okay," Lily said. "I'd be exhausted, too."

"It's fine," she said, shaking her head and smiling. "It's honestly been great, easier than I thought having two would be. Ella's about a hundred times easier than Jace was."

Lily could count the number of times that she thought Annie had been honest with her about married life and motherhood. But she believed her about Ella. When Jace was brand new, Annie called her all the time. Asked her, please could she come hold the baby while she took a shower? Would she mind taking Jace for a walk so that she could take a nap? Once, Lily had raced over to give Jace a formula bottle because Annie felt too ashamed about her dwindling milk supply to get out of bed. Another time, having been awake for two days straight, she'd called Lily in the middle of the night because she'd stolen Chris's phone to read his texts, to find out whether he'd really been working night shifts. When it turned out he had been, Annie had wilted into guilty, relieved tears. Lily, on the other hand, felt her anger grow hotter. If he could stay up for night shifts at the hospital, why couldn't he stay up for night shifts with Jace?

Annie had called her only once to come help with Ella. A part of her felt glad that Annie was coping better this time. A bigger part of her felt abandoned.

But she smiled and said, "I'm glad."

"You all done, cutie?" Annie asked Ella in baby voice. She pulled Ella off her chest and draped her over one shoulder, began to pat her back.

Lily had invited herself over that night, ostensibly to watch the new batch of *Love Is Blind* episodes, but really to talk to someone about Ben and Frances.

"So what will you do? If it's them? I guess it's not exactly like you can just, ask for their number, find out if they're single, because they're *not* single, are they?"

Lily rolled her eyes performatively so she wouldn't roll them for real. "Actually, it's exactly like that."

"Well," Annie said, pulling out her other boob and pressing Ella's face into it, "are you going to, then? Do you *want* to date them again? Or whatever?"

"I wanted to whatever them the whole time. It was them who stopped wanting to whatever me."

The hurt flooded over her as she said it. It surprised her, to find that it was still living in her, after all this time. She'd spent only one night with them, but it was one night that had come at the exact right time. She'd been bored with her boyfriend, living in her college town along with her college girlfriends. But Annie had been newly married, Tess had just started graduate school, Gracie had been wrapped up in her boyfriend.... Everyone had had other things to focus on. All *she'd* had was a growing pool of worry: Her father had started behaving strangely, her brother refused to talk about it, and her mother refused to see it. She had never felt more alone in her entire life.

And then they had appeared. Two beautiful, grown-up people who had wanted her! Her specifically! They'd wanted to learn about her—her interests, her friends. They'd hugged her, before and after. They'd felt (god help her) both like loving parents and like characters from some old-school porn who wanted to fuck her because she was young.

She'd had threesomes before, but always drunkenly, in a dorm room, with a girl who was just trying to please her boyfriend. This hadn't been like that. The way Frances had looked at her, like she was hungry. The way Ben and Frances had looked at each other, like they were sated. She was as attracted to their relationship as she was to either of them.

She'd felt that things were about to turn in her life, that the world might be about to open up in some big, intangible way. But instead, it had closed down. She'd been trapped in her home with her tepid boyfriend, trying and failing to teach her declining father how to use Zoom, for more than a year. And whatever care Ben and Frances had felt for her must have been in her head, some sad projection of her own desperation. Because they hadn't called, once they could, and she'd been too afraid of another rejection to reach out herself.

Annie knew all of this, but Lily laid it out again happily. She found it natural to tease out her thoughts, to probe them for new angles. She wanted to understand herself, and believed that she could do so only if she maintained a sense of inquisitive detachment—even mistrust—when she looked inward. She wanted to find out what she was hiding from herself, and bring it into the open, even if it was ugly or sad or embarrassing. Or perhaps especially if it was one of these things—because that would mean it was the truth.

"Look, look!" Annie said, pointing at the television. Two sets of doors were sliding open. The couple, who had gotten engaged without ever seeing each other, were about to meet. She watched as their eyes lit up, and the woman began to run toward the man. The people were always hot. Annie sucked in a deep breath. Lily reached for her hand, and squeezed it. "Soulmates," Annie said, squeezing back.

On her way out the door, Lily hugged Annie and said, "I'm sorry you're so tired. You know, it could be good to talk more about it. Get it off your chest."

Annie nodded, but quickly looked down at the baby, whose

eyes were beginning to close as Annie bounced her. "Yeah, I know. I've actually been working on a new article, to think through some things." Annie stopped working when she got pregnant with Jace, but she'd begun writing articles every now and then for mommy advice sites and mommy blogs that had corporatized rather than die after their boom in the aughts. Once, she'd written a series of posts for a prominent tradwife momfluencer on Instagram. ("She's gross," Annie had said, "but the job paid, like, *so* well.")

"Oh," Lily said, trying to keep her face neutral. "Well, good. But if there's anything you need to talk about, like, privately, you know I'm—"

"I know," Annie said.

"Just because I'm not sure you can really be, like, honest in those things."

Annie laughed, maybe bitterly. "I like writing them; I've *told* you that. It's nice to be part of a community; it helps me."

"I just mean, you have *me*, you know."

Annie let out a huge sigh. She looked so tired suddenly. Her eyes swollen with a lack of sleep, her hair greasy around its part. Lily looked down at Ella, now asleep. Ella had done this to Annie, *but so did I*, she thought. She wasn't sure why she always ended up picking on Annie, making her life harder.

"I love you," she said. "Go get some sleep while Ella's sleeping."

Annie nodded. "I love you, too."

As Lily was walking out the door, Annie said, "Lily." She ran her hand down the side of the door and continued, "Look, I know all of this looks really bad to you. I don't get to be as creative as you, or as free as you. But I'm happy. Really. This is what I always wanted."

Lily felt something rise up in her throat. Disbelief? Fear? Jealousy? She wasn't sure. She nodded and said, "I know."

* * *

Lily sometimes felt like a traitor, both to her generation and to the human race. Wedding photography, how patriarchal! How heteronormative! How capitalist! At the very least, she ought to be a nature photographer, traveling the world to photograph glaciers, or polar bears, or the myriad islands that would vanish if the ocean were to rise by a mere half-inch, which it would. She could travel by boat, reduce her carbon emissions, risk death by orca. Maybe photograph an orca, if its scarred and barnacled body would fit within the frame. Not that they needed her to preserve their memory; whales had survived four global mass extinctions. Her whole body could fit within a whale's lung.

She knew that the photographs she was producing amounted to little more than sentimental bits of paper that would be gathered, stuffed into a closet, and one day, thrown into the trash by grown-up children or grandchildren. And then they would wither away in a landfill until they were blown or washed away (choose your storm!) into the ocean, where they would be sucked up and eddied around by an ocean gyre like the North Atlantic Garbage Patch.

And yet.

How many times she had pulled out her parents' wedding album. Two twenty-three-year-olds with shiny skin, tanned one shade too dark, her mom with big hair and curly bangs, her dad with tortoiseshell glasses. How they smiled at each other, with wide mouths and uneven teeth. How they danced. How they smushed frilly white cake into each other's faces. They were so happy. Their personalities bubbled up through the paper, through the plastic sleeves in the photo album, and into Lily's imagination.

She felt drawn to those people in a way she never had to her physical parents, who were stiff and distant, even when she was a child.

And so here she was, a traitor to everyone but that little girl, trying to capture not just the visual, but the sensual. Before they became apocalyptic litter, her photographs, she hoped, would be little gifts for her clients, now older, less exuberant, with mysterious children. She hoped to give to them the memory of their own sensations: being hot, being cold, being nervous. The memories of what they heard: the pop of champagne, the bass of the DJ, the stupid, beautiful conversations of their drunk friends. Fragments of sense memory that might open up the fullness of a cherished and profound connection between themselves and the ones they once loved. She wanted her work to rupture the surface of the merely visual and reveal everything that lingered below.

Probably this was why she still had to wait tables to make ends meet, while her friends had marriages and full-time jobs and publications on *mommy blogs*—to Lily's mind, the fakest, most surface-level, shining bullshit that existed.

The night before the wedding, Lily went to see *Challengers* again. She knew all the beats by this point—the power plays, the overlapping desires, the exquisite cruelties—and so could let the movie wash over her, soothe her racing mind.

As she waited for it to begin, she opened Annie's new article on her phone.

> Let me level with you, my sweet baby. You're getting screwed over. You're the second child. When your big brother was growing in my belly, I had nothing but

> time to devote to him. He got a brand-new stroller and décor carefully selected to fit a green-and-gray nature theme. You don't even have a room of your own. What would Virginia Woolf say?

Lily smiled, skimmed down a bit.

> When you arrived in this world, my eyes and heart focused on taking in the miracle of you, but part of me was worried about your brother, how he'd cope with you, brand-new precious you, who

She closed the tab. It always turned into mishmash of sweet precious miracles.

"Sorry, I think this is us." Lily looked up to see a woman with a blond ponytail holding out her phone, which showed a movie ticket. "I didn't realize we were right next to anyone." The theater was only half full.

"Oh"—Lily giggled—"weird. No problem, though!"

The woman smiled and sat down. The man she was with followed suit, and then glanced over the woman to smile at Lily, too. What kind of a smile was it? Did it linger for a beat too long? She felt her breath catch. She'd gotten lucky this time. They were both attractive, maybe early forties, tall, fit. The man was blond, which Lily thought was deeply unserious, but at least it looked natural. She wondered if they had kids at home, a babysitter. She might have to invite them to her place. Or—she felt a tingle rise up her arm—maybe they'd pay for a hotel room.

Lily let herself sink into the familiar images on the screen. The big ears and the big mouths and the slow-motion shots of pooling sweat. She luxuriated in the unabashed, almost indecent horniness of the characters. And as the film progressed, she let her arm inch ever closer to the woman's, the blondish hairs on her forearm prickling. Her pinkie twitched, and brushed against the back of the woman's hand.

The woman pulled it away. Crossed her legs.

On her way out of the theater, Lily tried to remember exactly what they had looked like. They hadn't even stayed for the credits! A cardinal sin, as far as Lily was concerned. All of those people who had worked hard for the couple's enjoyment, never to be acknowledged by them. She huffed. They'd probably come for the tennis. Now that she really considered them, their looks bothered Lily. Sure, they were "attractive." But they were the kind of people whose bodies were collections of features rather than whole things. Straight white teeth. Nice arms. Defined eyebrows. Abs, probably. With nothing ugly and breathing to hold them together.

When she woke up the next morning, she was drenched in sweat. It took her a moment to come out of her dream, to realize she could throw off her covers.

She'd been back with them, Ben and Frances. It had begun as a memory: Frances pushing her onto the bed, drawing her hand down her stomach, licking up her thighs. As she had in real life, Lily turned her head as Frances ate her out, and looked at Ben, framed in the doorway, watching them, watching his wife, his breathing growing louder. He was beautiful, alone there, with desire in his eyes. She saved him as an image in her mind.

But suddenly, she felt their roles reversed. It wasn't Ben who was framed; it was herself and Frances. It felt as real to her as if he'd had a camera. She was the subject, the art. It occurred to her, briefly, to pose. But for some reason, she didn't. Let him have this picture of her, let Frances have this feeling of her, as a real person. So she had relaxed, let her stomach go, let her face go. When she came, she felt the world flash.

As she had in real life, she let herself be enfolded into Frances, let her face nestle between Frances's breasts, let her mouth then take one of Frances's nipples into her mouth. But when she looked up, in the dream, it was Annie's face above her. Annie's young, round, exhausted face. "I have enough for you, baby. I promise. I'm going to do better this time." Lily, swaddled, trapped, felt herself become greedy, and began to suck and suck and suck.

Lily arrived at the gardens early to get a sense of the space and lighting. It was late afternoon, and the sun glowed a light orange behind the rows of white chairs leading up to a delicate floral arch. The arch was covered in eucalyptus leaves and magnolia blooms, punctuated by spurts of untamed, bright snapdragons, delphiniums, and stargazer lilies.

She walked the edges of the gardens, taking photographs of flowers and bees. She zoomed in tightly to them, to capture the veins in their wings, the individual hairs on their fluffy backs. She moved her way up the plots, and then up the aisle to the arch, keeping her back carefully turned from the entrance, where she could hear the first guests arriving. It was tranquil work, but she was sweating.

As she framed a shot of a particularly unruly snapdragon, a voice just behind her said, "Lilies."

She jumped and turned, her camera raised. It was Frances,

tracing her fingers down a hot pink stargazer. Her face was flushed, her eyes shining.

"I was wondering if it was you," she said, letting her hand fall to her side. She was wearing a gauzy blue dress with a keyhole cutout just below her breasts, which were fuller than Lily remembered. "Is it you?"

"Oh!" Lily said. She still had her camera pressed into her face. She pulled it down. Frances was closer to her than she had realized. "It's me. I was also wondering if you were this Frances. Izzy's Frances."

"I am. Have been since college." Frances smiled, which made Lily smile, and she felt something grow between them, like a web. "It's good to see you. You became a photographer!"

"Hi!" It was Ben, walking toward them with his hand on a woman's arm—Allison's, Lily remembered. She felt herself bristle. She didn't like seeing Ben's hand on this arm, and not Frances's arm. She moved instinctively closer to Frances, but Frances was smiling at both of them, undisturbed. Allison broke off to speak to another couple, two men who had waved at them.

"Hi," Lily said to Ben, her voice chillier than she wanted it to be. His beard was grayer than she remembered, but it suited him.

"I—" Ben moved in closer to her, then took a step back, and said, "Sorry—I was going to hug you."

"That's good!" Lily said. So he stepped in and they hugged. It must have looked incredibly awkward, Lily thought, but it didn't feel awkward, once his arms were around her. She remembered that smell, his smell, like orange peels or black tea. Her frost melted.

"You're a photographer!" Ben said, too, sounding proud. It touched Lily, deep in her chest.

"You told us you wanted to be one," Frances said.

"I still wait tables sometimes, but yeah. I did it," Lily said, beaming. How easily she'd fallen into her role, she realized. The young woman. "What's, um, what's new with you two?"

They looked at each other and began to laugh for some reason. They pulled in close to each other. Ben put his arm around Frances's shoulders. *There we go*, Lily thought.

"We had a baby!" Frances said, like she couldn't believe it.

"A—what?"

"Henry. He's five months old."

"He's the best," Ben said, to Frances as much as to Lily.

"Wow," Lily said. Her heart began to beat faster. "Congratulations. I bet you guys are really good parents."

She felt the way she was looking at them change. Did they look tired? Older? She reassessed the gray hairs around Ben's mouth, tried to find them worrying instead of attractive. But she couldn't quite. So she looked at Frances's face. It was a bit thinner maybe, and with more distinctive lines around her eyes when she smiled. Lily looked down at her shoulders, broad and strong. At the brown hairs on her forearms. At her breasts and stomach and hips. All she could find was evidence of fullness, of softness. They liked having a baby. And for some reason, that unsettled her.

She felt something like the frisson of jealousy that had crept up her arms when she'd learned about Allison. Surely she wasn't jealous of a baby. Some baby she'd never met! What was wrong with her? She pushed it down.

"It's almost time," Lily said. "I need to move back so I can get Izzy coming down the aisle."

"Let's talk later," Frances said, and reached out to squeeze her hand.

She tightened her mouth to keep it from trembling, nodded, and moved out of the scene.

Lily had asked for her first camera when she was ten years old. Her parents obliged, but quickly became irritated by her new hobby. She brought her camera with her on errands, to church, to the dinner table. She took picture after picture of her mom and dad, all without warning, trying to capture their essential beings—that happiness, that silliness that their wedding photographer had seen. She tried to catch them off guard, finally putting her camera in front of her dad's face while he was driving, causing him to run off the road and demand that she get rid of the damned thing once and for all. She begged her mom to let her keep it, but it was no use. "Perhaps," her mom said, packing the camera into a cardboard box of Lily's old clothes to be donated, "it's better for you to stop distancing yourself. Don't you feel a bit on the outside of things, always on the other side of a camera?" Lily didn't have the language at the time to explain that the camera was a tool for finding her way *in*—into relationship with those warm, lively, curious people who she knew must be inside her mom and dad somewhere.

She never found them. And now her dad was losing his memory, years earlier than anyone could have expected. Last time she went home, she put the wedding album on his bedside table.

The sun had set, and the fireflies had come out. The air was still thick with summer heat, but a breeze had moved in with the night. Dangling bulbs had come on around the guests in the tent, circling them in soft light.

Lily stood outside. She was scrolling through the images she'd taken, making sure she got what she needed. Izzy walking down the aisle, beaming in her understated column dress. Her new husband, Jess, watching her from the archway, his eyes shining bright. The couple looking at each other, alone after the ceremony. Jess wiping a tear from his eye during his brother Daniel's best man speech. Jess brushing a strand of sweaty hair behind Izzy's ear on the dance floor. Frances squeezing Izzy's hand. Daniel dancing with his husband, Max. Izzy and her friends, Frances, Gina, and Hazel, hugging as a big group. Frances with her head on Ben's shoulder. Allison kissing Frances on the cheek as she left the dance floor, minutes before, and disappeared behind the house.

They were good, Lily thought. Really good. She should say good night to Izzy, let the lingering guests sing louder and more embarrassing songs. (Though could they top the "Mr. Brightside" they were all—each and every thirty- and forty-year-old there—yelling and jumping in the air to now? She framed a wide shot, and got a final picture.) She'd done what she came to do. She'd proven to herself—and to Izzy, she believed, who had asked to see a few photos minutes before and had squealed—that she could handle a wedding on her own. She'd get more contracts now, and would have Izzy as an excellent reference.

But instead of walking toward the tent to find Izzy, she turned and walked down the rock path toward the front of the house.

"Oh fuck!" Frances said as Lily walked up the steps to the front porch. "You scared me!" She was sitting on a rocking chair, a half-full bottle of white wine at her feet. Her dress was unzipped down the side. Lily's eyes lingered for a moment on that sliver of pale, freckled skin, remembering her own hands there, pulling at a black dress.

Her breasts were pushed up high, like she was in a Jane Austen adaptation, unable to be contained. She'd stuffed two electric, hands-free breast pumps into the front of her dress. Frances saw Lily's eyes on her chest. She turned toward her, instead of turning away, and breathed deep.

Lily had seen her friends use these pumps before, always somewhat shamefully, usually while folding laundry or loading a dishwasher. They were bizarre, these big mechanical cups. But something about the way Frances wore them was different. Her lack of shame about them made them sexy in an odd, uncanny way. Fembot, or maybe Madonna. Lily's body began to pulse.

"Sorry," Frances said, without meaning it. "I couldn't stand to sit in the bathroom on a night like this."

"It's beautiful out," Lily said, and walked over to sit at her feet.

"If you can believe it, I bought these because I thought they'd be discreet." Frances bent forward unnaturally so as not to spill, grabbed the wine bottle, and handed it to Lily, who took a gulp from it. She was off work now, she told herself.

"Not quite," Lily said, laughing.

"Not quite," Frances agreed.

Frances was a little drunk; Lily could tell. Her voice was slightly altered, her posture relaxed. Lily was glad; it made her less nervous around her.

"I didn't realize Jess and Izzy had only known each other for a year," Lily said, referencing Daniel's toast.

"I know," Frances said, like it was gossip. "But she fell for him practically on sight. I thought it was grief at first. For her first marriage, I mean. She arrived here like a hurricane, all torn up and scattered. She'd applied for a job but I never thought she'd take it. She and Liam liked Chicago." She shrugged and then smiled. "I'm not complaining! It's been great having her. I thought she'd be mad at me, but . . ." She trailed off. "That's Izzy. Plus, there were others. I think a lot of them."

Lily nodded, like she knew what Frances was talking about. She grabbed the bottle of wine from her and took another sip.

"Anyway! We had a little welcome party for her. Max and Daniel brought Jess . . . and here we are. They talked all night. It really happens that way sometimes."

"They seem really happy," Lily said. "I got some good pictures of them."

Frances smiled at her. "It's good to see you."

She felt her heart beat double. "It's good to see you, too."

The air had become heavy and still while they spoke. Frances's skin was dotted with pinpricks of sweat. The way the low light hit her made her glow. There was a long pause, and then Lily asked, "Can I take your picture?"

She laughed. "Like this?"

"Yeah. Not for Izzy, just . . . for me, I guess," she finished.

"Sure." She leaned back in the rocking chair, opened her legs just slightly, let her mouth fall into its natural slight pout, and looked directly into the camera.

"Just like that," Lily said as she framed the shot. "Yes."

She put down the camera, but Frances didn't drop the pose. Lily looked at her, and she looked back.

"What does it feel like?" Lily asked quietly.

"Pumping?"

"No," she said, feeling her face redden. Glad that the darkness would hide it. "To be a mother."

Frances sat up and knit her eyebrows together, as though she was trying to gauge how seriously she should take the question. "It feels . . ."

"Tell me for real, because . . . because I'm not sure I get it."

Frances looked at her so tenderly just then that Lily felt overexposed. She averted her eyes, but felt the heaviness of Frances's gaze on her skin.

"Have you ever been in love?" Frances asked, still looking at her in that way.

Lily laughed uncomfortably. She thought of Lucas, her college boyfriend. She had told him that she loved him, but she hadn't. *No*, she almost said. But then she thought of the other women whose beds she had slept in as much as she had her own. Her friends, Tess and Michelle and Gracie and Leah. And Annie. Her Annie. "Yeah," she said. "I have."

"You know when you're in bed with them, in the morning, and the sun is coming in, and they have pillow lines down their face, and their hair is all mussed, and their eyes are closed, and their cheeks look full and red, and you want to reach out and touch them so much but you don't want to wake them, because they seem so sweet and peaceful?"

Lily's heart was beating. She said quietly, "Yes."

"It feels like that."

"That's a lot."

"It's the biggest feeling. I feel . . ." She laughed, but then frowned and continued, "It feels so big sometimes, when I look at Henry, that I have to walk away. I can't seem to keep myself from walking away, to go wash the bottles or whatever, even though I want to be with him and keep looking at him. And then, when I'm gone, I think about how when he can't see me, he doesn't know I still exist, and how alone he must feel, and then I go back, and he smiles at me and makes this sound, it's, like, 'Ooh!'"—she smiled hugely as she did this, imitated her child, felt him in her body—"and I feel... I feel *so* happy. And then I want to walk away again. It's almost a compulsion."

There was a small silence as Frances shrugged and looked down at her feet. The pulses of her pump sounded to Lily like the clicks of her camera when she scrolled through pictures; each little blip contained thousands of images, layered and mixed and consolidated into a whole life. In her mind, she saw an eighteen-year-old Annie, hair stuck to her face, black mascara smeared below her eyes, sharing Lily's pillow. She smelled the spicy sweet of the tulip poplars that dotted her college campus. Michelle and Tess jumping into piles of autumn leaves, their sweatshirts poked through with twigs. The buckets of buttered popcorn, Lily's fingers yellow and oiled and salty as she snuck, with Gracie, from one theater into the next, unpaying and unseen. All the silly and embarrassing and small things rolled up into one big thing that she wanted to keep forever—and to pack away, out of sight.

Lily pushed up onto her knees, and then put her head into Frances's lap, her face pressed into one of her thighs. She breathed in the plain cottony smell of her hair, a plainness that reminded Lily of sitting on a warm, full couch. Frances ran her hand through Lily's hair, back and forth. "That sounds really hard," Lily said quietly.

"It's impossible to describe. Even what I said isn't quite right. I love him. Love him love him love him, my cutest, sweetest, precious little boy. There's no way to really say it, except like that. Which seems stupid and fake."

"It doesn't," Lily said, surprised to find she was telling the truth. Was this what Annie was saying when she wrote about her children? *My perfect little boy is a whole year old today! Smiling emoji. Crying emoji. Heart eye emoji.* What was so different about that?

"You'll understand one day when—"

Lily jerked her head out of Frances's lap. "I don't want to have kids. I never have."

"Sorry," Frances said. "I shouldn't have—"

"It's fine, don't feel bad." Lily shook her head. "It doesn't matter anyway, because my friends are married. My friends have kids. My whole life revolves around bedtime and nap schedules and all that shit anyway. I don't want to be alone, but the only way I can *not* be alone is by making myself fit into everyone else's lives, going to *their* houses, and waiting until *their* baby falls asleep, and... whatever."

Lily had never said this out loud before. She wanted to stop, to keep from revealing too much, but found that she couldn't. Her voice got louder as she continued, "So I'm forced to be this kind of adult that I don't want to be, and that I'm not, and I can't really do what I want because everyone thinks what I want is frivolous, but I think what they want is"—she searched for the right word—"*flattening.* I miss ..." She paused, and let out a mirthless laugh. "God, it's so boring. It's how everyone feels. Afraid of getting older." She shook her head, irritated with herself, and drained the wine.

"Say what you mean," Frances said.

"I mean...I miss being a teenager, when I could just pop over to a friend's dorm room or text them and they'd be free. I can't even find anyone to go to the movies with now." She looked down, and tried to hide the lump that had risen in her throat.

Was that it? she asked herself. Had she been unable to let go of Ben and Frances—or of her fantasies of them—because they would let her play young? Had she felt jealous earlier because, to some extent, she had wanted to be parented by them? To let them love and care for her? To have them as a do-over?

Maybe that was part of it. But it was also that she'd been reminded, once again, that there was a great big enormous kind of love out there that she wasn't a part of, as a daughter or as a mother. Or as a best friend.

Glancing back up, she saw Frances was still looking at her. "I'll go to the movies with you. If you want."

Lily laughed. "You don't have to do that."

"No, I...I want to."

"What about your baby?"

"Hello, he has a dad."

"All these other babies have dads, too." Lily thought about Chris, who had moved into the guest room so that Annie "wouldn't have to worry" when she fed the babies in the middle of the night. She thought about how Gracie said she couldn't go to Tess's bachelorette party because she didn't feel comfortable leaving the baby "alone" for a whole weekend. She thought about her own dad. Had he ever dressed her? Put her hair into pigtails? There had to be other kinds of dads. There had to.

"Well, Henry has a real one, and I have a real life."

"And a real Allison?" Lily asked, her expression suddenly accusatory.

"Well...yeah. But she's not, like, his caretaker. We wouldn't ask—"

"Do you sleep with her?"

Her voice came out harsher than she'd intended; Frances looked slightly taken aback. "With Allison?" She shrugged. "I have. But it's not really like that. It's more—"

"Why didn't you call me?" Lily hadn't meant to ask this. She felt instant shame. The question was so pathetic, so teenage. There was an uncomfortable silence, the only sounds the mechanical clicks of the breast pump.

"I think I... didn't I text you?" She took a drink of wine and reached down to adjust one of the pumps, for something to do.

"Text isn't the same as call."

That made Frances laugh for some reason. She caught herself and said, "No, it isn't. I'm sorry. I felt... It was the first time we'd done something like that. I felt surprised by... well, how I felt about it. About you. And then I thought, well, there was no way you cared about it as much as I had."

"What did you feel about me?"

"Oh, I don't..."

"Because I really liked both of you. Seeing you together. How you knew each other and liked each other. And how you... were to me. Sorry, this is coming out really stupid."

"No, it isn't," Frances said, looking at her again.

"And I liked you. How you looked at me. You made me feel like... fuck. Well, you made me feel like you cared about me. I didn't... I needed that then. I was really lonely. My friends all..." She sighed, and continued, "And then you didn't call. And then the world ended."

Frances looked at her, confused, and then burst out laughing. "Is that why, you think? Because I should have called you, but I didn't?"

Lily shrugged, smiling. "It's a better explanation than a lot of the other theories out there."

"Well, fuck. I guess I owe a lot of people an apology." She let out a final snort of laughter, and then grew serious. "I should have called. I'm sorry." She meant it, Lily could tell.

"It's okay."

"I liked you, too. We both did. I didn't really know then that it was okay to like someone else."

"Okay," Lily said, pouting. "Yeah."

"But I'm not scared of that now. And I'm less... well, I'm less needy now. I'm not looking for someone else to fill this big..." She spread her hands out wide, letting them speak for her.

In the silence, Frances's pump went off abruptly.

"Look!" Frances said, and pointed over her shoulder. Behind Lily's back, a family of deer materialized.

Two of the deer galloped off, frightened by the sight of them, and vanished into the enveloping dark. But one lifted its face to them, an inky leaf in its mouth. Lily turned back to Frances, whose eyes grew wide.

"So cool," she said, and stood to approach it.

"Deer are everywhere." Lily shrugged. "There are actually too many around here, relative to what the environment can support. They wreak havoc on vegetation."

"Whatever," Frances said, and she began to walk toward it. As she got to the edge of the porch, she missed the step, and there was an odd sloshing sound. She caught herself on the railing. "Fuck!"

The deer ran off, and Lily saw that the front of Frances's dress was soaked. Frances looked down and laughed. "Oh well. I was going to dump it anyway. It's *horrible* when you spill it, otherwise." She reached into her top, pulled out one of the cups, and poured the remaining milk over the edge, into the grass. Her top was draped low on one side, her strap halfway down her arm. "God," she said.

"It smells like a Four Loko. Henry's heart would explode if he drank this."

"And it's only available for a limited time," Lily said, smirking, her eyes on Frances's collarbone. "Like Four Loko."

"There's no way you've ever had one. Those were a thing when Izzy and I were in college."

Lily shrugged.

Frances pulled out the other cup and let her other strap fall down her shoulder. "Wanna try?" She held out the cup. With her other hand, she held on to the front of her dress, but didn't rezip it.

"Have you ever tried it?" Lily took a step toward her.

"Oh yeah. It's not bad. Well, *this* stuff is probably bad."

She made to dump it, but Lily said, "Wait."

She had been struck by the image of Izzy and Frances in college. Had they drunk Four Lokos and acted dumb and gone to frat parties and then shared a bed, as she and Annie had done? If this were Annie in front of her, holding out something stupid and gross for her to drink, wouldn't she do it? Hadn't she done it—Jell-O shots, watermelon vodka, cherry moonshine—hundreds of times before?

"No. Really?" She even looked a little like Annie then, her mouth quirking to the side mischievously. Though Annie had always been more elfin, more nervous in these moments. Lily's heart ached to see this version of Annie again.

"Sure. It'll make me big and strong," Lily said, walking toward her.

"That's such a weird thing to say," Frances said. But Lily noticed the way her eyes focused in on hers. Lily had fascinated her. Her curiosity felt heavy and insulating.

Lily took the cup from Frances's hand. It was warm from

where it had been pressed against her breast. They looked at each other, and she could tell that Frances was breathing as hard as she was. She tilted it and opened her mouth.

"Oh fuck!" Lily said, her face twisting. "It's *sour.* Ugh!"

The heat that had built between them broke, and Frances began to laugh a loud, open laugh. "Spit it out! You don't have to!"

"Oh my god. Your kid drinks this?!"

"Pour it out! It's poison!"

"Holy fuck," Lily said, dumping the rest in the grass. "That's so gross."

"I can't believe you drank that."

"I can't believe you produced it."

"Well," Frances said, and laughed again. "It's better from the source, you know. Pump and dump milk isn't really... you know..."

"I'll take your word for it," Lily started to say, but Frances interrupted her, grabbed her hand. It was back, that heaviness between them, pulsing like fireflies in the humid air.

Still holding on to her dress, she said, "We could try again sometime. I'd like to."

"I'd like to, too," Lily said in one fast breath.

"Okay." She smiled. Then Frances said, "Could you help me with this?" She shrugged her shoulder to indicate her dress.

Lily took the zipper down at Frances's hip and pulled it, slowly, up Frances's rib cage. Frances lifted her arm and Lily slipped the hook into the eye. Then she let her hand trace the same path downward.

And then Frances kissed her on the mouth, hot and soft and sour and spicy and wet. Lily closed her eyes, opened her mouth. She ran her finger along Frances's collarbone, and had to stop herself from doing it again and again. It was as though her body felt that it could make the hundreds of times she'd imagined touching Frances real, all in this one moment. She wanted the tips of her fingers to hold those sense memories. Maybe even more, she wanted Frances's body to hold the memory of her own.

The rush of feeling brought into piercing focus how untouched Lily had been lately. How quietly she moved through her days. It astounded her, suddenly, how much she wanted to be known, cared for, tended to. She wanted this from Frances. But she wanted it from Annie, too. She felt a low, deep ache to recover what she had let herself lose in her desperation to preserve it, unchanged.

She would call Annie tomorrow, tell her what had happened. And then she would ask her about her day, and try to listen without picking it apart.

Frances pulled away. She ran a hand down Lily's face and said, "Do you want me to call you?"

Yes, Lily thought. *Please, yes*. She heard herself say, "If you want to."

"Yes," Frances said, smiling at her. A wide, toothy smile. "I really want to."

Acknowledgments

Thank you to my wonderful agent Alexa Stark for your sharp advice and early support of this novel. I so appreciate you holding my hand and being a strong, decisive voice throughout the publication process. Thank you to the whole team at Writers House, especially Maja Nikolic, Sofia Bolido, Cecilia de la Campa, Peggy Boulos Smith, and Tom Ishizuka for the work you've done to ensure that this novel reaches an audience far and wide. Thank you, too, to my agents at WME, Hilary Zaitz Michael and Nicole Weinroth.

I couldn't have asked for more thoughtful editors than Reagan Arthur and Federico Andornino. I'm so grateful for your insightful guiding questions and for your enthusiasm for this story and these characters. I feel incredibly lucky to have found a UK publishing home at Sceptre. Thank you, especially, to Kitty Ollard for facilitating the publishing process, and to Louise Court, Ella Young, and Emily Harrison for your marketing and publicity expertise. Thank you for treating *Skin Contact* with such care!

For the beautiful design of this book, thank you to Saffron Stocker. And thank you to Jenna Gribbon for allowing me to use her painting "Lunch Touch" for the cover.

Versions of several of these chapters initially appeared as stories in literary magazines. Thank you to *The Missouri Review, Electric Literature, SmokeLong Quarterly, Grist, Orca,* and *The*

Lumiere Review for giving them homes. Thank you to the editors who selected them, especially Evelyn Rogers, Kylan Rice, Wynter K. Miller, Christopher Allen, Titus Chalk, Joe Ponepinto, and Jessica Kim. Your early input made these stories stronger.

Thank you to all the booksellers and reviewers for reading and sharing your thoughts about this novel. Your early support is invaluable to me. Thank you, especially, to Gwen Kirby, Kevin Wilson, and Ada Calhoun, who dropped everything to read this manuscript and offer early blurbs; and to the booksellers at Flyleaf Books who have gone above and beyond to support my work.

Thank you to everyone in my workshop at the Sewanee Writers' Conference, particularly Holly Goddard Jones, Erin Swan, and Laura Maylene Walter. This novel would not be where it is without your incisive critiques and professional advice. Thank you, too, to Natalie Edwards, who I met in Sewanee and whose interest in early forms of this novel gave me the confidence to pursue publication.

Thank you to Victoria Dillman, the first person to read "Motherlove" when it was just a story. And thank you to Abby Muller. You taught me how to edit, and you saw promise in my writing before anyone else.

Thank you to my friends, who are my ideal readers. Joanna Klager, Anna Spears Tuell, Anneke Schwob, Hayley Joyce, and Kevin Joyce read the first version of this manuscript the moment it was finished; your enthusiasm and love gave me the confidence I needed to get to this point. My book club—Emily Poe-Crawford, Rachael Perrin, Sara Duffus, Cubbie Ditmore, Janie Miller, and Jess Girault—was available at all hours to troubleshoot crucial issues like the title, the cover, celeb references, and more. Becky Price, Travis Tillman, Seema Vennam, Reed Tomlinson, Jenny Robb King, Sam Amick, Hope Leray, Hayley Summs, Emily Noggle, and Ashley Clay have read, supported, questioned, hyped, shared, and improved my writing for many years. Thank you to all of you; you shaped me and how I see and write about the world. Any jokes in these pages are for you.

I could never have written this book without the love, support, and influence of my family. Thank you to Tom Heflin, Cornelia Heflin, and Mary Catherine Heflin for reading and taking pride in my writing, and for counting me as one of your own. Thank you to my dad, George Faison, for placing such a high value on my education and access to books. Thank you to my sisters, Emmy Faison and Eva Marie Faison, and to my honorary sister, Elizabeth Clifton, for being my most enduring readers, champions, and friends. Your unwavering love is unspeakably precious to me. Thank you for being the people I turn to, to share my wins and my losses.

I feel so very lucky to have had Lois Faison as a grandmother. Hanky, you remain my favorite storyteller. Thank you for teaching me how to be funny and curious; and thank you to Laura Faison for telling me that you saw some of Hanky in my writing. Much of this is written in Hanky's memory, and in the memory of her sister, Judith Alter.

Thank you to my mom, Sharon Thomas Faison, who made me in every possible way. Thank you for sharing your love of literature with me. When I think about you, this is what I remember most: reading with you, and knowing I was loved.

Thank you to Morgan and Judy, who came into the world and helped me to see it differently. You taught me to feel more deeply and to love more fully. Being your mom is my proudest accomplishment.

And finally, thank you to Wil Heflin, who knew I was a writer before I did. Thank you for being with me for every word of this novel. I didn't know it was possible to believe in someone the way you believe in me. Thank you for making this book what it is—but mostly, thank you for sharing your life with me.

RAISING READERS

Books Build Bright Futures

Dear Reader,

We'd love your attention for one more page to tell you about the crisis in children's reading, and what we can all do.

Studies have shown that reading for fun is the **single biggest predictor of a child's future life chances** – more than family circumstance, parents' educational background or income. It improves academic results, mental health, wealth, communication skills, ambition and happiness.[1]

The number of children reading for fun is in rapid decline. Young people have a lot of competition for their time. In 2024, 1 in 10 children and young people in the UK aged 5 to 18 did not own a single book at home.[2]

Hachette works extensively with schools, libraries and literacy charities, but here are some ways we can all raise more readers:

- Reading to children for just 10 minutes a day makes a difference
- Don't give up if children aren't regular readers – there will be books for them!
- Visit bookshops and libraries to get recommendations
- Encourage them to listen to audiobooks
- Support school libraries
- Give books as gifts

There's a lot more information about how to encourage children to read on our website: **www.RaisingReaders.co.uk**

Thank you for reading.

hachette UK

[1] OECD, '21st-Century Readers: Developing Literacy Skills in a Digital World', 2021, https://www.oecd.org/en/publications/21st-century-readers_a83d84cb-en.html

[2] National Literacy Trust, 'Book Ownership in 2024', November 2024, https://literacytrust.org.uk/research-services/research-reports/book-ownership-in-2024